## THE ONLY THING MORE DANGEROUS
## THAN A LIE IS LOVE

Scotland 1455 – The Douglas clan is at war with their king. To protect his lands from confiscation, Lord John Douglas, the dying Earl of Kildrummond, must find an heir that doesn't carry his name.

A landless knight, Lachlan Ramsay expects no more of life than battles, blood, and the occasional warm bosom. But when Lord John makes him his heir, Lachlan has a chance at something he never dreamt of—a home. There's just one condition: He must marry the earl's bastard daughter, the fiery, eccentric Moira MacInnes.

Lachlan has no desire for a headstrong, sharp-tongued wife. Moira has no need for an arrogant, too-handsome husband. To save Kildrummond they will marry and seek an annulment immediately upon the earl's death. But deception is never simple, and passion once inflamed is impossible to ignore. Soon they will no longer be deceiving the earl but themselves.

# A NOBLE DECEPTION

## Veronica Bale

www.BOROUGHSPUBLISHINGGROUP.com

PUBLISHER'S NOTE: This is a work of fiction. Names, characters, places and incidents either are the product of the author's imagination or are used fictitiously. Any resemblance to actual events, locales, business establishments or persons, living or dead, is coincidental. Boroughs Publishing Group does not have any control over and does not assume responsibility for author or third-party websites, blogs or critiques or their content.

A NOBLE DECEPTION
Copyright © 2015 Katherine Ellyse LeGrand

ISBN 978-1-942886-82-2

*To my Christopher. You inspire me every day, wee man.*

# ACKNOWLEDGMENTS

I would like to express my thanks to many people who made this book possible.

To the team at Boroughs Publishing Group: My sincere gratitude for everything you've done to make my book possible. A special thanks to Jenni Hendriks, my amazing editor. Your expertise has been invaluable, and your commitment to, and enthusiasm for, my story is deeply appreciated.

To my family and friends: Thank you, every single one of you. Your support has meant the world to me. To my husband, Jeff, and my son, Christopher: My book would not exist if it wasn't for the both of you rooting me on…and more-than-occasionally picking up the slack at home when I'm in my "Can't talk; writing" mode.

And finally to my readers. You mean more to me than words can express. My gratitude to you all is boundless.

# CONTENTS

# A Noble Deception

## *Prologue*

A sudden, stiff breeze, heavy with the scent of summer heather, careened over the hills. For a brief instant it lifted the dragonfly caught in its wake higher; when it passed, the creature touched down on the leaf of a young fern, bravely poking its feathery head through a tangle of scrub. The dragonfly's wings vibrated once, then twice, then stilled.

Behind the fern at an unobtrusive distance, a pair of blue eyes, round with fascination, fixed on the creature. Slowly, ever so slowly so that she wouldn't disturb it, Moira raised her disheveled head. Her heart thrummed excitedly within her tiny chest as she crawled towards the fern, on hands and knees that were scuffed and scabbed from play.

She moved with patience (oh, she was *ever* so patient), creeping into prime pouncing position like a cat, graceful and deadly. Another ell more—only the distance from elbow to fingertips—and she'd have the wee mite.

Slowly. Slowly. Almost there…

A sharp throb in her bladder made Moira clench her small thighs. Oh no…she had to pish-pish. Reacting instantly, she bounced up and down, which rustled the heather around her.

As quick as a wink the dragonfly lifted itself into the air and flew away to safety.

"Fie!" she cursed.

Shoving herself out of her crouch, she stomped her foot with all the fury that a lass of four years could. Then she batted the wrinkles from her freshly washed leine of homespun wool.

"Double fie!" She'd smudged the garment with grass and dirt.

Mama had insisted so strongly that she stay tidy. What would their visitor think if he saw her this way? He'd come to see a fine young lady; instead he would be greeted by a filthy, rumpled faerie.

Mama would be so cross, but Moira simply hadn't been able to help herself. The urge to explore the hidden, magical places of her new home had been too acute to ignore. Why, there were caves and braes, foxholes and burrows.

And hills, oh, the hills! Emerald and violet, hills as far as the eye could see and not a soul within miles. Their old borderland village had been nothing like this.

As if instinctively sensing her daughter's disobedience, Moira's mother called to her. "Moira, ye'll come in now. Our visitor is here."

There was no help for it. Her mother would see her soiled leine. She would see her tangled hair. She would punish Moira. No cakes for a fortnight; never again to the glen; no more wonderful—

Her bladder convulsed again. Moira ran the short distance to the hut, praying that her pish-pish would stay up there just a wee bit longer. She'd meet the gentleman quickly, and then she could run for a tiddle.

Her mother greeted her at the doorway. Her long, fawn-colored hair was bound in a simple plait and draped over her shoulder. She was clad in her best gown—though with only two gowns to speak of it meant her mother wore the one without the tear at the sleeve. Still, Moira had never seen her so beautiful. Her cheeks were flushed and her eyes sparkled with a radiant, inner light.

"Och, lass, what have ye done to yerself?" the lady chided as Moira sauntered into the one-room hut, their home of a little more than a sennight.

Moira trotted over the threshold, her hands clasped to her belly to keep the pish-pish in its place. She opened her mouth to tell her mother that she needed to go wee, but the sight of the gentleman standing in the middle of the hut brought her to a halt.

He was a man of great importance; that much was immediately clear. His ermine-trimmed robe, a luxurious umber velvet, covered his broad shoulders and was fastened at the neck with a braided gold clasp. The tunic beneath was of fine quality and adorned with golden chains and pendants set with dazzling gems.

The man exuded wealth and status—a noble, surely. Moira had never seen one in person before; she'd only heard of such men from the children in her old village.

She studied him through eyes narrowed to slits. The gentleman was old—perhaps not as old as MacEachern, Beth's grandfather, but old enough. His dark hair and beard, both neatly combed and trimmed, were streaked with grey, and though he was not fat (at least she did not think he was fat, though it was hard to tell since he was covered with so much fine clothing), he had the larger, thicker frame that many robust elders had.

The gentleman gazed down at the lass with a smile. Something in his expression made Moira pause. People were always smiling at her, as people do with children, but this man regarded her with something more than passive indulgence. It was as if the sight of her filled him with joy. And awe.

"Ye must be Moira," he said, his rich voice gentle.

Her mouth slightly agape, Moira nodded. The pish-pish throbbed ferociously at her tiny bladder; she resumed her foot-to-foot shuffling.

"A gae fine lass ye are. As beautiful as yer mam."

Upon saying so the man raised his eyes above Moira's head to her mother. The tender look in his eyes was of little interest to the wee lass. Unable to hold her pish-pish anymore, she whirled around and bounded for the door.

"Mama, I have to tiddle," she called over her shoulder before she fled for the hills.

A deep, throaty chuckle followed her.

Out of sight of the dwelling, she crouched in the scrub and relieved herself. As she stared blankly ahead, relishing the glorious sensation of her rapidly emptying bladder, the same dragonfly fluttered past her in erratic bursts of flight.

"I'll get ye next time," she vowed. "I canna catch ye right now, though. I'm busy."

Teasing her, the dragonfly flew closer before rising high in the air and out of sight. Moira sighed regretfully. Such a handsome dragonfly he'd been, too.

Finished with her personal needs, she traipsed back to the hut. The thought of entering again was not particularly appealing. The gentleman had been kind, to be sure, but something about the way he looked at her made Moira uncomfortable.

Like he knew her, though she did not know him.

Instead, she stooped beneath the only window at the rear of the dwelling and seated herself on the grass. Her mother and the gentleman were talking, and from her position below the window, Moira could hear them well enough.

"John, I dinna ken about this," came her mother's melodic voice.

"Hush, love. Ye're here now."

"Nay, this isna right. I should go home."

"*This* is yer home, sweetling. Wi' me."

There was a gap of silence, and then something uttered in a low, muffled tone, which Moira couldn't hear. Then the gentleman spoke again.

"Lilian, I'd marry ye this instant if I could. Ye *ken* that. But—"

"But ye've a *wife*."

"Och, dinna be that way. I have ye now, isna that enough? We've a beautiful, bonnie daughter together, and God willing, we'll have more children."

"John, I—"

"And I'll recognize each and every one of them, I promise ye. Stay. This is yer home. Ye'll never want for anything."

Another pause followed, and then the sound of footsteps on the grass outside. Moira glanced over her shoulder to find her mother approaching.

Lilian crouched beside her daughter. Her cheeks were even more flushed, and there was a reckless, almost daring glint in her amber eyes. Her plait had been pulled loose and her locks caressed the contours of her face and neck. Moira gasped, enchanted by her mother's unprecedented beauty.

"Will ye go play in the hills for a while, love?" Lilian brushed her fingertip over her daughter's cheek. "Why dinna ye go to the village for a while? See if Niall is about."

"Yes, Mama." Obediently, Moira stood and trudged away in the direction of the village.

"Stay away from the brae," Lilian called after her.

Moira didn't much feel like going to the village to play with her new friend Niall, the local brewer's son, nor to the brae whether she was permitted or not. She didn't much feel like doing anything, in fact. So she curled up in the heather a short distance away.

She did not understand her mother's reason for sending her away, but instinctively she knew she must not return any time soon.

Overhead, large, fluffy clouds raced across the sky, casting fast-moving shadows onto the green and violet hills below. Moira watched them, following each patch of shadow until it went beyond her line of sight.

Eventually she dozed off.

# *One*

*Moray, Scottish Highlands, 1455*

The brittle crunch of hooves on gravel echoed off the stone walls of the bailey, announcing the party of travelers that charged through the gatehouse of Glendalough Castle. Leading the procession was Lord Edward Douglas, Earl of Albermarle, whose arrival had been expected.

The earl was a familiar sight at Glendalough, for not only was he kin to John Douglas, Earl of Kildrummond, but Lord Albermarle's lands of Kinross nestled Kildrummond on its northern border.

A flurry of activity stirred within the bailey. A flock of ghillies, who had been sent to the cobbled courtyard to receive the earl, hastened forward to take the horses' reins. Servants streamed from the castle to unload the travelers' trunks and other belongings from the single carriage that followed.

"How is he?" inquired Lord Albermarle of the ghillie that came to take his gelding.

"Lord Kildrummond is rather poorly today, yer Lordship," the boy answered with a voice that was in the awkward, crackling middle ground between child and man.

"I am sorry to hear it. Perhaps I should see him on the morrow; let him rest this night."

"Oh, nay, my lord. His Lordship were quite insistent ye be shown to his bedchamber as soon as ye'd arrived. If yer Lordship be willing, that is."

"His bed chamber?" Lord Albermarle raised his heavy, dark eyebrows. "I hadna realized he were *that* poorly."

"Aye, my lord. He is abed more often than no' these days."

Lord Albermarle pursed his lips, concerned by this unanticipated news. "He'll no' thank me if I dinna visit him now, the stubborn old ram," he murmured to himself. Then to the ghillie he instructed, "Have my men's horses seen to, aye?"

"Certainly, my lord." The boy bowed.

Lord Albermarle entered the castle, sweeping importantly through its hallways and passages on his way to the keep. Glendalough was not a large fortress by any means, but neither was it small. Lord Albermarle had admired it ever since he was a young lad. Many a time had he run amok in this castle when his father had taken him along for a visit. It had a certain, indefinable charm to it.

Glendalough, as well as the earldom of Kildrummond, would be his one day—and by what the ghillie had told him, it looked as though that day might be sooner than he'd expected. Lord Kildrummond and his wife, Lady Glinis, had not produced any children from their union. As the earl's next closest kinsman, the title and the lands would pass to Lord Albermarle.

Approaching the heavy, oaken door of Lord Kildrummond's bedchamber, Lord Albermarle rapped soundly.

"Aye, come," called a gentle, feminine voice from within. Lady Glinis, the earl's wife of six-and-twenty years.

Pushing aside the door, Lord Albermarle stepped through to the grand chamber. His wide, stately shoulders barely made the width of the threshold.

Within, Lord Kildrummond was propped up in his bed and wrapped snugly in furs. A large fire blazed in the hearth, making the room so warm that Lord Albermarle was forced to remove his fur-lined cloak lest he drown in perspiration. He'd been chilled by the brisk, mid-March air on his ride and had been eager to warm himself, but the heat of this room was too much for any man in good health.

Lord Kildrummond was obviously not in good health. He'd withered since Lord Albermarle had seen him last. His face was gaunt, and deep shadows smudged the pale skin beneath his eyes. A man who had never looked his seventy-odd years before, the earl looked every one of them now. And more. It pained Lord Albermarle to see his once strong, virile kinsman so diminished.

Glinis Douglas, Lady Kildrummond, was seated in a cushioned armchair pulled to his bedside. Born of the Ramsay clan, the lady had the fine, regal bones and dark, silky tresses that were a common feature among her kinsmen. Her emerald velvet surcoate illuminated her delicate complexion and onyx eyes, and though she appeared somewhat drawn (owing to her husband's illness, no doubt), she was still breathtaking.

"Well then, John, how be ye this fine day?" Lord Albermarle enquired cheerfully. "Only, the lad that received me in yer bailey said ye were poorly."

Lord Kildrummond smiled. He opened his mouth to speak, but was overcome by a wet, rattling cough.

"I am no' so poorly I canna have a visit wi' my closest kinsman," he declared when his cough passed.

"Ye should be resting," Lady Glinis put in.

"Lady Kildrummond," Lord Albermarle addressed her, bowing, "ye're lovelier every time I have the pleasure of seeing ye. If ye're no' careful, ye'll be tried for conjuring, for no woman can be so beautiful wi'out possessing the powers of a witch."

"Such flattery," Lady Glinis returned playfully. "I'd advise ye be careful wi' yer attentions, my lord, lest I tell yer Rosamund that her husband's a shameless flirt. Nay, I am haggard, and ye well ken it."

"Haggard my eye," Lord Kildrummond snorted. "Ye behave as though ye've aged twenty years since my illness. Ye're only one-and-forty, and ye're as beautiful as the day I married ye."

The earl's flattery surprised both of his companions, for he was not a man to praise his wife often. His flattery was reserved for his beloved Lilian, dead these two years past. The earl had taken the woman as mistress shortly after it was discovered that Lady Glinis, then a young bride of fifteen tender years, could not sire an heir.

"I thank ye, my lord," Lady Glinis replied, unsure of how to receive her husband's compliment. A glance to Lord Albermarle confirmed they shared the same thought: the earl was growing softhearted in these, his ending days.

"Perhaps I should come back later when ye've had a rest," Lord Albermarle offered. "My men and I plan to enjoy yer hospitality at least a few nights; I willna be returning to Glen Craggan immediately."

"That would be kind of ye," Lady Glinis said.

"Ye'll stay where ye are," Lord Kildrummond objected. "What I must speak wi' ye about canna wait. It may take some time to orchestrate, and I'd rather go to my grave knowing it's been seen to."

Lord Albermarle flashed a lopsided, indulgent grin at his kinsman. To Lady Glinis he whispered conspiratorially, "We'd best no' distress the old man, my lady. If I'm to believe him, he has one scraggly leg in the grave already."

"I do—as good as, anyway. Now, leave us be, wife. I'd discuss wi' his Lordship in private."

Tossing her hands in defeat, Lady Glinis gave a long-suffering sigh. "Be it so then. I'll take my leave, my lords." To Lord Albermarle she added, "Do send someone to fetch me if he requires anything."

Once she departed the chamber, Lord Albermarle took her chair, adjusting its position to accommodate his larger legs.

"She's devoted to ye, John," he noted. "The word at Glen Craggan is that she's attended ye faithfully since ye first took ill. That's a fine woman ye've wed."

Lord Kildrummond shrugged his frail shoulders, and his lined face reflected a twinge of regret. "Aye, I ken it. She's been handed a difficult lot in life, yet she's weathered it wi' grace and dignity."

"She'll always have a home here at Glendalough. I promise ye that."

At this, the old earl's expression turned guilty. Averting his eyes, he cleared his throat and pushed himself straighter against the pillows. "Well, er, that is what I wish to speak wi' ye about, Edward."

"Lady Glinis?"

"Nay...Glendalough."

"What about Glendalough? Ye dinna owe the Crown on the estate, d'ye? I'll no' have to dig into my coffers to keep my inheritance, I hope."

"It isna that. These being dark times, ye can understand that I'd worry about the place."

"Dark times, aye." Lord Albermarle nodded reflectively. "It doesna seem like he's been gone three years, does it?"

"It doesna."

But it was. Three years ago their kinsman William, the eighth Earl of Douglas and chief of the vastly branched Douglas clan, had been brutally murdered by King James the Second at Stirling Castle. In a fit of rage, the monarch had stabbed Lord Douglas more than twenty times after the earl refused his demand that he sever his powerful alliance with Alexander Lindsay, Earl of Crawford, and John of Islay, chief of Clan Donald. Since that time the existing feud between the Black Douglases, as the clan had become known, and the Scottish king had grown dangerously heated.

The king's rash and violent act also fuelled the rumors that the fiery birthmark upon his cheek was a mark of his fiery temperament. Thereafter, references to King James as "Fiery Face" became even more commonplace—when he was not around to hear it.

"And now there is the matter of the lands being forfeit to the Crown," Lord Kildrummond added, referring to the recent seizure of Douglas lands and the imprisonment of William Douglas's successor.

"Who kens what further lands Fiery Face intends to seize? The name of Douglas isna a friend to the Crown right now, that's for certain."

"That," Lord Kildrummond stated with an odd, uneasy look, "is what I wish to speak wi' ye about, Edward."

Lord Albermarle assessed the old earl with an odd, uneasy look of his own. "Why do I have the feeling I'll no' like what ye have to tell me?"

"I daresay ye willna…because I have decided ye'll no' be my heir upon my death. Glendalough will go to another."

"Ha!" Lord Albermarle chuckled. "Ye nearly had me there, John. 'Tis no' a funny jest, that."

"I agree, 'tis no.' 'Tis also no' a jest, Edward. I willna be leaving Glendalough to ye."

The younger earl's face fell serious. "By God, why? What have I done to displease ye so?"

Lord Kildrummond knew his kinsman well, and recognized the need to proceed with caution. Though Lord Albermarle had not shouted or grown angry, there was a steely edge to his calm, controlled manner. He was a man of great power and influence, after all, accustomed to leading men and giving orders.

He was not accustomed to being denied the things he wanted.

"Ye've done nothing to displease me, Edward. I plead wi' ye to hear me out, for I ken—we *both* ken—that ye can easily protest my decision wi' the king. And ye'd probably win yer petition, too, for ye are the rightful heir to Kildrummond. I dinna dispute that."

Lord Albermarle stared at the old earl, frail and ashen beneath his furs. A muscle worked at his jaw as the silence lengthened. Eventually he answered, "Go on, then. I'm listening."

"My decision, Edward, is only for the good of Kildrummond. While I've no doubt ye'd be a fine steward of its people, ye *are* a Douglas."

"As *ye* are," Lord Albermarle observed tersely.

"That is my concern. Who kens whether the king will take more Douglas land in the course of this wretched feud? Who kens whether he will decide to take Kildrummond?"

"'Tis speculation. Ye dinna ken anything is at risk. This feud may blow over by the end of the year."

"And it may no'. Edward, I havena much time left on this earth. I dinna care to go to my grave worrying about what the king may or may no' do. It isna as if ye need Glendalough's coffers to add to yer own. Ye've lands and wealth enough as it is. I beg ye, Edward: let my title and my lands pass to another. For the sake of the great name of Douglas; for the sake of the clan. If James is set on making enemies of us all, we must do what we can to protect our own."

Lord Albermarle considered the old man's proposition in palpable silence. He did not like it. In all his adult life he'd thought of Glendalough as his, had measured his own wealth with the inclusion of Kildrummond coin. These lands had a significant advantage over his own: where Kinross was a landlocked parcel of territory, Kildrummond possessed a valuable seaport on its northern edge. It was a prime acquisition, not only in terms of economy, but also military strategy.

Yet old John Douglas's logic could not be ignored. All the military and economic advantage of Kildrummond was for naught if King James seized it. This feud between the Crown and the Douglas clan was carrying on far too long, and many a noble speculated on the king's sanity—what monarch in his right mind would brutally murder one of his subjects by his own hand? In view of witnesses, no less, for indeed the pair had not been alone that night. There was no telling how far he planned on carrying this quarrel.

After several long moments, he spoke. "If no' me, then who?"

"Lachlan Ramsay," Lord Kildrummond stated.

A shout of laughter burst from Lord Albermarle's barrel chest. "Lachlan Ramsay? *Now* ye must be jesting. Lachlan Ramsay, as in Viscount Strathcairn?"

"Aye, the very same. He is my wife's nephew, but more importantly he isna a Douglas. The king willna have any grounds to take Kildrummond, if it comes to that, because it will be in the hands of a Ramsay."

"So ye'll hand over yer earldom and all it entails to an insignificant young viscount—wi'out lands of his own, I might add—over yer own Douglas kinsman." Mirth still tugged at the corners of Lord Albermarle's lips. "All right then, John, I concede. Pray, tell me, what other reasons have ye for this mad scheme of yers? Nothing ye've ever done before had only one purpose to it."

Lord Kildrummond chuckled as well. "'Tis tied to the first reason, I admit. Ye see, Edward, ye're married. Ye've a beautiful wife in yer Rosamund, and ye've been devoted to her since the day ye wed. Lachlan Ramsay, on the other hand, isna married. Or at least he wasna the last time I inquired."

"I'm certain he still isna," Lord Albermarle put in dryly. "From what I remember of the lad, he isna the type to settle into matrimony wi'out being dragged to the altar." When the old earl's eyes sparkled mischievously, he added, "Ye dinna mean to drag him to the altar. *Tell* me ye dinna mean to drag him to the altar, John. I'll have no part in that."

"Of course not. Ye said it yerself; the lad has no lands of his own. He'll drag himself there, I'm certain. For the earldom of Kildrummond, and its lands and wealth, he'll do it."

Lord Albermarle's eyebrows knitted together as he worked out the old man's plan. Then a wave of understanding swept over him.

"Ah, I see. Ye wish for him to marry yer Moira."

"I wish for him to marry my Moira. I want to ken my daughter is provided for when I'm gone. I want to ken she'll always have a home in Kildrummond. I owe it to my Lilian to do this for our lass."

Lord Albermarle groaned. He could have contested his kinsman's wish to preserve Kildrummond from the king's greedy hand, and maintained an easy conscience. But not this, not Moira's security. Edward Douglas, Earl of Albermarle, was a father several times over himself. Illegitimate or no, Moira was still the dying earl's only child.

"I'll think on it," he said evenly.

In truth, though, he knew how that thinking would go.

## *Two*

The wide, dual doors to the stables at Slains Castle in Aberdeenshire stood ajar. Daylight seeped lazily through the entrance, weakened by a sky that was heavy with the threat of snow. It cast a colorless pallor over the lone bay gelding housed within and the figure stooped beneath it. The rhythmic melody of a hoof pick scraping against an iron shoe was the only sound to be heard.

It was this peaceful atmosphere that greeted William Hay, Earl of Erroll, as he stepped into the doorway across the path of the grey daylight.

"Lachlan, ye've a visitor." His cultured voice echoed off the low, slatted wood walls.

Lachlan Ramsay's gelding whickered at the noise, and pulled its front hoof from its master's hand. A puff of steam emitted from the animal's snout, condensing against the sharp chill in the late winter air. Rather than fighting, Lachlan let the leg go and stroked his bay's thigh reassuringly. When the beast settled, he peered around its rump to determine the source of the voice.

The Earl of Erroll peered back at Lachlan, a look of pure distaste on his noble face.

"I shall never understand why ye insist on doing that yerself," he stated, nodding at the dung-coated scraper that Lachlan held in his hand. "Yer squire should be doing that for ye."

Lachlan chuckled. Lifting the bay's hoof again, he resumed his scraping. "There's a great many foul tasks I leave to my squire, my Lord. This task I keep to myself. My mount and I, we have a bond. One which I nurture so that he willna fail me in battle."

"He hasna failed ye yet."

"I havena let a squire near him yet." Finished with the hoof, Lachlan focused on the Earl. "I have a visitor, ye say?"

"Ye have. He waits for ye in my private chamber."

"If I may, my Lord, why have ye come to fetch me yerself? Dinna mistake me I am flattered, but why not send a servant for me?"

"I wasna doing anything so important that I couldna deliver the message to my best knight in person. Besides, yer visitor is of great

power and wealth. I were obliged to see his summons safely
delivered."

Lord Erroll's statement, infused as it was with a playful sense of
mystery, piqued Lachlan's curiosity. He raised a dark eyebrow
inquiringly.

"'Tis Edward Douglas, Earl of Albermarle," Lord Erroll
explained.

"The Earl of Albermarle is here to visit *me*, my lord?"

"Aye, I could hardly believe it myself, but 'tis so. I've seen it
wi' my own eyes. Do wash yer hands before ye come, though. I'd
wager ye'd no' want to bring the smell of horse shite wi' ye when ye
meet him."

Lachlan released the gelding's hoof, and whispered a kind,
gentle word to the animal, which responded with another steamy
snort. Then he stepped out of the stall into the long, central corridor,
and bent to the bucket of water that his squire had placed there less
than a quarter of an hour ago. Already the liquid, which had been
searing hot when the lad had delivered it, was uncomfortably chilled;
it stung Lachlan's chapped hands, and he was forced to make quick
work of removing the offending muck from his fingers and under his
nails. When he was finished, he shook off the excess ice water, and
followed the earl out of the stables and over the grounds to the castle.

Overhead the sun had broken through the slate of cloud, and
patches of golden light streamed onto the snow-covered hills below.
A frigid wind stirred, biting at Lachlan's cheeks and the tip of his
nose. He pulled the upper swath of his plaid over his black hair and
around his face so that only his dark eyes could be seen.

Inside Slains Castle the cold did not recede. Nobles, knights and
servants alike were bundled in all manner of garments as they
wandered the corridors on their way to and from heated chambers.

When they reached Lord Erroll's private chamber, a guard
posted outside the room opened the door. Lord Erroll stepped
through first, followed by Lachlan.

Indeed, as Lord Erroll had announced, Lord Albermarle of
Kinross waited within. He was seated at a center table of imported
Scandinavian ash wood—a luxury Lord Erroll could well afford. A
pewter goblet was clutched in the visiting earl's jeweled hand, both
of which rested on the polished surface of the table in an easy
manner.

It had been many years since Lachlan last saw the Earl of Albermarle, and when Lord Erroll had announced his presence in the stables, he recollected vaguely the image of a regal and intimidating figure.

Confronted with the man in the flesh once more, he was every bit as formidable as Lachlan remembered. His thick, dark hair, which drifted to his shoulders and pillowed there, was elegantly streaked with silver threads. A fine fox-fur cloak was fastened across his breast and drawn back to reveal a stylish tunic of pearl-crusted black velvet. He smiled when Lachlan approached.

"Viscount Strathcairn," he acknowledged with a slight teasing tone.

"Yer Lordship," Lachlan answered, bowing. "To what do I owe this pleasure?"

Lord Albermarle sat forward in his chair, releasing his grip on the goblet. Assessing the young viscount's tall, lean form he said, "I come wi' summons."

"Wi' summons, my lord? Who summons me?"

"Lord Kildrummond; he requests an audience wi' ye."

"My aunt is no' ill, is she?"

"Nay, lad. Lady Glinis is well. As beauteous as ever."

"I am glad to hear it. If it isna my aunt, then what other reason can Lord Kildrummond have for summoning me?"

A secretive smile passed over the earl's lips, though it did not quite reach his eyes. "*That*, Lord Strathcairn," he said enigmatically, "I canna tell ye. As much as I'd like to, the old goat forbade me to breathe a word of it. Says he wants to speak wi' ye personally. And I, being the loyal kinsman I am, have acquiesced in consideration of his health."

"I'd heard he were poorly. He'll recover though, nay?"

Lord Albermarle glanced to Lord Erroll, a shadow passing over his handsome face. "Nay, he willna."

"Oh...I see." Lachlan shifted from one foot to the other, unsure of the proper response. Lord Albermarle and Lord Kildrummond, he knew, were close. Not only in proximity, for theirs were neighboring lands, but each man was in high esteem of the other. The pain in Lord Albermarle's statement was thick. Almost tangible. He looked like a man deeply affected by his kinsman's impending death.

He also, Lachlan thought, looked like a man that would *not* appreciate an offer of condolences from a lowly viscount such as himself. Wisely, he decided to keep quiet.

"Given that there isna much time left for Lord Kildrummond, ye'll come wi' me on the morrow to see him," Lord Albermarle concluded. "If ye be willing, that is. And also if Lord Erroll be willing to part wi' ye."

"Of course I am," Lord Erroll answered.

"My lord, are ye sure this is the best time? Wi' things the way they are at present—"

"Dinna worry about all that, lad. We're no' on the eve of war just yet. I havena given Moray my answer. Indeed, he'll no' have it any time soon, for I wish to consider it in great detail."

"Moray?" Lord Albermarle questioned. "Ye mean to say that Douglas seeks the support of Clan Hay? So he's determined to keep the feud wi' old Fiery Face alive then, is he?"

Lord Erroll shrugged. Lachlan looked between both men, confused. "I thought James Douglas were the ninth Earl of Douglas."

"He is, lad," Lord Albermarle replied.

"Then who is Moray?"

"*Archibald* Douglas. James's brother, and the Earl of Moray."

"Isna Lord Albermarle from Moray?"

Both lords laughed heartily at Lachlan's naivety.

"Edward Douglas, Earl of Albermarle who ye see before ye, holds the lands of Kinross which are *in* Moray," Lord Erroll explained. "Just as *John* Douglas, Earl of Kildrummond, holds lands which are *also* in Moray. But that isna to say that either is the *Earl* of Moray. Honestly, Strathcairn, ye'll need to learn who's who in this business wi' the Black Douglases where ye're going. And soon."

"Lord Douglas—that is James, the ninth Earl of Douglas—seeks support in his opposition against King James, since he doesna seem to be getting any help from John of Islay." Lord Albermarle clarified gently. "Islay, that is the chief of Clan Donald, is the last pillar of the triad alliance wi' William Douglas, murdered by Fiery Face himself, and the Earl of Crawford—Alexander Lindsay—dead these two years past."

"Aye, I ken all that," Lachlan's cheeks reddened.

"Dinna take offense, lad," Lord Erroll put in. "Ye havena had the benefit of court and noble society since ye've been in my employ. We dinna hold that against ye; 'tis only a bit of fun."

"I took no offense, my lord," Lachlan assured. It was truth—he was not offended. He was *embarrassed*. His lack of political understanding was a product of his landless title, and it humiliated him at times.

Shooting a knowing look at Lord Albermarle, Lord Erroll said, "Perhaps this journey comes at a fortuitous time." When Lachlan raised his brows questioningly, the earl answered, "Aye, lad, I ken the reason for the summons. Lord Albermarle has told me, for I insisted on knowing why my best knight were being taken from my service. 'Tis worth yer while to go, I promise ye. Ye'll take a man of yer choosing wi' ye, of course."

Lachlan knew immediately whom he wished to take. "If yer certain, my lord, then I'd request Sir Alexander MacByrne."

Lord Erroll groaned. "Of course he'd have to ask for my second best knight. All right, so be it. I'll send word to MacByrne that he is to pack his belongings."

"And ye canna give me even the smallest hint why I'm being summoned?"

"Of course I could," Lord Albermarle answered, "but I willna. Ye'll ken the reason soon enough. For now, see to yer affairs; we leave at first light."

"Yer Lordship," Lachlan acknowledged, bowing to Lord Albermarle. Then doing the same to Lord Erroll he repeated, "Yer Lordship."

He exited the chamber, and the guard outside closed the door behind him. The solid thud of oak colliding with stone, followed by a metallic click as the door latched shut, echoed along the corridor. Within the chamber deep male voices hummed in resumed conversation. Lachlan longed to press his ear to the door that he might hear what was being said, but when he paused, seriously considering it, the guard eyed him discouragingly. Raking his fingers through his thick, dark hair, Lachlan strode away.

He was not sure what to make of this journey. On the one hand he was wary of leaving Slains. He rather liked the life he'd carved out for himself here. A nobleman without the benefit of lands (thanks to his grandfather for pishing away the family's wealth and vast holdings), Lachlan, like his father before him, had been forced to take a knighthood with the Earl of Erroll. One needed food, coin and shelter, after all.

Under William Hay's leadership he'd risen in the ranks, proving himself a trusted and worthy servant. His life was by no means luxurious. But it was comfortable.

On the other hand he did not like that the feud between King James and the Black Douglases had reached Lord Erroll. Lachlan liked the action of training and battle as much as the next man, but this was different. If Lord Erroll were pulled into the fray, the earl would be siding against the king.

Which meant *Lachlan* would be siding against the king.

Which meant treason.

Perhaps, then, this summons to Kildrummond had come at a fortuitous time, as Lord Erroll said. It was a notion which his friend, Sir Alexander MacByrne, agreed with.

"I've no wish to fight the king," Alex said as the two knights sat together in a tavern later that evening. "I've heard that Lord Erroll considers standing wi' Douglas."

"He didna outright deny it when he and Lord Albermarle discussed the matter earlier," Lachlan confirmed. "I'd think that, were he a mind to keep out of the quarrel, he would have said so."

He regarded Alex with a sidelong glance; a sense of guilt prickled at the back of his neck. Alex had been his friend since childhood. It was Lachlan who had brought him to Lord Erroll— when he'd sought a place in the earl's guard, Alex had followed. It was Lachlan's fault; Lachlan was the reason Alex faced the possibility of conflict with the king. He took a long draught of his ale to silence his conscience.

"I find that the more I think on it, the more eager I am to go. Lord Kildrummond is a hospitable man, and I am curious about the purpose of this summons."

Alex twisted his own goblet of ale in his hands, his head bent as he reflected on this turn of events. His golden hair was tied at the nape of his neck in a queue, but a lock at his forehead had fallen over his right eye.

"I dinna recall meeting yer Kildrummond kinsmen," Alex observed.

"I dinna think ye have. My aunt, that is, my father's youngest sister, were married off at a young age to the Earl of Kildrummond. 'Twas my grandfather's hope to revive his squandered wealth wi' the union. As ye can see, that didna go so well for him." He held his arms out, displaying himself to illustrate the point.

"Ye poor soul," Alex responded dryly. "Having to make yer way in the world like the rest of us. How *do* ye manage?"

Grinning, Lachlan caught the eye of the serving wench that wended her way through the tables. Tipping his chin to her, he lifted his goblet and wiggled the stem back and forth between his fingertips.

Though other customers also awaited a top-up to their goblets, the serving girl made straight for Lachlan. She was a buxom lass, with shimmering, copper-colored hair, inviting grey eyes and a plump, pink mouth. It was a mouth which Lachlan knew intimately.

God's bones, it was a mouth which intimate parts of his *body* knew intimately.

She bent over the table unnecessarily as she filled his goblet, presenting the pillowy mounds of her bosoms to him. Lachlan gazed at her unabashedly.

Or perhaps it was Alex to whom she presented her bosoms. The two friends did not make sport of comparing their bedmates, but Lachlan did know that Alex had carnal knowledge of her, too. In fact, there were probably very few men in this tavern who *hadn't* had a turn with the comely, copper-haired lass.

"Ye dinna mind coming wi' me, d'ye?" Lachlan asked when she'd gone. "If ye'd rather no', I'll bring MacAndrews in yer stead. 'Tis no trouble."

"Nay, 'tis fine. I wouldna mind some time away."

"I'm glad to hear it." Lachlan downed his ale in one swallow and, stretching his arms above his head, peered across the room to the serving wench. "Well then, Alex, I'm off to bed."

Alex followed his gaze. "Ye go on, I'll send her yer way when her work here's done. I think she were after ye, anyway."

*****

Warm in his bed, the serving wench from the tavern asleep against his chest, Lachlan thought of the journey ahead. He had not seen his aunt in a very long time and would enjoy the reunion.

Of her husband, Lord Kildrummond, he remembered little. He only recalled that he had a similar, regal appearance to Lord Albermarle. Both men, if he remembered correctly, were tall and broad, with commanding, handsome features and a firm but gentle countenance. Both men were greatly respected.

Of the happenings at Kildrummond he remembered even less. His father had not taken him there often, neither as a boy nor in later years. The details were hazy, but Lachlan seemed to remember there had been a mistress. A very public mistress, which caused Lady Glinis great shame. Indeed Lord Kildrummond had settled the woman into a hut close to Glendalough Castle so that he would have regular access to her.

It was a wonder he didn't just set her up in the castle proper, since he was so determined to flaunt her.

The mistress, Lachlan knew, was the reason his aunt usually came to visit them, instead of the other way around. He did not blame her; he felt deeply sorry for her, in fact.

Glancing at the sleeping lass by his side, her bare, creamy shoulders and naked breasts so appealing in the whispering light of the fire, he was afflicted by a stab of guilt. For with a bounty of beautiful maids wherever he went, Lachlan wasn't at all certain he wouldn't do the same if he were in Lord Kildrummond's place.

It was just as well that he had no intention of ever marrying.

## *Three*

Moira was a patient lass. It was something she prided herself on. She could sit at a tapestry for hours on end, working by even the poorest of light, and concentrate on the most delicate embroidery with not a whimper of frustration.

But even she had her limits, and her patience had just about worn thin. The icy March wind had stolen the last whisper of feeling from her fingertips; her nose trickled like the nearby brae; her heels refused to dig into the trampled, ice-slicked snow beneath her feet.

Muttering an unladylike curse beneath her breath, she braced herself one more time, closed her eyes, and heaved with all her might.

Her bloody, stubborn cow would not budge!

Mocking her futile effort, the beast lolled its horned head and emitted an insufferable bleat.

"Fine, freeze out here, ye stubborn wench," Moira tugged at the cow's long red fur in retaliation then directed her scowl to Niall. Her dearest, closest friend in all the world leaned against his old grey-and-white speckled mare, which was tethered to the side of her hut, and took in the spectacle with mirth.

"Please, dinna feel obliged to help me at all," she shouted.

Niall shook his head, his sandy hair swaying loosely over his brow. "She doesna like me."

"Excuses."

"'Tis no'. Last time I tried to help ye, she horned me in the arse."

"Perhaps if ye had some padding on yer arse it wouldna have been a problem, ye twig!"

"Ye're one to talk," Niall taunted with a laugh. "Ye're as lanky as I am."

Moira conceded, throwing her willowy arms into the air. She pondered her dilemma before deciding there was only one course of action left—one which earned the animal a furious glower.

"I didna want to do this," she muttered.

Stomping the short distance to her hut, she retrieved her pot of treacle from its shelf above the oven. Removing the fired clay lid, she wistfully admired the meager dollop of sweet, dark syrup. It was all she had left, and she'd been hoping to make a treat for herself this evening. Market was not for another four days, and even if it were sooner, she didn't have the coin to waste on frivolities this time.

Now she'd have to use her precious treacle to coax the cow into its pen, for it was far too cold outside to leave the beast there. Though she deserved to freeze, the damnable thing.

Moira snatched a fresh handful of rushes from the animals' stall and, with a final gaze of longing, scooped out the last of the treacle. Marching back outside she shoved the sticky-sweet syrup under the cow's muzzle.

The animal tilted her shaggy, red head, lured by the scent of the treat. Lumbering forward she followed Moira, who guided her with backwards steps.

"That's it, come on ye big stupid beast," she encouraged.

The cow followed happily, intent on the treat in the lass's outstretched hand. Once she'd been rewarded and secured in her stall Moira went back out for the sheep.

"Ye can help me wi' them at least," she called to Niall, who was still leaning against his mount.

"Aye, all right."

Working together they herded the sheep into the hut and closed the door against the winter chill. Moira removed her cloak and took Niall's from him, then hung them on the makeshift peg, which her mother had lodged into the mudded walls long ago.

"I dinna believe ye gave her the treacle," Niall lamented. "I was looking forward to this special treat ye said ye'd be baking."

"What makes ye think ye'd be getting any of it?" Moira snorted. "Ye've a mother of yer own to feed ye."

"Ye're right, I forget sometimes yer on yer own now, wi yer mam gone and all. Ye couldna share a piece of bannock, could ye? I'm half starved."

Moira slanted him a long-suffering look, but his impish grin softened her. The devil; she could never be annoyed with him for long.

"Oh, go on." She fetched him the heel of the loaf she'd made the previous morning. Taking the stale offering eagerly, Niall bit firmly into it, ripping the hardened bread with his teeth like a wolf with fresh meat.

"That's grand, that," he sighed, chewing loudly.

Moira placed a portion of the loaf into her own mouth, then took a seat on her worn, wooden stool by the fire. Niall took the single armchair beside her, his customary spot, and stretched his hands and feet towards the warmth of the flames. It was a scene that had replayed itself regularly since they were children. The only difference was that, where once Lilian labored over the tapestry, it was Moira who now held the needle and colored thread in her chapped, raw fingers.

The particular piece that she was working on had been commissioned for the Countess of Leslie. Since the lady's husband had only held the newly-created earldom of Leslie for ten years, the lady had made it a priority to accumulate possessions. As if an abundance of *things* would somehow substantiate the family's inherent nobility. It was commonly known that the tapestries and needlework of Moira MacInnes were particularly exquisite, and Lady Leslie appreciated the lass's creativity and fine hand. Moira was only too happy to oblige.

But the coin from her last commission had nearly run out. If she did not sell some of her ready-made pieces at market, the days ahead would be lean indeed. Since she could not count on that, she'd been burning the wick at both ends for nearly a sennight just to finish Lady Leslie's latest tapestry.

"When does she want it finished?" Niall inquired, tossing another log of turf onto the modest fire.

"In a month. But she's offered a bonus if I finish early." Holding the tapestry to the light of the fire, Moira inspected the stitches where she'd left off before taking up the pattern again.

"Why dinna ye draw the curtain," Niall suggested.

"Aye, I shall. I just need a wee while to warm my fingers first."

There was a stretch of companionable silence, punctured only by the occasional shuffle of the animals against the rushes, before Moira spoke again. "Ye havena mentioned Janet's name in a while. How d'ye fare these days wi' her?"

"I have given up on the lovely Janet," Niall answered heavily.

"I dinna believe for one second that ye've fallen out of love wi' her."

"What purpose is there in being in love wi' *her* when she'll never fall in love wi' *me*?"

"Ye dinna ken that."

"But I do. She's too busy chasing after Dougall MacFadyen. Next to him, I've no' a chance in heaven of winning her heart. The only time she kens I'm alive is market day when she buys her da's ale from us."

"Next to Dougall MacFadyen ye're pig fodder," she agreed, recalling the handsome captain of Glendalough's guard.

"Thanks for yer support," he retorted.

"Nevertheless, I dinna believe ye've no chance of winning her heart. First of all, Dougall MacFadyen wouldna look twice at her. Lovely as she is, Janet's nowhere near the most beautiful lass in the village—never mind what *ye* may think. And Dougall sees many other villages besides Kildrummond almost daily, wi' all *their* lasses too. If she's after him, she'll soon discover he'll no' be interested.

"Second," she continued, "yers isna the only ale stall at market, yet she comes to ye time and again. She kens full well ye're alive, at least."

"No' that it does me any good; she doesna look twice at me."

Moira exhaled and dropped her tapestry to her lap. "If she doesna look twice at ye, it's yer own fault. Ye never say anything to her when she does come except "cask of bitter?" For heaven's sake, the lass probably doesna even ken yer name. As much as ye'd like to, ye canna blame *that* on Dougall MacFadyen."

Niall brooded over the accusation briefly. "Ye're probably right," he shrugged.

"I *am* right," Moira asserted. "Ye go and speak to her. Let her ken how ye feel, and see if she doesna pay ye more attention."

"Aye, I can do that. I can tell her how I feel."

"Next market day."

Niall hesitated. "Maybe the one after next."

"Coward."

Chafing his hands on his plaid, Niall stood. "I'd best be off, then, while I've still got the light. Ye coming into the village tomorrow?"

"Perhaps, if I have time. Depends on how this tapestry comes along tonight."

"If ye do, there's a fresh batch of mead waiting for ye. Mam's been given the last of Glendalough's honey to brew, but it isna due to be collected until Thursday."

"Ye'll come by if I dinna make it out?"

"Of course."

Setting aside her work, Moira walked her friend out to his mount. As Niall untethered the reins, they both glanced to the horizon, where a lone figure on horseback made a leisurely course straight for them.

"Ah, speaking of Dougall MacFadyen," Moira murmured.

"Lady Moira, how be ye this aft?" the captain greeted her when he was close enough to be heard. A fur cloak covered his shoulders, and the upper portion of his plaid was wrapped around his head to keep his ears warm. Even bundled as he was, Dougall MacFadyen was unnaturally handsome.

"I am fine, thank ye, Dougall. Can I hope one day ye'll stop calling me 'Lady Moira'? I dinna recall ever giving the impression I were a lady."

"Ye are yer father's daughter. Yer a lady whether ye like it or no'." He teased her affectionately, as an older brother might tease his sister. "Sir Niall, how be ye?"

"I am well," Niall answered, awestruck by the captain. Moira snickered for all the disparaging of Dougall the young brewer did behind his back.

"Will ye come in and warm yerself?" She gestured to the hut.

"Thank ye, lass, but I'll no' stay long. I'm here to deliver a message."

When he hesitated, Moira prodded, "And the message is?"

Dougall sighed, his massive shoulders rising and falling beneath his cloak. "If I tell ye, ye must promise ye'll no' go off on me the way ye do. All right…yer father requests that ye attend the evening meal on the morrow. And he bids that I beg ye to wear the fine silk gown he purchased for ye on yer birthday last, for 'tis a grand occasion."

His message was received with round, innocent eyes. "What d'ye mean, go off the way I do?"

"Ye canna be serious. The last time I were sent to invite ye to the meal, ye gave me a right piece of yer mind about how ye'd no' be ordered about. Bloody hell, I've never been so frightened of such a wee lass in all my life!"

"Honestly, Dougall, as handsome as ye are, ye've no idea about a woman's whims. The last time ye delivered my father's message, ye said he *requires* me to attend. Since ye've said he *requests* it this time, then I shall of course oblige. But I beg ye tell him in return that I'll wear my own gown, the one that I purchased wi' my own coin."

"Aye, by working *his* land, and taking *his* coin when ye've none of yer own," Dougall countered with a devious wink.

Moira reddened. "I'm no' so daft as to refuse a gift when it's sorely needed. I'd imagine ye wouldna be either, were ye in my position."

"Och, I'm only teasing. If I were in yer position, I'd be lodging at Glendalough, not stubbornly clinging to this peasant life ye're so fond of." When she scowled, Dougall added, "Come, now, my lady. We ken ye're entitled to much more, and his Lordship would happily give it ye—if ye'd only let him. But we also ken how hard ye work to support yerself and we admire ye for yer determination."

"She kens that, Dougall," Niall said eagerly. "Ye ken that, aye Moira?"

"Aye, I ken," she allowed begrudgingly.

"Well then, that's settled. I'll report back that ye'll be there. That should please him. What about the gown?"

Moira shook her head. "No gown."

"Well, no one can say I didna try. Take care, lass." Dougall turned his mount, but before he nudged the beast onward Moira stopped him.

"D'ye ken why it is my father wishes me there?"

Dougall glanced backwards over his shoulder. "I'd tell ye if I could, my lady, but I dinna ken that myself."

Once he was a distance away, Niall put in his opinion. "He's right, ye ken. If I were in yer place I'd take advantage of what was on offer more than ye do. Ye do ken what kind of food they have there every night, aye? Ye're here fretting about the last of yer treacle while they eat it by the barrel up there."

"The difference between ye and me, Niall MacCormack, is that I dinna think wi' my belly."

"Canna argue wi' that one." He grinned, untying his own mare and hopping up into the saddle. "But if ye do happen to find yer way to Glendalough tomorrow evening, see if ye canna snatch a few bits for me, hmm? Maybe some cakes or pastries."

"Oh, be off wi' ye." Moira slapped at his shin. But as always, where Niall was concerned, she could not stay put out at him for long.

# *Four*

The journey from Aberdeenshire to Moray had been long and painfully cold. Intent on reaching Glendalough before evening, Lord Albermarle had pushed the party onward. He allowed minimal stops, only what was necessary to feed and water the animals. It was of no concern to him that his companions were rendered miserable by his ambition.

To make the going worse, the wind had not been kind; it gusted steadily over the open ground, raking the travelers unforgivingly and without respite. Though they were well wrapped, furs and woolens layered atop one another, the wind still found its way through gaps and seams to slice at fragile flesh, and bite into weary bones.

They reached the castle as the last light of dusk faded into the inky night sky. Every member of the party—including the horses— looked utterly wretched. Earning sympathy from the servants who received them, they were immediately shown to private chambers in which fires, hot broth and other comforts had been readied well in advance.

Huddled now in front of his own cozy hearth, a cup of spiced, hot wine pressed to his lips with both hands, Lachlan bathed in the heat of the flames. The deep, bone-racking shivers, which had come upon him had, for the most part, subsided. But every now and again he would be taken by another round of them, and would have no choice but to wait until the uncontrollable vibrations had passed.

It was nothing new; being cold was a condition to which he'd grown accustomed. The life of a knight was not one of comfort, and training was undertaken in the entire spectrum of weather: rain, heat or violent snowstorm. On top of that, his chamber at Slains was abnormally drafty and the small hearth inadequate for the space.

The chamber in which he was lodged at Glendalough was far more luxurious than anything he'd previously experienced. Lachlan was awestruck by the rich furnishings and generous proportions. And though such things had never been of interest to him before, he found the tapestry that hung on the wall opposite the bed rather stunning.

Abandoning the comfort of the fire, he crossed the room to study the workmanship of the piece.

The skill of its master was extraordinary, the stitching worked, no doubt, by a remarkably fine hand. Threads of muted greens, browns, and yellows blended together so exquisitely it was as if the color palette were the product of some divine or magical dream. As natural and complex as a real-life forest or loch. The tapestry depicted a woodland scene: deer played effortlessly with each other in a border that circled the central figure of a noble hunter. Lord Kildrummond, likely—unless the tapestry pre-dated the earl. Lachlan did not think so, for the threads had not yet faded with the passage of time.

A knock at the door interrupted his musings.

"Come," he called.

The door swung wide, revealing the shapely figure of his aunt, Lady Glinis Kildrummond. Lord Albermarle had not exaggerated; she was as beauteous as ever, though her ordeal with the earl's illness had etched strain onto her lovely features. She smiled as she stepped into the room and closed the door after her. Her rich, dark eyes were warm and eager.

"Lachlan, my dear nephew." She opened her arms to him.

"My lady." Equally as eager, Lachlan wrapped her in a firm embrace, lifting her feet off the floor as he did.

"I am so glad ye've come," she declared when he'd set her back down. She rubbed his back affectionately, as if he were still a lad, rather than the broad, hardened viscount knight he'd become. "Ye look well."

"And ye." Lachlan pulled back, holding Lady Glinis at arms' length. "Though ye look tired. Are ye certain ye're no' ill as well?"

"Och, 'tis no such thing. Besides, I'd hardly complain given the state his Lordship is in." Gesturing to the fire, Lady Glinis took the chair that Lachlan had just vacated. Lachlan pulled a footstool next to her.

"Is it as bad as Lord Albermarle says?"

She lifted her delicate shoulders. "I dinna ken what Lord Albermarle has said, but if ye've been told his Lordship will die, 'tis true."

"How long does he have left?"

"He doesna leave his bed much anymore, though he can if he must. And he's still in good spirits; that, at least, is a blessing. I reckon he'll no' make it to spring. Or if he does, 'twill only be just."

"A month then, maybe two," Lachlan reflected. "Is he in pain at all?"

"It depends on who ye ask. *I* would tell ye that his pain is considerable at times."

"What would *he* say?"

Lady Glinis smiled begrudgingly. "He'd likely tell ye he's fit as a bear and to mind yer own affairs."

Lachlan barked a laugh. "I dinna recall much of him, but that seems fitting wi' what I do remember."

"At least we can say his illness hasna changed him."

Without warning, the door to the chamber swung open, interrupting the conversation. Lachlan and Lady Glinis turned, both startled by the intrusion. In strode Alex, a half a piece of manchet bread in his hand. The other half-chewed piece was lodged indelicately in his cheek.

"Lachlan, ye must have a look in the kitchens, I've just—" He stopped abruptly at the sight of Lady Glinis. Frantically he chewed his mouthful and swallowed before speaking again. "I apologize, my lady. I thought the Viscount Strathcairn were alone."

Lady Glinis rose, and turned her eyes to Lachlan. "I'll leave ye be for now, but we shall speak later at the meal, aye?"

"Of course." Lachlan bowed to his aunt. She returned a curtsy, and nodded to Alex on exiting the chamber. Alex bowed his respects, hiding the half-eaten piece of bread behind his back.

Once the door was firmly shut, and the echoes of Lady Glinis's retreating footsteps gone, Alex straightened. He looked at Lachlan, his eyes wide.

"By the stars in heaven, who were that lady?"

"She is my aunt, the Countess of Kildrummond."

Alex gaped. "*That* is yer aunt?"

"Aye, what of it?"

"When ye spoke of yer Kildrummond kin, I pictured yer aunt...er...more advanced in years."

"Why would ye think that? I told ye she were married at a young age."

"For all I kent, that could have happened fifty years ago."

"She were married at the tender age of fifteen. Lord Kildrummond were closing in on fifty years himself at the time. As the earl is now in his seventies—"

"That is a little more reasonable," Alex pondered. "Still, if she be forty-odd years, she doesna look it. She is the most beautiful woman I've ever laid eyes on."

Lachlan studied Alex, his eyes narrowed to slits. "Whether she is or isna is no concern of yers. I hold ye like a brother, Alex, but I'll no' hesitate to pound ye black-and-blue if ye think to make bed sport of my aunt."

Alex reddened. "Dinna pay me any mind. I'd considered no such thing, I were only saying. Anyway, will ye have time to show me the grounds before the evening meal?"

Lachlan's glare held firm a second or two longer, in which pause Alex innocently bit into another chuck of his wheat bread. Satisfied that his warning had been heeded, Lachlan answered, "I could manage it, I think. I'll take ye as far as the brae to the south. Give me an hour more to warm myself, and then I'll fetch ye from yer chamber."

True to his word, Lachlan fetched Alex within the hour. His friend, too, was enjoying the luxury of a chamber that was far grander than what he was accustomed to.

"Did ye see?" Alex boasted excitedly when he opened the door. "I've a bed big enough for two! And look: six strides from wall to wall." He backed up to the far wall and took six long paces to illustrate his point. A silly grin spread across his face from ear to ear. "In my chamber at Slains, I could stretch myself on the floor and touch wall to wall wi' fingers and toes."

"Ye daft fool, dinna let anyone see ye behaving so, else they'll take ye for a peasant in knights' clothing."

"I'm sorry. 'Tis only that I canna believe I've been granted a guest chamber such as this. Surely it were meant for noble visitors."

"Ye're probably right," Lachlan agreed. "I did tell ye Lord Kildrummond were hospitable."

"Aye, but I figured ye meant we wouldna be thrown in wi' the chattel."

"D'ye still want me to show ye the land or would ye rather I leave ye here to pace yer chamber like a madman?"

Alex grinned sheepishly. "Och, give over." Removing his cloak from the wardrobe, he added, "Did ye see? I've a wardrobe fit for an earl!"

Lachlan started with a tour of Glendalough itself, guiding Alex around parts of the castle he had not seen—which was just about everything not directly en route from his chamber to the kitchens. Female servants young and old stopped and stared at the two handsome knights, blushing and curtseying. They made a striking pair. Both were tall, lean and well proportioned from their extensive training, but their complexions contrasted each other: Lachlan's dark hair, even darker eyes and fair skin complemented Alex, who was blonde, green-eyed and had the sun-kissed coloring of his Norse ancestors.

Neither minded the attention. In fact, they rather enjoyed it—though neither would admit such a thing to the other.

Once their tour of the castle was completed, they headed to the stables to fetch their awaiting horses, which had been fed, watered and rested. From there, they headed through the gates of the curtain wall and into the village.

A variety of shops and other trade establishments, interspersed by individual dwellings, expanded westward from the immediate castle grounds. The buildings were by no means opulent, but they were in good repair. Modest and sturdy, simply but practically constructed and adorned.

The people of Kildrummond were a living mirror of the village's dwellings. They too were modest and sturdy, simply dressed, but appeared to enjoy a comfortable, well-nourished existence. And they were friendly. They welcomed their visitors with smiles and warm greetings. Especially the women, who were all taken with the handsome young strangers.

"There isna a tavern," Alex lamented when they'd completed a cursory round of the village's main body.

"Aye, but there's plenty of ale and mead at the castle."

"These comely lasses here in the village willna be at the castle."

"On the contrary," Lachlan argued, "I'm given to understand that many of them are called in to serve when there are guests." He nodded flirtatiously to one particularly bonnie specimen, who giggled and curtsied in return.

From the village they cut south, heading to the brae that, in the summer months, burbled and wended its way through Kildrummond, dividing it nearly in half. In the grips of a March wind, however, the frozen brae was as far as they were able to go before they were forced to turn back.

They met only one other living soul on their return: a young lass, wrapped in layers against the bitter cold. She kneeled at the stream, scooping a peasant's bucket through a broken patch of ice. She glanced up, a pair of large, blue eyes fixing on the two men with an expression that was somewhere between curiosity and annoyance.

Lachlan met her gaze, nodded politely, and continued on his way. She was not particularly beautiful, her face merely pleasant. And despite the bulk of her simple garments, hers was clearly a scrawny, unappealing frame.

Almost as soon as he'd noticed her, Lachlan forgot her.

\*\*\*

The great hall of Glendalough was joyous and lively that night. Plentiful quantities of roast meats, baked pastries and even the last of the castle's preserved fruits were displayed for the guests to sample. The feast was accompanied by bottomless pitchers of wine and ale. Musicians threaded through the esteemed members of Clan Douglas, both local and visiting.

Lord Albermarle was present with his lovely wife, Rosamund, who had journeyed to Glendalough to join her husband on this momentous occasion. Even James Douglas, the ninth Earl of Douglas after his murdered brother William, availed himself of Lord Kildrummond's hospitality. Indeed, the head of Clan Douglas travelled all the way from his Lanarkshire estate, close to the Scottish Borderlands.

As lively as the feast was, and as bountifully as he was enjoying everything on offer, Lachlan could not seem to work out *what* the particular occasion *was*. Excitement and merriment filled the hall, yet no one seemed to know why they were so excited, so merry.

Adding to the confusion was the fact that Lord Kildrummond had not joined in the feasting. Talk circulated that he was not well enough this night to attend, and remained in his bed, with Lady Kildrummond at this side, through the entire meal.

Lachlan did his best to put it all out of his mind and simply enjoy the event. He almost succeeded; his enjoyment was hindered only by the nagging curiosity of why he'd been summoned to

Glendalough in the first place. But there were enough lovely lasses to overshadow his private concerns. He threw himself into enjoying them as well, enjoying their rosy cheeks, their glances and smiles, their curves and pillowy softness.

Alex, too, was in high spirits. The knight indulged himself in the ale, which flowed freely; by the time the platters were cleared away he was quite in his cups.

"Lachlan, isna this fan—fantastic?" he hiccupped. The jerk of his body caused him to spill ale over the rim of his cup.

"Easy there, man. What's gotten into ye? Ye act as though ye've never been to a feast before."

"I ken, isna it grand? I've no' had so much fun in years."

"I'll no' begrudge ye yer fun," Lachlan conceded. "Things have been tense of late. 'Tis good to shake it off for a night."

"Aye." Alex bobbed his head vigorously. "Aye, 'tis. Tonight I am content to forget about old Fiery Face, to forget about Slains, about Lord Erroll and the whole Hay clan. Tonight I'll drink myself daft, find myself a nice, soft lass, and forget all about the troubles that await us when we return."

"I'd say ye're halfway there."

Alex squinted into his cup, examining the dregs intently. "Ye're right. Halfway isna good enough. Wench!" He raised his cup above his head and lifted his chin to a nearby serving lass.

The maid approached and filled both men's cups, encouraging their flirtations as she did. When she'd gone, Alex gazed across the room, furrowing his brow at something that caught his attention.

"Isna that the lass we saw at the brae this aft?" He pointed, sloppy and tactless.

Lachlan followed his finger to the rear of the hall. There, indeed, was the lass from the brae. She remained seated at one of the few trestle tables that had not been removed, and conversed mildly with two elderly clanswomen.

"How in the blazes of hell did ye make her out when ye could hardly see the bottom of yer cup?" he demanded, incredulous.

Alex winked. "I've a gift when it comes to comely lasses, I do."

Lachlan snorted. "Comely my arse! She's the body of a young lad, flat as a board. She isna even dressed finely."

Alex pursed his lips, considering the lass's plain tunic of umber wool, and her simply bound hair, which was a bland, colorless kind of light brown in the surrounding torchlight.

"Perhaps. But she's lovely eyes."

"I think that's the ale speaking. Besides, ye'll no' be looking at her eyes if ye get her into yer bed. *That's* when the shape of a woman counts."

Alex flipped a hand dismissively and drank from his fresh cup. His gaze moved on to other, lovelier maids.

Lachlan, though, could not redirect his attention as easily as his friend. The presence of the unexceptional lass in the unexceptional clothing intrigued him. It was then that he noticed others seemed to be talking about her. He watched as eyes darted towards her and then quickly away, as lips were hidden behind hands to shield unkind whispers and giggles.

The lass noticed, too. Knowing this, Lachlan wondered if the conversation she kept up with the two elderly women was for the sake of her pride.

His interest was a brief aberration, and it passed eventually. Soon he and Alex were talking of other things, and indulging in the atmosphere once more.

Just as the merriment was winding down, in the wee hours of the morning, they were interrupted by Lady Glinis. She approached their table gracefully; all eyes in the immediate vicinity followed her with admiration. Any that did not know who she was at least recognized her importance.

Upon noticing her, Alex jumped up; he swayed a little as he bowed. Lachlan bowed as well, though being less inebriated, he did not wobble like his friend.

"Nephew, I am sorry I didna have the chance to speak wi' ye at the meal as we said we would."

"Dinna think on it, my lady," Lachlan assured her. "I ken ye're busy wi' his Lordship. How is he this evening?"

"He does poorly, though in truth I've seen him worse. He has just woken, actually, and wishes to speak wi' ye now."

"There is no rush. It can wait to the morrow."

Lady Glinis lowered her eyes. "'Tis best ye see him now. Not only because he bids ye, but because there is no guarantee that he will be any better on the morrow."

"Of course. If that be his wish." Tossing a wink to Alex, he said, "I'll tell ye all on my return."

He followed her out of the hall and to the keep. It escaped his notice that Alex had not taken his eyes off the lady for a single moment.

## Five

The instant that Lady Glinis entered the hall, the skin at the back of Moira's neck began to tingle. It was as if she had some sort of innate awareness where the Countess of Kildrummond was concerned. Moira observed from the corner of her eye, careful not to let the lady see her watching, as she approached the two visiting knights and ushered the dark-haired one away.

Only when Lady Glinis had gone was Moira able to release the tension that had crept into her shoulders. Oh, how that woman made her uncomfortable. Never a smile, never a kind word did she offer. Ever since childhood Moira had known, on some level, that her very existence offended Lord Kildrummond's wife.

As she grew older she came to understand the reason. To sympathize with the unfortunate lady, even. Were she in Glinis's shoes, Moira would probably feel the same way. What woman could tolerate such close proximity to the bastard offspring of her husband's mistress, after all?

There were many reasons why Moira avoided Glendalough; Lady Glinis was one of them. It was for her sake that Moira had declined Lord Kildrummond's offer that she live at the castle when her mother died (not that the lady appeared in any way grateful, or even appreciative). In fact, Moira would have preferred to avoid the meal tonight, too, if she could. If she hadn't felt guilty about denying a dying man's request.

"And how is that young lad of yers these days?" The elderly clanswoman with whom Moira had been chatting cut into her silent fretting.

She studied the woman, her brows knitting together. "*My* young lad?"

"Aye, that tall, gangly one. What be his name?"

"That'd be Niall MacCormack." Her companion tapped her wrinkled finger on the slatted table board, adding authority to the statement.

"Ah yes, young Niall MacCormack. Will ye be announcing yer wedding soon? I'm sure it'd make his Lordship happy to ken ye'll be looked after. He does love ye so, even if ye are a bas—er, well, that is to say 'twould make him happy, is all."

Moira pressed her lips together and forced a smile. "I'm sure it would. But unfortunately Niall MacCormack is only a friend. He and I willna be announcing our wedding plans any time soon. I *guarantee* that!"

"Oh, well that's a shame. 'Tis no bad thing to be the wife of a brewer. They do a decent trade, they do."

Eager to end this particular line of conversation, Moira racked her brain for something else to talk about. Thankfully she was relieved of her predicament by the reappearance of Lady Glinis—and the fact that Moira was relieved to see Lady Glinis emphasized how uncomfortable her predicament was.

Glinis towered over Moira, who had to lift her chin to meet the lady's steely gaze. "His Lordship wishes an audience wi' ye."

A chill ran across Moira's shoulders at the countess's veiled hostility. She refused to let Glinis see it, though.

"If ye'll excuse me." She smiled brightly to her companions. Rising from the bench, she followed Lady Glinis who glided from the hall with not a single backwards glance.

The lady proceeded through the lower corridors of the castle, and on to the keep. Reaching the staircase, she lifted the hem of her pale blue silk gown. The grace with which she moved enchanted Moira, who in turn bunched the fabric of her own simple gown in her fists and lifted the hem just enough that she wouldn't trip.

Their manner was just one aspect of a world of difference that existed between the two women. Their hair, their clothes, even their shoes told of that difference in status. Lady Glinis wore exquisite slippers of satin, which had hardly been worn at all. Next to such finery, Moira was slightly ashamed of her rivelins, which she'd made herself from her own stock of rawhide and laced together around her feet with leather thongs. The footwear of a peasant.

Not for the first time Moira wondered what it might be like to give in, and let his Lordship provide her with financial stability, a comfortable life. It was a hope the earl had not abandoned despite Moira's persistent rejection. She rejected the notion even now, for as a child she'd resolved never to be at the mercy of a man the way her mother had. She would not open herself up to the derision of others.

Not that it did much good; the highborn Douglases looked down on her with derision anyway. But at least she had not invited it, not the way her mother had.

Ending the uncomfortable silence in which the pair travelled, Lady Glinis halted at Lord Kildrummond's bedchamber. Moira felt her heart pick up speed; she had not seen the earl since he'd taken to his bed with his illness. A pang of guilt pricked her conscience over that. Despite what her personal resolutions were, the man *was* her father, and he *did* love her.

As if divining her thoughts, Glinis shot Moira a warning glare. *Behave*, her eyes seemed to say. Then she rapped curtly on the door. Without waiting for an answer she pushed it open and stepped through. Moira trailed in after her, her entrance meek.

"Yer Lordship." Lady Glinis curtsied, and immediately her countenance softened. A warm smile came to her face as she took in the men in the room.

Moira cringed, for she had not expected such an audience. Besides the earl there were also Lord Albermarle and Eamon Douglas, Glendalough's steward.

A third man stood against the far wall, the dark-haired knight that Lady Glinis had led from the hall not long before she'd returned to fetch her. Moira recognized him immediately as one of the riders she'd seen earlier that day by the brae. He'd been too far away in the hall for her to see his face clearly, but she saw now that it was, indeed, him.

The man looked at her now with passive curiosity. A shot of hot pride bolted through her. She knew his type: full of himself and his good looks. Thought he could get any beautiful lass he desired. She disliked his kind thoroughly.

Moira lifted her chin and stared coolly back. She was determined that this stranger would be of as little consequence to her as she so obviously was to him.

"Yer Lordship." She curtseyed properly to the ailing earl. A touch of hurt came to Lord Kildrummond's eyes at the formal greeting, which Lady Glinis noticed. She pursed her lips disapprovingly.

"Moira, my sweetling. I'm glad ye've come." The earl's voice was raspy, and his breathing labored, as if he'd worn himself out by those few words alone. Alarmed, Moira glanced uncertainly towards Lord Albermarle, with whom she enjoyed a friendly companionship.

"Aye, ye didna think he were so far gone, did ye?"

"Perhaps ye might come more often now," Lady Glinis added crisply.

"Hush now." Lord Kildrummond held a hand up for his wife. To Moira he said, "Will ye have a seat?"

The only available seat in the room was the bedside stool. Gingerly she moved towards it, noticing, as she arranged herself on it, that she was the only one sitting. Lady Glinis probably wasn't too happy about that, she though miserably.

\*\*\*

Standing, as he was, outside the group, Lachlan surveyed the interaction between the others present. He maintained an impartial expression, though curiosity tickled beneath the surface. Who was this lass, this plainly dressed, plain-faced lass, who seemed to be afforded such courtesy?

"I'd first like to thank ye for making the journey here this evening," the earl addressed Lord Albermarle and Lachlan. "As ye ken, I've no' long left in this world; I'll be meeting my maker soon enough."

"No' too soon, we hope," Lady Glinis spoke earnestly.

"Nevertheless, I've an immediate concern wi' making sure my lands and family are taken care of. Now we all ken what trouble the king makes for Douglases, and wi' these recent confiscations of Douglas lands, I've a concern that Kildrummond might come into his sights. We are no' a wealthy people, but my lands are prosperous enough, and my people live in peace. I willna rest easy until I ken it'll continue this way after I'm gone."

"Lord Albermarle will see to that, yer Lordship," Lady Glinis assured him. "I've no doubt he'll manage the lands well enough."

Lord Albermarle exchanged a glance with Lord Kildrummond.

"As it happens, my dear, I've spoken wi' Edward already, and he accepts my decision that I'll no' be naming him my successor."

This shocked everyone in the room. Except for Lord Albermarle, who lowered his eyes.

"If no' Lord Albermarle, then who—" Lady Glinis broke off, her eyes widening excitedly. "Ye dinna mean our Lachlan, d'ye? Is that why ye've summoned him?"

"Aye, 'tis. Viscount Strathcairn, the title and the lands are yers upon my death, if ye want them."

Lachlan stared at the earl, his jaw hanging slack. "Yer Lordship? Why would ye choose me? I'm no'—"

"Ye're family," Lord Albermarle put in. "But no' *Douglas* family. If the lands are no longer in Douglas hands, Fiery Face will have a difficult time confiscating them should this feud continue the way it is."

Lady Glinis clapped her hands together gleefully. A slow, baffled smile spread across Lachlan's face.

"There is one condition, though," Lord Kildrummond continued.

"Anything."

"As these things go, there must be a tie stronger than the law; there must be a tie made by God. I'm sure it'll come as no surprise to ye that I wish ye to marry my daughter. Keep a little Douglas blood in the place, aye?"

"Yer daughter, my Lord?" Lachlan glanced questioningly to his aunt, whose elation had turned to disbelief. "Who be yer daughter?"

"I am," the plain-faced lass interjected shakily. She looked shocked, as though she might faint, and simultaneously so outraged that she might very well pound through the masonry with her bare fists.

Lachlan's confusion cleared swiftly. The mistress—of course. This lass was illegitimate. Studying her now, he saw the resemblance between her and Lord Kildrummond, though she was much more feminine than the earl. They had the same rounded jaw, the same high forehead. The eyes, too, were of the same wide shape and the same shimmering blue.

Chafing under the intruder's scrutiny, the lass scowled. "I'll do no such thing," she vowed, and stood abruptly.

"Now, Moira," Lord Kildrummond urged.

"Ye'll mind yer tongue and do as yer father says," Lady Glinis argued.

"My dear—"

"Nay, I'll no' hear it. Ye indulge that lass too much. Ne'er before have I seen a daughter behave so terribly towards her father. I would have been flogged in the village square if I dared speak to my own father in such a manner."

Lachlan said nothing, though in truth he, too, was appalled by the lass's brash outburst.

"Ye're in no position to defy him, Moira," Lord Albermarle added gently. "Ye live on his lands, free of rent—often enough," he amended when she shot him a challenging glare. "Ye're dependent on him for yer coin, too. Even when ye dinna take a direct offer, most of yer goods are sold at market to Douglases and Kildrummond tenants."

Moira opened her mouth. Unable to think of any argument, she closed it again. "I'll no' live on his lands, then. I can find another place to live, far away. I'll head north, or I'll find somewhere in our old border village. I can live anywhere, I dinna have to live in Moray."

"And struggle even harder than ye are now?"

"Moira, love, I think only of yer best interests," Lord Kildrummond promised.

Moira stared hard at the earl; then she turned her head to Lachlan. "What the bloody hell are *ye* looking at?" she spat. "Ye can forget about it. I'll no' be marrying the likes of ye!"

Then, before anyone could speak further, she whirled and bolted from the room.

"Moira!" Lady Glinis shouted after her. "Moira ye come back here this instant."

But the lass was gone. Exasperated, the lady dropped her hands to her sides. "Ye should have her dragged back here. That's what any father would do wi' a daughter so insolent."

Lord Kildrummond nodded, resigned. "Aye, I should. But I canna."

"Ye've ne'er been able to discipline that wee terror."

"My lady, she is in a state," Lord Albermarle said. "I agree wi' ye, that kind of behavior shouldna be tolerated, but give the lass a bit of sympathy. She'll come round."

"But what about Lachlan? Will ye still offer him Kildrummond if Moira runs off and he doesna marry her?"

"My lord, if I may," Lachlan put in. "Give me the morrow to speak wi' the lass. Perhaps I can bring her round to the idea."

"Aye. I'd be grateful if ye'd try." Lord Kildrummond smiled sadly. "I only want her safe. I only want to ken that my Lilian's lass is looked after once I'm gone."

Lachlan noticed the hurt and betrayal that crossed Lady Glinis's face. It was only there for a second, and in another flicker it was gone, smoothed out after years of practice.

He had never felt more sorry for the lady in his life.

## *Six*

No sooner had the weak light of the winter morning spread across the snow-covered land than there was a furious thumping at the door of the MacCormack family's hut.

"Can ye believe it?" Moira demanded as soon as a bleary-eyed Niall opened the door. "He's only gone and said I must marry."

"Good morning to ye, too," he yawned.

Moira threw him a frustrated look and began pacing the narrow doorstep. Niall knew well enough not to interrupt her when she was angry. Instead, he folded his spindly arms over his chest, leaned against the doorframe, and prepared to wait out her tirade.

"He's decided—ye'll never believe this—he's decided that no Douglas will inherit the earldom of Kildrummond. He's leaving it instead to a Strathcairn. Lachlan Ramsay is his name, and he's a landless viscount. But the man willna have Kildrummond unless he marries me. I mean, honestly Niall, who does that man think he is, giving my hand away like that to a perfect stranger?"

"Who does that man think he is? He's the Earl of Kildrummond, *and* yer father. If one of those conditions doesna give him the right to give yer hand to whomever he chooses, then the other certainly does."

"Ah, but how do we ken for certain he's my father?" Moira pointed accusingly, as if it were Niall that were guilty of a crime. "The only reason we think that is because my mother said so. But how do we ken she's told the truth?"

He shot her a pointed look. "Careful, Moira. That be yer mother ye're talking about. I'll no' have ye speaking ill of the dead, *especially* no' of Mistress Lilian."

Chastened, Moira lowered her glare to her feet, scrutinizing them as she trod back and forth over the same, narrow strip. "Ye ken I didna mean that. No' truly."

"I do. Now will ye come inside? Ye'll wear a pit into the ground if ye keep up that pacing, and *I'll* be the one my mam'll expect to bail out the water every time it rains."

"This is serious, Niall. I willna be forced to marry. I'll flee before that happens. Ye dinna think I will?" she challenged when he raised his brows.

"On the contrary, I'm sure ye will. But then ye'll expect me to come wi' ye, and then *we'll* have to be married, and I'd rather no', if it's all the same to ye."

Moira stared at him, her mouth agape. "I wouldna—" she stuttered before she saw his teasing grin. Defeated, her shoulders slumped. "Niall, what will I do?"

"Ye'll come in out of the cold, for a start. A man could freeze to death while he waits for ye to finish yer ranting." He stepped back, and when Moira crossed the threshold he closed the door after her.

Compared to Moira's lowly dwelling, Niall's family home was far more comfortable. Being the best and most sought after brewer in the village, Master MacCormack provided an admirable level of prosperity to his wife and children. Their main dwelling was sectioned into three distinct parts. The family area where they ate, cooked, slept and lived was situated at a distance from the stalls where they kept their modest collection of chattel. It was a luxury for which Moira inwardly yearned—the sounds and smells of animals sleeping could, on occasion, make for a long night.

The third section of the MacCormack family's dwelling was a secure room where the fermenting barrels of ale and mead were stored until they were either collected for the castle, or ready to be sold on market day. Master MacCormack spent his days in the alehouse, a separate outbuilding behind the main dwelling, but the finished goods were not kept there for fear of thievery.

As she stepped through to the family's living space, the rich, sour-sweet smell of yeast wrapped her in calm. It was a scent which she associated with the happy atmosphere of Niall's home, for Niall's home was indeed happy. Mary MacCormack, Niall's large, robust mother was seated by a central fire pit. Her ruddy complexion and matching hair glowed in the firelight as she bent over, tending to a loaf of the family's daily bread.

Beside her, Niall's youngest sister Imogen smiled demurely at Moira. The nine-year-old was busy grinding oats into flour on the worn, circular grindstone. Moira returned the lass's smile, cursing herself that she'd not done her own grinding yet. She'd been too preoccupied with the surprise her father had sprung that she'd rushed over to Niall's to unburden herself.

"Moira, love," Mary MacCormack greeted. "Come sit a while."

"Thank ye, Mistress MacCormack. I am sorry to be upon ye so early wi' my problems." Moira crossed the space and took a spot beside Imogen. "Shove over," she instructed the younger lass. Taking the handle of the stone from Imogen, she carried on with turning the half-ground grains into barley flour.

"Hush, now. We've been up wi' the sun—well, all of us but Niall here. I must say, though, I dinna see what ye've got to be all worked up over."

"Ye think his Lordship's right, then?"

Mary MacCormack shrugged her soft, round shoulders. "Whether 'tis right or no, 'tis his Lordship's right to give yer hand to whichever man he chooses."

Moira slumped, and her hand paused in her work. "I dinna want to marry."

"I ken, child. But ye canna pretend to be surprised. Ye're of a marriageable age—past a marriageable age, actually—and the daughter of an earl. That ye live the way ye do now isna common, ye must ken that. His Lordship affords ye quite a bit of independence that ye've no right to expect."

Moira hated the truth in what she said. She did not want to be any man's property. She despised that the law of the land declared it so.

"Niall, how about ye fetch the lass a cup of mead?" Mary suggested to her son, who stood back from the fire, still half-asleep.

"Aye, get her bladdered. That'll change her mind."

Moira snickered, and Mary slapped at his knees as he sauntered into the aleroom. When he returned, he handed Moira a half-filled wooden cup and took the remaining space on the bench so that they were all nestled snugly together.

Moira let go of the grindstone handle to accept the beverage. Pressing her palms to the outside of the cup, she raised it to her lips. The mead had been spiced with cloves and thyme. She sipped at the sweet, luxurious flavor. There was a reason Master MacCormack was known as the best brewer in Moray, and his products sought exclusively by Glendalough Castle.

"Last of his Lordship's honey, that," Mary McCormack noted.

"Aye, Niall told me. Ye sure his Lordship willna mind?"

"Will his Lordship mind me offering a touch of his mead to his own daughter? Really, Moira!"

"Think on it as payment for making ye marry," Niall jested, nudging against her playfully. "In fact, ye should demand a whole barrel. Ye and I can drag it down to the brae. We'll get ye so drunk ye won't even ken ye're being wed. Problem solved."

"Ye'll do no such thing," Mary objected. "Feeding his Lordship's daughter mead is one thing, but letting her freeze to death down by the brae because she's too drunk to help herself is quite another."

"Give over, Mistress MacCormack, we wouldna freeze," Moira joined in the jesting. "We'd have enough liquor in our blood to keep us warm."

Mary snorted. "I feel sorry for whoever has been promised yer hand, for he's been given no lady, that's for sure."

A brisk knock at the door interrupted the easy chatter. Prompted by a nod from her mother, Imogen went to the door. Dusting her hands on the front of her homespun gown, she opened it only a crack, just enough to peek her head through.

"Odd child," Mary MacCormack muttered, shaking her head at her youngest daughter.

Low murmurs continued between the girl and whoever was on the other side. When Imogen was satisfied, she removed her head from the opening and peered back into the dim space.

"Mama, there's a man here to see our Moira."

"To see me?" Moira frowned.

She stood with Niall as Mary MacCormack bustled over to the door to see for herself who was outside. Pulling it open she stared, shocked, at the towering figure of Lachlan Ramsay.

"Can—can I help ye, sir?" she questioned.

"Yes, Mistress. I am Viscount Strathcairn. As I explained to yer wee one here," he gave Imogen a silly grin that set her giggling, "I've come to have a word wi' Lady Moira MacInnes."

"Viscount? Oh, sir, please ye come in, and forgive my daughter her ill manners." Flustered by the handsome knight, she waved her arm vigorously.

"I thank ye, Mistress—"

"MacCormack," a red-faced Mary informed him with pleasure. "I am Mary MacCormack, and this here be my eldest son, Niall."

"How did ye ken I were here?" Moira demanded acidly as soon as the door had closed again.

"Moira," Mary reprimanded, horrified by her poor manners.

Moira scowled. Then, overly-polite, she amended, "Ye'll forgive my rudeness, my lord. May I enquire as to how ye'd discovered where I were?"

Lachlan tilted his head, an unintentional grin playing at his lips. "When I didna find ye at yer own home, I asked about the village where ye might be. I was told I should come to the brewer's home to find ye."

"And how did ye ken where my dwelling is?"

"His Lordship told me."

"Er...Mama, why dinna we leave Moira to speak wi' her visitor?" Niall suggested when his mother continued to ogle the comely viscount with a daft grin.

"Nay, there is no reason for ye to go," Moira objected.

Mary shook her head. "No, no, lass. Niall is right. We'll just step outside for a touch, perhaps visit wi' Mistress Douglas next door. Take yer time."

Her eyes still trained on Lachlan and a silly grin still plastered across her face, Mary MacCormack curtseyed and pulled her daughter towards the door. Then she gave a commanding nod to Niall before slipping out of sight. Niall tossed Moira a devilish wink and departed after his mother and sister.

"Niall, no," she hissed, but he closed the door. She stared blankly at door for long seconds before her eyes swung warily to the viscount knight across from her.

"Will ye sit, sir?" she mocked, bouncing a half-hearted curtsey.

Lachlan laughed, amused by her obvious effort to be contrary. He accepted her offer, and sat himself on the bench. She responded by rounding the fire and deliberately taking the stool on the other side.

He studied Moira's determined scowl. "I've a question." When Moira said nothing, he added, "May I ask my question, my lady?"

"By all means, my lord," she returned, syrupy sweet. "I dinna have a say in my own fate, after all. Why should I have a say in which questions I may hear and which I may no'?"

He ignored her provocation. "Very well, then. My question is this: have I done something to make ye hate me so thoroughly?"

This startled Moira. She pressed her lips together, relenting. "I dinna hate *ye*," she sighed. "'Tis only that I dinna like being told what to do and who I must marry. Ye just happen to be caught in the middle of it all."

"Let us be at ease wi' each other then," he suggested, offering her his most charming smile. When that seemed to put her off even more, he opted for frankness. "I can assure ye that I had no idea of Lord Kildrummond's plan. And, as a matter of fact, I dinna like the idea any more than ye seem to. I'll have ye ken I'm no' the marrying kind."

"Then I dinna see what there is to discuss."

"On the contrary, we've much to discuss, my lady."

His mocking tone matched her own from earlier. Moira sensed she was being toyed with. She narrowed her eyes, assessing her adversary. "And that is?"

"Kildrummond, of course. Ye see, if I dinna marry ye, I dinna get Kildrummond. And if *ye* dinna marry *me*, ye risk losing yer home if King Fiery Face decides to confiscate it as Douglas holdings. I'd say that puts us both in a quandary, wouldna ye?"

Moira glowered at the dirt floor beneath Lachlan's boots. She hated to admit it, but the man's logic was undeniable. "That may be. But I dinna see what could be done about it, if neither of us is inclined to marry the other."

"Dinna play daft, lass. What's to be done about it is that we marry." When she snapped her head up with fresh anger, he pressed, "Consider for a moment, will ye? If we marry, it will be in name only. We'll pretend to live as man and wife until such time as his Lordship passes. We'll refrain from having…er, carnal knowledge of each other. When his Lordship passes, and I am made Lord Kildrummond in my own right, we'll have the marriage annulled."

"That's all well and good for *ye*, sir, but what about me? What do I get in all of this?"

"I would have thought it were obvious. In return for yer cooperation, I promise ye that once the marriage is annulled, ye'll be allowed to remain in Kildrummond for as long as ye wish—the rest of yer life, if it pleases ye."

"Give over," Moira dismissed.

"I am earnest," Lachlan promised. "Ye can even stay in the castle, though I think ye prefer yer wee hovel, if I'm no' mistaken. Ye'll have all the benefits and comforts ye have now, and they'll be guaranteed for the remainder of yer lifetime. We'll part friends, and never have to spend time in one another's company again."

"I dinna ken." Moira chewed her lip. "How do I ken ye'll do as ye say?"

"Ye'll have to trust me. Ye have no choice, lass."

"I do so have a choice," she contested hotly. "I can run. I can leave Kildrummond."

"Moira," Lachlan exhaled softly. She stiffened, wary at the softness in his voice. "I dinna ken ye very well, but I believe ye love yer home. Leaving Kildrummond would break yer heart."

The pain look in her round, cerulean eyes confirmed he'd hit a nerve. "Think on it," he urged. "Come to me this evening and let me ken yer decision."

Then, leaving her to contemplate his proposition, he let himself out. She would be a fool not to jump at his offer, and this lass was no fool.

At least, he hoped she wasn't. He needed her cooperation as much as she needed his.

## *Seven*

The subtle onset of a headache surged behind Lady Glinis's brow. She'd awoken with it, but until now it had been mild, and she'd been able to overlook it. Pressing her thumb and forefinger to the bridge of her nose, she moved gracefully through Glendalough, travelling from the lower corridors of the kitchens up to the main level of the castle.

She still had so much to do—a day's work was never enough to complete the mountain of tasks required of the mistress of a castle. But she would need to lie down if she were to get any of it done. Should this headache grow worse it would render her immobile for the rest of the evening.

Moira! The lass was always, in one way or another, the cause of Glinis's headaches. Why John couldn't simply put his foot down where his bastard offspring was concerned, Lady Glinis would never know.

The unkind sentiment stirred a twinge of guilt; she hated that even more. It would be so easy if she could simply hate the lass, could despise the whore Lilian's child without a second thought.

But for whatever reason she could not dismiss the fact— inconvenient though it might have been—that Moira was not at fault. The girl was not to blame for the wretched farce that was Glinis's marriage.

Lilian, on the other hand…She could happily loathe the woman to the center of her core.

Curse them, John Douglas and Lilian MacInnes both! They'd done this to her, turned her into the bitter, hating woman she was now. Did they know, or care, how damned hard it was to put a smile on her face every day so that no one would know how much it hurt?

Ahead of Glinis, the sound of voices at work echoed from the great hall. Before she took herself off to bed, she decided to peek in and make sure the servants didn't need anything for the next hour or so. Stopping in the entrance she saw that the tapestries—not Moira's thank the heavens; Glinis had insisted on that—were being taken down from the walls for their scheduled beating.

But instead of a Douglas servant perched on the ladder to remove the cast iron rods from their mounts, it was Lachlan's companion. Sir Alexander MacBride…or MacBurns….or Mac-Something-Or-Other. He stood on his toes as far up the ladder as he could go, one hand gripping the very top of the wooden support pole and the other reaching for the tip of the rod above him. Glinis grimaced; that particular tapestry had always been a nuisance to remove when it needed cleaning.

My, but Sir Alexander was a handsome man, she reflected. Similar in stature to her nephew, Viscount Strathcairn, he was tall and strong, though more lean-limbed than Lachlan. Broad, sculpted shoulders sloped to a narrow waist around which his *feileadh mhor* was snugly belted. The plaid's colors were unknown to her.

Also in contrast to Lachlan, with the fair skin, midnight eyes and raven black hair that marked the Ramsay line, Alexander Mac-Whoever-He-Was had been endowed with a richer complexion. As though he'd spent time serving in warmer, sunnier climes. Golden hair, braided back from his temples and hanging loose over his shoulders, hinted at the possibility of Norse blood in his lineage.

She did not watch for long; Glinis rarely indulged in the sight of silly, handsome young men—though for their part they seemed more than willing to fall at her feet (even now, when the days of her youth were far behind her). Intent on retiring, she drifted away from the door.

But not before she was spotted by one of the servants, who called out to her as she departed.

"My lady, if ye dinna mind, can ye tell me—"

Alerted to Glinis's presence, Alex swiveled his head to catch a glimpse of her—an action which upset his balance on the ladder. As he slipped from the rung on which he perched, his fingers nudged the tip of the rod. With a clatter he fell to the stone floor below and the heavy rod fell on top of him.

Grumbling under her breath, Glinis rushed to assist the prostrate knight. Her head throbbed under the sudden rush of movement. Oh, but she did *not* need this right now!

Reaching Alex, she knelt at his side. He was shaken, but otherwise all right. A gash in his forearm, however, was visible, sliced open by the sharp end of the tapestry's rod. Dark red blood seeped from the wound.

"Ye clumsy fool," she tisked. Then to the servants and clansmen gathered round she instructed, "Send to the kitchens for a pitcher of hot water and clean linen strips."

"Aye, my lady," answered the servant woman who had inadvertently caused the commotion. Dipping a curtsey, she scurried off.

"*Ye*, come sit." Hoisting Alex by the elbow, she led him to one of the benches that decorated the perimeter of the room.

Obediently, Alex yielded to her authority as the servants dispersed to resume their tasks. When she sat, he lowered himself next to her. He was so close that his sculpted thigh (which she could clearly see, despite the cover of his plaid, was indeed admirably sculpted) grazed hers.

Deliberately, she inched away from him. He certainly was brazen! Glinis knew better than to acknowledge the indiscretion; these young whelps were all the same. Nor did she look up to meet his eyes, which she knew instinctively, were alight with amusement. To do so would encourage him, and Glinis was far too wise to encourage the attentions of a shallow, young man.

Once, perhaps, she'd entertained the desire and had allowed one or two of them into her bed. But it had only been for sport, and no harm had come of it. John had neither noticed nor cared—and had no right to complain even if he had.

Those days were over, now. And reminiscing about them was a useless exercise.

"I do wish ye'd be careful while ye're here, sir. I'd rather ye no' burden our people wi' the task of caring for yer injuries. We've limited resources as it is." She examined the wound closely, her slender fingers prodding gently at its edges. "A clean slice, at least. 'Twill leave a scar, but I doubt 'twill give ye any lasting trouble."

"I think I'll live, my lady," came the smooth, rich voice from above her head. "Especially with the administrations of one so lovely as ye."

A warm glow flickered to life in her belly, which she immediately doused. Once it was under control, Glinis raised her face to his. Her instinct had been correct: his green eyes radiated amusement, and his lips were cocked with a hint of a smile. Intent on keeping her head, she gazed coolly back.

"Ye'll mind yer tongue. Ye're speaking to the lady of the castle."

"Of course, my lady," Alex nodded solemnly. It was obvious he was not the least bit chastened.

Inexplicably unnerved and far too aware of the young man at her side, she stared hard at the entrance to the great hall. "What is taking so long?" she wondered testily. Then, because she didn't have anything else to do until the water and bandages arrived, she reluctantly engaged Alex in some light chatter.

"I am sorry, Sir Alexander, I didna catch yer family name. What clan be ye from?"

"I am of the MacByrne family."

"Mac*Byrne*." So that was it. "I dinna ken the name. Come ye from a Highland clan?"

"Nay, MacByrne is an Irish name, though I've no ties to that land nor its kin. My own kin have existed in Scotland for as long as anyone can remember. Landless, titleless, and no significant lineage to speak of."

"So ye're a lowly knight, hiring yer skills to whatever lord will have ye?"

Alex chuckled, the sound husky and inviting. An unexpected shiver skittered down Glinis's spine. She straightened her shoulders; she'd be damned if she let this foolish whelp know he'd had such an effect on her.

"No' just any lord, my Lady. William Hay, the great Lord Erroll."

She rolled her eyes. "I've nothing against the man, but I've never heard him described as great. And dinna tell me ye offer him yer services because ye find him all that great."

"No? Why, pray?"

"Because I ken full well ye followed our Lachlan there when *he* went to Lord Erroll. He told me as much."

Alex closed his eyes and pressed his unwounded hand to his heart. "Ye've seen through my lie, and have exposed me. Pray, dinna tell Lord Erroll, though."

Did she imagine it, or had his subtle emphasis on the word *exposed* been intentionally inappropriate?

What a bold, infuriating young man!

She had a mind to knock the wind from his sails, but she was diverted when, at long last, a kitchen lass appeared. A porcelain pitcher of steaming water was anchored in her hand, and strips of clean linen were draped over the same arm. Her other hand gripped her skirts, raising them above her ankle that she would not trip in her haste.

"Here ye are, my lady," she said in a light, efficient voice, and deposited her burden on the bench next to Glinis. "Will ye be needing anything else?"

"Nay, this is fine. Thank ye."

Once the kitchen lass departed, the lady focused on her immediate task. Dabbing a square of linen in the pitcher, she began cleaning the blood from the wound. Alex sucked in a sharp hiss through his teeth at the first touch of the hot cloth, but suffered the administrations patiently.

Her touch was firm and confident—she'd become well versed in attending to such minor injuries over the years. But her subjects had never before been anything but that: *subjects*. Sir Alexander MacByrne, however, affected her concentration. She could not help but marvel at the feel of his satiny forearm beneath her fingertips; at the golden hue, which in the dimmed light of the hall, shimmered faintly.

A strange urge niggled beneath her skin. A desire to trace the bluish lines of his veins on the inside of his wrist, and to follow the contours of the nicks and scars he'd accumulated from his trade. It was a yearning she'd experienced before, with other, insignificant men. And one which she expertly ignored now.

Wrapping the wound tightly, she tied the bandages off in a knot. "There ye be," she said, mildly patronizing. "Mind ye're careful wi' yerself from now on."

She stole a glance once more at Alex's face—and nearly faltered. His striking green eyes were fixed on her intently, as though he could see into her soul and read his effect on her. Raising her chin, Lady Glinis stood and strode purposefully away. It would not do for him to believe that he'd be in her thoughts beyond this encounter.

Though God knew he would.

\*\*\*

Bundled against the icy wind, Moira pushed her mare onward through the deteriorating weather. That morning, she had set her mind on making it to Glendalough by mid-afternoon (Highland wind be damned). She wanted to leave well before the evening meal to avoid being guilted into staying.

Except now, she was starting to regret her zeal; her new priority was to simply reach the castle's walls before dark.

One way or another, she would confront Viscount Strathcairn. After a considerable amount of thought, she'd made up her mind.

She would *accept* his proposal—sweet heaven above, she couldn't even think the words without gritting her teeth!

As much as she detested the arrangement, for however brief a time it may be, she had to concede that it was logical. As long as he was willing to uphold his end of the bargain and have the marriage annulled when the time came—and Moira had no choice but to trust that he would—then she would agree.

And why wouldn't he make good on his promise? A man like Lachlan Ramsay wouldn't want a plain, simple lass like Moira for a wife under more natural circumstances. Any more than *Moira* would want a vain, over-confident, self-important brute like *him*.

Vain he certainly was!

Well, he probably was, at any rate. All men that good looking were.

"Come on, then, Beauty," she encouraged, patting her horse affectionately on the neck. The mare snuffed great spurts of steam, and obliged her mistress.

Beauty. It was the perfect name for this particular mare. On the outside, she was anything but beautiful, with notably squat hindquarters and a long, marring scar that crossed over her left eye to the bridge of her muzzle. Moira had traded a sack of raw wool for the beast at market last year. Given the animal's unattractiveness, Master MacCormack had taken it upon himself to inform her that she'd not gotten the bargain she thought she had.

Moira had named her Beauty anyway. And no name could fit her better for she had a lovely, gentle soul. After all, wasn't that what made a person beautiful? That which existed on the inside?

Take Lady Glinis, for instance. Outwardly she was ravishing. Her figure was unparalleled, even when compared to ladies half her age. Her eyes, deep and black as coal, gazed out at the world as though they guarded some mysterious secret. Long, flowing, raven-black hair complemented a complexion that was as iridescent as pearls.

Yet the lady was a miserable wench. Cold and uncaring towards anyone that was not noble, a condition caused by nearly a lifetime of disappointment thanks to Lord Kildrummond and his Lilian. Not even her uncommon beauty could thaw the lump of ice that was her heart.

If being beautiful on the outside meant being bitter and unable to love on the inside, then Moira would much rather be beautiful where it mattered. It was why she shared such an affinity with her mare: neither was particularly attractive, but both knew what it meant to feel love in all its forms.

Not that Moira knew love in *all* its forms; she certainly loved the MacCormacks well enough, each and every one of them. She loved them like they were her very own kin. And she enjoyed the company of the villagers. *Most* of them, anyway…the ones that didn't frequent the castle and talk about her behind her back.

Yes, though she was far from beautiful, Moira knew what it was to love her fellow man.

As to the form of love which she had still yet to know—not love for her *fellow* man, but love for *one* man in particular—perhaps one day she would have the opportunity to learn. She was not against marriage, necessarily. If she could find a man whom she could love, and who could love her in return…then yes, she was quite confident she had the ability to love in that respect, too.

Lachlan Ramsay, Viscount Strathcairn, however, was *not* that man!

"Come now, old girl, no use getting yerself all worked up," Moira muttered. Beauty let out another snort, agreeing with her mistress.

By the time the towers of Glendalough came into view, the sky had transformed, taking on a hue that was a blend of rose-and-gold, peppered with rich, rounded clouds of greyish-blue.

"My Lady Moira," called a familiar voice from the gate.

Glancing up, Moira waved to Dougall MacFadyen, who leaned over the crenellated parapet of the tower gate. He peered down at her, a warm smile on his handsome face.

There, she thought. Sir Dougall MacFadyen was a prime example of the coexistence of beauty both without *and* within. He would make some lady a fine, devoted husband one day.

"Dougall, good evening," she responded.

"I didna ken his Lordship were expecting ye. Shall I send word ye've arrived?"

"Nay, thank ye. Actually, I have come to speak with the Viscount Strathcairn. Is he wi'in?"

"Aye, he is." Dougall had to raise his voice to be heard over the clatter of the wooden gate as it was raised to admit her. "I'll fetch him."

"Dinna trouble yerself, I'll find him." Moira nudged Beauty with her heel and trotted the beast into the bailey. Reaching the main doors she hopped deftly down to the cobbled courtyard. Handing the reins to an awaiting ghillie, she stepped through to the inner corridor of the castle.

"Where might I find Viscount Strathcairn?" she inquired of a passing servant, a village Douglas woman whom she knew.

"Em...I am no' certain, Moira dearie—er, that is, my lady. If he be no' in the great hall, then ye might wish to try his chamber."

"Dinna call me *my lady*, or I'll never speak to ye again," she teased.

"Cheeky lass," the woman responded affectionately.

Taking the servant's advice Moira proceeded to the great hall. At this time of day it was being set up for the evening meal, and the air was alive with the bustle of preparation.

Lachlan wasn't there. Moira muttered an un-ladylike curse. She'd been hoping to avoid his chamber. Though she may have made up her mind to marry the man, such an intimate space need not be shared prematurely.

Reluctantly she set out for the keep, stopping once more to enquire exactly which chamber the Viscount Strathcairn was in. Finding it, she paused outside his closed door, and breathed deeply to settle her nerves. Then, raising her hand, she rapped decisively.

The sound of shuffling feet from within seeped through the oaken door, but no one came to open it. Had she been heard? Should she knock again? She leaned closer, pressing her ear to the wood.

Before she righted herself, the door was pulled back. She stumbled slightly, her wide-eyed gaze falling upon the full figure of

Lachlan Ramsay. His legs and feet were bare, and his linen tunic had been pulled from his belt, and hung loosely over his hips.

Fie! She'd disturbed his slumber.

"Oh—er, excuse me, sir," she stammered. "I didna mean to disturb ye when ye were—"

"Nay, my lady, 'tis all right. I were meaning rise anyway. Will ye come in?"

She peered uncertainly into the dim chamber. Someone might see her enter, which would certainly set tongues wagging more than they already were. On the other hand, the matter before them had to be settled.

Eyeing the threshold as if it were a pit of horse dung, she crossed it.

"Leave the door open, then. We dinna want anyone thinking there's anything untoward happening in here."

"Heaven forbid that a soon-to-be-married couple engage in activity that might be considered *untoward*." Nevertheless, he obliged, and left the door ajar.

"Please," he said, indicating the leather-padded chair by the hearth.

Moira accepted and perched tentatively on the edge. With no other option—it was the only chair or bench in the chamber—he sat on the edge of the bed, tucked his shirt back into his belt, replaced his plaid on his shoulder, and pulled his boots back onto his feet. Moira tried not to notice the rippling definition of his muscles, visible beneath the linen of his tunic; tried to ignore the heat that crept into her stomach.

"Sir, I have thought about yer proposition," she stated once he'd settled himself.

"I am glad."

"I'd prefer ye didna tease me. This isna a light matter."

"On the contrary, I may tease, but 'tis wi' the highest respect to the serious nature of our conversation."

Moira frowned. "Are ye always this glib?"

"Only when my company is as drab and serious as ye."

He was testing the limits of her patience. "I am no' drab and serious," she retorted. "And even if I am, I think I have reason enough to be."

Lachlan cocked an eyebrow, but waited for her to resume. That infuriating grin of his remained on his lips; her hands itched to smack it from his irritatingly handsome face. She breathed, reining in her control.

"As I was saying, given the circumstances of our predicament, I see no way around yer proposition. I've no desire to leave Kildrummond, and though I could run if I wished to—"

"I've no doubt."

A warning glare silenced him. "Though I *could* run," she repeated, "I love Kildrummond, and the friends I have here. If yer suggestion that we marry be the only way out of his Lordship's design, then I've no choice but to accept yer offer. *But*," she stressed, leaning forward intently, "ye've promised that we may have the marriage annulled once ye've taken on the title of earl in yer own right, and to allow me to remain in my home for as long as I live. I expect ye to uphold yer end of the bargain when the time comes."

Lachlan peered at the lass, an unexpected stir of respect forming in his breast. She had a strength about her; it was not something he often encountered in the women of his life, especially women with ties to nobility.

Then again, he'd never encountered a woman with ties to nobility so brash and ill-mannered as she—even the illegitimate ones, for she was not the first he'd known.

He regarded her with begrudging approval. "Dinna fret, Lady Moira. I've no intention of keeping a wife—*any* wife. Just as ye obviously have no intention of keeping a husband."

It was Moira's turn to be surprised. And offended. He thought she never wished to take a husband...did he think her a shrew?

"I've no intention of taking the husband his Lordship chooses for me. I've no intention of being a man's property, if I can help it. That doesna mean I've no wish to marry."

"Aye, I've heard ye value yer independence. But tell me: how do ye reconcile yer wishes, as you claim here and now, wi' the fact that once ye marry, ye'll be a man's property?"

Hmm...he'd taken the conversation in a direction she hadn't anticipated. He'd challenged her logic, but unlike all the self-important men who had done so before (it being their God-given nature, she knew from experience) he'd not spoken condescendingly. He'd not treated her like a silly woman with silly opinions.

This was a rare trait in a man, one she'd never before seen in the flesh. She was not entirely certain that she liked it.

"I wish to find myself an equal," she answered honestly. "A man wi' whom I can enter into matrimony, and who will belong to *me* as much as I would to him. I do value my independence, that is true. No' just independence as a *status*, but independence of the mind. I dinna seek love, but if I find it, I believe it will be for someone who respects my right to use my mind. Who respects my right to make the decisions that will affect the course of my own life."

Lachlan stared poignantly at her. His impression of Moira MacInnes had taken a turn in a direction he hadn't anticipated. The reports he had of her willfulness were accurate enough, but they hadn't been fair. For beneath the stubbornness there was a keen intelligence, and a passionate nature.

It was a rare trait in a woman, one he'd never before seen in the flesh. Despite himself, he rather liked it.

"Then I wish," he said solemnly, "that when all this is over and done wi', ye find someone who'll love ye as ye desire."

Moira was astonished by a sudden rush of respect for the man standing in front of her. She lowered her eyes to hide her pink cheeks. "Aye…well, then I suppose we're finished here. I assume his Lordship will handle the details of the wedding?"

"Wait, dinna go yet." Lachlan held out a hand. "Pray, stay and talk wi' me a while?"

She glanced out the window at the fading light. "I had hoped to be home before dark."

"Ye could stay for the meal and take a bed here until morning."

"That is what I hoped to avoid. Besides, I've no' prepared my animals for an overnight absence." Sensing his disappointment, she relented. "Perhaps I can have someone escort me home before the meal commences."

"Allow me. I shall be more than happy to see ye safely home. Even if it is dreadfully cold."

"I think that would be fair. Seeing as how I suffered the cold to get here, *ye* can suffer the cold to get me back."

Her jest earned a laugh from Lachlan. She smiled back. She had a glorious smile, he decided. The simple expression lit up what was otherwise a plain face, transforming it into something rather pretty.

He could very well learn to like this lass a great deal. If he had to be married to her, even for a short while, it might not be such an intolerable experience after all.

"Since we're being so open and honest wi' one another," he continued, "may I ask why ye refuse to accept the help that his Lordship is willing to offer? Why eke out a meager living when ye dinna have to? And for that matter, why do ye insist on calling yer own father *his Lordship*?"

Moira leveled him with her clear, blue eyes. "Did ye no' hear? I'm stubborn, ill-mannered and ungrateful."

"I had heard. However, I'm beginning to think that what I've heard may no' be the whole story. I'd rather hear yer opinion on the matter, if ye dinna mind—since we're to be married and all."

"Since we are to be married *briefly*," she corrected. Then, with a slight lift of her shoulders, she prepared to speak of things she'd never before needed to tell.

It occurred to her, in the brief moment before she began, that everyone in Moray knew of her tale, from Kildrummond in the north to the mountain of *Beinn MacDuibh* in the south. But they didn't *really* know. No one ever asked her what *she* thought of the illicit affair between her mother and Lord Kildrummond.

Yes, people knew of the deeds, but they had no idea of how it had shaped Moira as a person—well, perhaps Niall and his family did, but that was about it. She should not have felt the need to defend herself, to *unburden* herself to this perfect stranger. Yet that is exactly what she found herself doing.

"As ye may ken, Lord Kildrummond fell in love wi' my mother only a few years into his marriage to Lady Glinis—" she frowned when his brows drew sharply together. "Aye, of course ye ken that. Anyway, when my mother fell pregnant wi' me, she ran away to a village just east of Berwick, and that's where I were born. She thought she'd never see his Lordship again, for what man of noble blood ever wants anything to do with the illegitimate child he's sired? She didna think he'd be any different, and she had no desire to remain in Kildrummond and be a burden to him. Nor had she any wish to be a pariah to the villagers.

"As it happened, Lord Kildrummond was devastated when she left. He loved her so much that he searched far and wide for her. When finally he reached Berwick and heard word of us, he begged her to come back to him, and promised to take care of her and the child—me—for the rest of our lives. He couldna marry her, ye see, and they both kent that. But he was prepared to keep her as his mistress. Wife and clan be damned."

"It's a wonder that his Lordship didna just move her into the castle," Lachlan observed testily.

"I think he tried, actually," she admitted. "But his close kin came to Lady Glinis's defense, made him see that what he was doing was bringing enough shame on her. To have his mistress in the castle, invading the rightful Countess's home…well that were too much."

"That's hardly better. So he doesna parade his mistress around at the castle, but instead he installs her a short distance away where the whole village can witness their adultery. Sorry," he relented when he remembered whom they were speaking of. "I forget this is yer mother."

Moira sighed heavily. "Perhaps, but ye do speak true. In any case, that is precisely why I work so hard to separate myself from him, from them both. Ye canna imagine what it's like to grow up knowing yer own mother is despised by her people. And I were despised right along wi' her. She traded her happiness for mine, what else can be said? I've worked long and hard to make sure people around here know I'm no' standing here wi' my hand out, waiting for Lord Kildrummond's charity. I canna change my origins, but I can make my own impression. And I think I've done that…in the village, at least. The people here at Glendalough still dinna think very highly of me."

"I admire ye for yer courage. And ye're right: the people of the village do hold ye in very high esteem."

Moira scrunched her face in disbelief. "And how would ye ken that, sir?"

Lachlan raised his shoulders dismissively. "I've made a few inquiries. I've also learned that ye were expected to marry yer Niall MacCormack before this business wi' me arose."

She barked an exasperated laugh. "I dinna ken how many times I can say it—Niall and I will never be getting married."

"Is he that objectionable, then?"

"Nay, he's my best friend." Her smile grew wistful, and her gaze turned inward. "Ach, I give him a rough time—no harder than he gives me, mind—but he's my best friend in all the world, and I dinna ken what I'd do wi'out him."

"That is like Alex and me—Sir Alexander MacByrne," he clarified, when Moira lifted an eyebrow.

"Ah, the one wi' whom ye've traveled here."

"That'd be him. We grew up together. The both of us were from poor families, looking to better our lot in life. The only difference between us is that my father had a title…for all the good it did him. Anyway, I, too, dinna ken where I'd be wi'out him."

"What happened to make a viscount take on a position as a knight? Since we're being so open and honest wi' each other."

She'd parroted his own words back to him. It made Lachlan laugh. "Since that is so, I'll make it clear now that ye're no' marrying a man wi' an abundance of wealth—in case ye thought to marry me for my coin. My grandfather were the last Viscount Strathcairn that had any measure of wealth to his name. And he pished it all away—pardon my crudeness. So I am as landless and as wealthless as ye, Lady Moira. But unlike ye, I'm no' about to sniff at an offer to remedy that condition."

"Indeed," she reflected. "Perhaps then this little arrangement of ours is more important than either of us thought."

"Aye. I must say, I'm glad I've had the chance to speak wi' ye about it. Perhaps we might start afresh, find our way forward as friends, instead of enemies?"

Moira grinned sheepishly. "Perhaps we can. I'll allow that ye might no' be the arrogant villain I imagined ye to be—I said *might*, ye understand."

"And ye're every bit the ill-mannered wisp I imagined *ye* to be. But 'tis no' my place to try and change ye. And besides, I find ye rather refreshing."

"Well then, I shall consider it my mission to tire ye of the notion soon enough."

She was incredible! Lachlan threw his head back and roared heartily. "I daresay ye'd try, lass."

## *Eight*

Because of Lord Kildrummond's rapidly failing health, it was imperative that the wedding be arranged without delay. A priest was sent for from the abbey at Inverness to perform the ceremony, and during the sennight it took for him to travel to Moray, Lachlan and Alex used the opportunity to settle their affairs in Aberdeen for good.

It pained Lord Erroll to learn that he was to lose not one, but *two* of his best knights. Being the honorable man he was, the chief of Clan Hay released them both from their obligation to Slains. He wished them a sincere farewell, and left Lachlan with the promise of Clan Hay's political alliance if ever he had a need of it.

Moira, on the other hand, spent the sennight until the priest's arrival dreading the event of her marriage, farce though it was.

Perhaps it was *because* the event was a farce that she found herself a bundle of nerves on the eve of her wedding. She spent her last hours of matrimonial freedom huddled before the fire in her own, modest dwelling. There she pondered her future, the ever-faithful Niall at her side. The pair sat in silence, their mutual affection requiring no words.

No matter how hard she wished it, Moira could not halt the relentless march of nightfall.

"Ye should get going before ye lose the light," she told Niall reluctantly.

Niall sat forward, and idly crinkled the piece of straw he held in his fingers. After a moment he tossed the piece into the fire.

"Nah, I'm all right."

"Ye sure ye dinna mind looking after the place for me while...while I'm gone?"

While she was gone. While she waited for her father to pass, more like. The poor lass, she couldn't bring herself to say it. Niall knew his lifelong friend well: this sort of trickery was not in her nature, and it was eating away at her conscience.

"One of us will be out here at least once a day," he reassured her.

"Of course I'll be out as much as I can, too. I expect I shall be able to come out at least a few mornings each sennight."

"Aye, so ye've said."

Moira glanced sideways, chagrined. "I *have* said that before, havena I?"

"Ye have. And if ye say it one more time, so help me I'll tip ye into the brae."

"I'm sorry. I'm just—"

"Ye dinna need to explain anything to me, lass. I've kent ye almost yer whole life, and I ken how to read ye. 'Tis an enormous burden ye've agreed to bear here, even if it's a lie."

She was silent for a long while, her blue eyes following the flicker of flames. When she spoke, her words were so meek Niall could hardly believe they'd come from her.

"Am I making a mistake, Niall? Is this lie an unforgivable sin?"

He studied her small, frightened face and quivering lips. A deep sigh filled the cavity of his chest. "I dinna ken, lass. That's something ye'll have to work out yerself. On the one hand, ye *are* lying to yer own father. Ye've an obligation by the law of the land to do as he bids, and it's his right to determine whom ye marry."

"So *ye've* said," she quipped morosely.

"*But*," Niall pressed, "all his Lordship has ever wanted for his only daughter is that ye be happy, and that ye're looked after. Now, perhaps his notion that a marriage will make ye happy isna quite to yer liking—nor to Viscount Strathcairn's liking, for that matter—but it's always been *ye* he's thought of."

"He thinks to keep Kildrummond from the king's hand," she argued.

"And whose sake d'ye think he does that for above all else? *Yers*, Moira. He wants Kildrummond preserved, first and foremost, for *ye*. But as I was saying, even though ye'll be ending yer marriage to Lachlan Ramsay when the old man passes, in the end, what he wanted for ye will come to pass: ye'll remain in Kildrummond, and ye'll be protected and looked after for the rest of yer life. His wish for ye will, one way or another, come true."

"Aye…perhaps. I still feel wretched for deceiving him so."

Niall shifted in his chair so that he was facing her fully. "I dinna blame ye for feeling that way. But it may be that some good can come of yer guilt."

Moira gazed back, her expression wary. "Go on."

"He's wanted nothing more than to love ye, Moira. To love his daughter and to have his daughter love him in return. Could ye no' see yer way to being the daughter he's always wanted? Ye've no reason now to be so cold to him. As far as all of Kildrummond kens, ye're marrying a nobleman and Glendalough will be yers—well, through yer husband, anyway. The independence ye've sought so hard to maintain is for naught now."

She straightened. "Ye take that back, Niall. It isna!"

"Settle yerself, lass. We both ken that ye've avoided a relationship wi' him all this time because ye dinna want people thinking of ye the way they thought of yer mother: that ye take advantage of his Lordship's love in exchange for gifts and goods. But like it or no', sweetling, that's exactly what they think of ye now; now that ye're to be wed to a nobleman and given Kildrummond. And ye'll no' change their minds, either, them that willna see ye as anything other than Lord Kildrummond's bastard offspring—dinna look at me like that. I'm only saying what they think, and it isna anything ye dinna already ken yerself."

He gazed searchingly at her. "They'll look down on ye no matter what. Ye canna change them, so ye might as well forget about them. Why no' put yer father's mind at ease, hmm? At least in this last stage of his life."

He was right. She hated to admit it, but Niall had a point. She'd capitulated; she'd allowed the earl to determine her future; she'd been dragged into Kildrummond's noble sphere by that Viscount Strathcairn and his little plan. It was what she'd been fighting against all her life, to be cast into the same light as her mother. God's bones, she shouldn't have listened to Lachlan Ramsay; she should have kept on fighting.

But she hadn't. And it was too late to change her mind now. Groaning, she dropped her face into her hands.

"I'll think on it," she grumbled into her palms.

And think on it she did. All the next morning, though her wedding—her *marriage*, for heaven's sake—was mere hours away, it was what *Niall* had said about the earl that occupied her mind. His words played over in her head, and with each revolution she found it harder and harder to deny their truth.

She could no longer deny his Lordship—no, not "his Lordship," her *father*—the paternal relationship he desperately craved. If she did, she would regret it until her dying day.

And so, with the ceremony less than an hour away and the chapel filled with Lowland and Highland Douglases alike, Moira visited the Earl of Kildrummond's chamber.

*Without* having been summoned. For the first time in her life.

Halting in front of the door, she took a breath. Then, raising her hand, she rapped a knuckle against the heavy oak. Long moments passed in silence; she was certain her breath was so loud it echoed down the corridor. She was about to knock again when the earl's man pulled the door open. Seeing Moira standing on the other side, he gazed quizzically at her for a brief instant. Composing himself, he stepped back to let her pass.

Inside, the earl was seated in front of his dressing table. Though his body had withered in its illness, he still looked every bit as regal as he always had. His silver hair had been combed and lay feathered over his shoulders, emphasizing how narrow they'd grown. A robe of deep black velvet was latched over the stark cords of his neck, and cascaded down his back like a ribbon of midnight sky.

His blue eyes, so much like hers though they were now sunken into his gaunt face, sparkled with enthusiasm. A smile that was almost childlike spread across his wan lips when he caught her reflection through the polished tin mirror.

"Moira, lass. Ye look positively lovely. Every bit as beautiful as yer mother."

"Yer Lordsh—er…Father." She curtseyed awkwardly. "Should ye be out of bed?"

Lord Kildrummond coughed. The sound of wet phlegm rattling in his chest was so pronounced, both Moira and the earl's man winced.

"I wouldna miss it for the world, seeing ye married," he answered when he'd recovered enough to speak.

"Ye'll be there to make bloody sure I marry, more like."

Warmth infused his eyes as he took in her stubborn grimace. "Such spirit; such life. I've been called a fool for neglecting yer upbringing, for not checking yer manners when ye were young. But I ask ye: how could I? I could no more change ye than I could tell the hills no' to bloom wi' heather. Yer mother's spirit shines in ye, lass."

His wistful tone at the mention of Lilian dredged the last of her buried guilt. She lowered her eyes to the floor. "Aye, well…I'm sure she's grateful to ye for all ye've done for me."

"I would have done more, lass, if ye'd have let me. And what I do now, this marriage to Viscount Strathcairn, 'tis only yer welfare I think of. Ye'll see, 'tis for the best."

Her exhumed guilt twisted sharply in her gut. She glanced warily at Lord Kildrummond's man, who stood unobtrusively to the side.

"We need no' speak of it anymore. 'Tis done. I only came to see how ye were before things get underway. Ye look as if ye need to rest."

"Ye're right. The effort simply to prepare has tired me. I'll rest now, but I'll be counting the minutes until I can see ye again."

Moira shifted uncomfortably. "Er—aye. Until then." She bounced on the balls of her feet once or twice, itching to flee the room and silence the angry sting of her conscience. But the proud light radiating from Lord Kildrummond's face brought the echo of Niall's words into sharp clarity.

*Why no' put yer father's mind at ease? At least in this last stage of his life…be the daughter he's always wanted.*

Cursing silently, she stepped to the earl's side and placed a kiss on top of his thinning hair. He started, caught off guard by her sudden affection. His eyes shining with tears, he raised a withered hand and patted her arm.

God's blood, those tears would haunt her for the rest of her life!

As it always does, time marched on, and the final hour passed; it was time for the ceremony to begin.

Bound and constricted by the pearl-colored silk of her wedding gown, and her hair yanked into an elaborate plait, Moira waited outside the great hall with Lord Albermarle at her side. It would be he that gave her hand to Lachlan Ramsay, since Lord Kildrummond was physically unable to claim that particular honor.

The earl's rest had restored him, though—enough, at least, that he could make the journey from the keep to the hall with the aid of two sturdy clansmen. They held his elbows, bearing his weight with patience as he scuffled his feet along the flagstone floor. Lady Glinis hovered at his back, ready, it seemed, to catch him if his knees should buckle suddenly. Though what she could do in that instance that the two burly clansmen at the earl's side could not was anyone's guess.

Not once did she glance in Moira's direction. In fact, as she passed the lass, her chin raised a notch in blatant dismissal of her presence. Her dark eyes smoldered with quiet hatred. Nor did Lady Glinis offer a glance for Lord Albermarle, who took the slight in stride. He knew the reason for it. When he felt Moira stiffen at his side, he patted her elbow.

"Dinna think on it, lass. 'Twill soon be over."

There was little pause between the time Lord Kildrummond was taken into the hall and the ceremony began. Before she knew it, Moira was being pulled across the room on Lord Albermarle's arm to where Lachlan stood waiting for her on the dais.

Curse the brute; *must* he look so handsome? His chin had been scraped smooth, emphasizing the regal tilt of his jaw. Odd that such a simple change should alter his face so noticeably.

Or perhaps it was not his face that was altered, but rather some indefinable quality behind it. When rough and whiskered, it was a touch savage. But now, the battle-hardened knight had been transformed into the noble viscount by nothing more than a scraped chin.

His eyes, however, still retained a wisp of that savagery, still looked out on the world from a warrior's perspective. It was a chilling duality, a dangerous one.

An inexplicably *sensual* one, too.

Moira pressed her lips together, annoyed with herself for even having entertained the thought.

Catching her grimace, Lachlan cocked an eyebrow in question, and raised his shoulders ever so slightly. For heaven's sake, she was being ridiculous. He probably thought she was scowling at *him*. If she were not careful she might just start muttering to herself. Unclenching her teeth, Moira drew a calming breath and glanced around the hall to distract herself.

She knew many faces in the crowd. And liked almost none of them. The only guests she could truly count as friends were the MacCormacks, invited at her special request and only *because* of her special request, for they were not important enough to be in attendance otherwise. Mary MacCormack looked at her with something akin to motherly pride. Next to Mary was Master MacCormack, tall and wiry like his eldest son, who stood on the other side of him. The remaining four members of the MacCormack clan stood in front of their parents and eldest brother: Niall's two younger brothers, nineteen and seventeen respectfully, and beside nine-year-old Imogen was a second sister, thirteen years old.

Knowing his friend's outward composure was a lie, Niall crossed his eyes, jutted his bottom teeth forward and pulled the most atrocious grin.

His timing couldn't have been worse. Under the weight of her frazzled nerves, Moira's ribs began to vibrate with a silent chuckle.

Which turned into a barely contained giggle that shook her shoulders.

Soon she was laughing out loud with such force that tears blurred her eyes and her stomach hurt. A twitter of astonishment flitted through the crowd, mingling with murmurs of disapproval; Lord Albermarle had to pull on her arm to quiet her.

Yet still she had trouble keeping a solemn face. By the time she reached the altar and Lachlan had taken her arm she was trembling with another round of incomprehensible laughter.

Which—God forgive them both—affected the bridegroom as well.

"Ye bloody fool, look what ye've done!" Mary MacCormack reached across her husband and gave Niall a whack in the stomach.

"Give over, they're getting their vows out," Niall protested, chuckling himself at the hilarity he'd caused.

"Barely. Ye can hardly hear what the Viscount Strathcairn is saying, he's shaking so hard."

The priest fixed the blasphemous pair with a stern look as he pronounced them man and wife. Chastened, Lachlan leaned over to kiss his bride with a herculean attempt at gravity—an attempt which was shattered the moment their lips touched, for his new wife accidentally let out the most unbecoming snort that echoed off the masonry.

"I am sorry," she apologized to Lachlan later at the feast. "I dinna ken what came over me."

Lachlan's eyes swept over the crowd at the trestles below. Folding his arms on the tabletop, he turned his face to her. His lips were upturned in a conspiratorial grin. "I were no better. Besides, it weren't yer fault. I saw what yer friend Niall did to set ye off."

Moira grimaced. "That scoundrel. I must whip him good when next I see him."

"Would ye like me to whip him for ye?"

"Dinna ye dare! Niall may be a scoundrel, but he's *my* scoundrel. No one lays a finger on him but me."

The meal wore on, course after course, and the air was appropriately festive. As usual, Moira took less joy in it than the other guests did, but for once it was not because she was the outsider, the object of ridicule. Surprisingly, she was sorry Lord Kildrummond was not there. He'd had to retire as soon as the ceremony concluded. His place at the center of the dais had been set, but remained untouched. It was a sad reminder that his absence would soon be permanent.

Lady Glinis occupied her usual place next to Lord Kildrummond's. She picked disinterestedly at her meal. Only once did her eyes meet Moira's; she stared at the lass with such undisguised loathing that Moira was forced to look away.

Once the tables had been cleared her mood lifted somewhat. She danced with Niall most of the time, with Lord Albermarle for one song, and with Lachlan for only those dances that were customary of the bride and groom. Each time she danced with him he was noticeably drunker.

"Careful now, man. Ye'll no' be able to raise yer staff if ye keep drinking at that rate," one of the Kildrummond Douglases snickered as the newlywed couple finished one of the dances.

It was a fair observation, for Lachlan had nearly fallen over twice. Even still, her eyes bulged at the man's audacity, and she opened her mouth to tear a strip off him.

Lachlan circled his arm around her narrow shoulder and squeezed. "Dinna fret, my friend. I've no doubt of my capacity to drink and perform as I ought to."

The crowd of men surrounding them roared with laughter. They missed his emphasis on the words *as I ought to*.

But Moira didn't. They both knew that the only task he *ought* to perform that night was to sleep. And for that Lachlan could be as drunk as he wished.

No one had any reservations about getting as drunk as they wished that night. Including Niall. And when Niall was in his cups, he tended on the morose side. Moira saw it coming even before it had started. When he finally sauntered off on his own to sit at a peripheral table and brood, she tactfully gave him some time before joining him.

"How is yer ale doing?" she queried cheerfully. "In need of a top-up?"

Niall tore his eyes away from the lovely young Janet who was at that moment serving the knights flanking Dougall MacFadyen on the other side of the hall. He looked down to his cup and then back to the object of his lovelorn desire.

"Ye've dirtied yer sleeves," he mentioned casually as he drained the dregs.

Moira lifted her forearms and examining the expensive, but plainly cut, pale silk that wrapped them. Indeed, he was correct. The juniper berry jelly that had been served as a garnish for the roast meat was smattered along the bottom to the elbow.

"Ah, bollocks!" she cursed. "I were hoping to sell it after this is all over." When Niall's pout cracked into a reluctant smile she leaned into him. "Come on, now. It canna be as bad as all that."

"As all what?"

"Well, if the face ye've got on ye says anything, ye're either hopelessly in love, or ye've eaten a mouthful of something foul and ye canna spit it out."

She'd hit her mark. Niall pressed his eyes shut and his shoulders trembled with inebriated laughter.

"That's better," she proclaimed. "Here, yer ale's gone now. Why dinna I call her over?"

Niall assessed his empty cup through a fierce squint. "Why no'?"

Glancing across the room to Janet, who had moved on to another table, he made to raise his hand. But something stopped him, and his eyes darted away. Curious, Moira searched for what he'd seen.

Finding it, she ground her teeth, furious.

At a section of tables close to where Dougall sat was Lachlan. Flanking him were Sir Alexander MacByrne and several more knights and warriors who had travelled to Glendalough for the occasion.

Firmly seated on the viscount's newly-married lap was a shapely serving wench. Moira recognized her from the village, though she did not know the lass personally. She did, however, know that this particular wench, with her fresh, rosy complexion and plump lips, was not as innocent as she was pretending to be at the moment. Indeed, she played the innocent well, flirting coyly with the men—and worst of all, with Lachlan, fresh from the altar.

*Coy my eye, the harlot*, Moira thought caustically.

The audacity of the lass she might have been able to overlook, but Lachlan's behavior she could not. He shamelessly entertained the wench's flirting, returning it in the most obvious of manners. He tickled her curves, pulled his arms tight around her as she feigned struggling from his grasp. He even pressed his face into the crook of her neck every time she tipped her head back to laugh gaily.

Foolish, conceited man! She'd judged him correctly the first time.

She was not about to let Niall know how irked she was, though. Forcing a look of indifference, she sniffed.

"What do I care? This isna a real marriage, after all. Let him do as he pleases, I dinna mind in the least."

"Of course no'," Niall agreed, no more fooled by her bravado than she was herself.

"What I *do* care about is yer ale." Catching the lovely Janet's eye, Moira waved her over.

"Ye daft mare, stop," Niall hissed, tugging at her sleeve. Too late, for Janet was soon upon them.

"Are ye all out then?" she sang, her voice rising above the festive din.

"Aye," Moira answered before Niall could. "My friend here is in dire need of a tip."

"Is that so?" Janet turned her sparkling eyes on a red-faced Niall. When his open mouth failed to make a sound, she added, "Does he no' speak, my Lady Moira?"

"Aye, he does. Most of the time."

"Only I'm nae so sure he does. Why, he never utters a sound when I see him at market. I took him for a mute." She grinned teasingly as she filled his cup. Satisfied that he'd been taken care of, she reached out and tapped him on the bridge of his nose with a long, pink forefinger. "That's ye sorted. If ye finish that, ye give me a wink, aye?"

With a conspiratorial nod to Moira, she dipped a curtsey and wended her way back through the crowds in search of more empty goblets.

"Would I be correct in guessing ye're never washing that nose of yers again?" Moira teased.

"Bloody right!" Niall vowed, a latent smile spreading from ear to ear.

She'd been so distracted by Niall's happiness that Moira had forgotten about Lachlan. But an accidental glance in his general direction reminded her anew of his shameful behavior.

Next to the table at which the viscount and his companions were stationed, a trio of Lowland Douglas lasses watched Moira deliberately. When she glared back, they giggled and whispered amongst themselves. They didn't even bother to hide their mouths.

*She's a bastard*, Moira read from their lips.

## *Nine*

It was well into the wee hours of the morning when the celebration finally came to an end. The exhausted groom and his bride, followed by the most important members of Clan Douglas's many branches, trudged up to their newly prepared bedchamber.

Moira glowered the entire way—at any noble Douglas who dared meet her eyes. Who in the blazes of hellfire did they think they were to be escorting her to her marriage bed? She was not chattel, whatever they might think!

When she made to protest, Lord Albermarle gave her a sharp jab in the ribs.

"It's their right by rank, lass," he warned, whispering into her ear that the others would not hear. "Ye'd best be getting used to it now that ye're to live at the castle."

When they reached the marriage chamber, a small, fat Douglas pushed his way to the front of the group. Leaning close, he scrutinized Moira with small eyes set deep into a ruddy face. He was a Lowland Douglas, a lesser baron of an unimportant seat. But he'd been sent as representative of the ninth Earl of Douglas, who himself was unable to attend. That, as well as the man's state of intoxication, gave this Lowlander a sense of entitlement over the other, nobler Douglases there gathered.

"Now lass, ye ken the importance of yer duty this night, aye?" His booming voice echoed down the corridor, accompanied by a waft of alcoholic fumes. "I tell ye now, Lord John doesna like the idea of this union, what being that Viscount Strathcairn isna a Douglas and all. But as ye, lass, are a Douglas *of sorts*, he'll no' take a petition to the king about it so long as ye put out male bairns—"

His drunken rant was cut short when Lord Albermarle swatted the man over the head. "Shut yer gob, Arch. If ye've anything to take home to John, let it be a reminder that his relations wi' the king are hanging by a thread as it is. Ye tell him he has more important things to worry about than the inheritance of Kildrummond by a non-Douglas and his illegitimate Douglas wife."

A shout of laughter escaped Lachlan's lips, which he lamely attempted to mask with a cough. The Douglas baron sputtered, his pebble eyes bulging from his head. Lord Albermarle glared down at him from his far greater height and stature. When Lachlan looked to Moira, however, to share his mirth, the laughter died on his lips.

The poor lass was fighting a surge of tears which pooled at the base of her lids. Humiliated, angry tears.

Moved by pity and, oddly, a sense of protectiveness, Lachlan took her by the elbow and spun her towards the chamber door. He couldn't bear to watch her suffer the even greater humiliation of the lords seeing those tears spill down her cheeks.

"If ye'll excuse me, my Lords, we'll be off to bed," he announced. Nodding respectfully to the noble Douglases, he opened the chamber door, ushered his bride through it, and closed it firmly behind them.

Even now, safely tucked away from prying eyes, Moira strained against her tears. She stared at the window, her pale skin burning scarlet as she ordered the tears back from where they'd come. Her tattered pride, along with her desperate attempt to cling to it, affected Lachlan. A tender spot just below his ribs bloomed as he took in her struggle.

"Dinna pay them any mind," he said, his voice huskier than he'd meant it to be.

"Easy for ye to say." She scrubbed away an errant tear with the palm of her hand. "A cartload of buggers, all of them. I'd rather they—"

"Shhh, mind yer voice," Lachlan interrupted quickly. "D'ye no' hear them on the other side still?"

Moira listened. He was right. The quiet murmur of deep voices drifted to her from the other side of the door.

"Oh, for pity's sake. Why dinna they shove off?"

Lachlan stared at her speculatively. Did the lass really not understand? Humiliating her further was the last thing he wanted to do, but she was not making this easy. He had no choice.

"They wait," he informed her, a note of apology in his tone. "They'll no' *shove off* until they're certain the marriage has been consummated."

"So they'll stand there all night and listen?" When he nodded, she added, "And what happens when they hear nothing? Do I need to remind ye that we'll no' be consummating anything, ye and I?"

"'Tis no matter." He gestured dismissively with his hand. Striding the length of the chamber, he took hold of the bed's footboard and began to rock the frame against the wall. The solid oak structure made great, loud thumps against the masonry.

"Ye're out of yer bloody mind," Moira accused.

"On the contrary, I'm very much in control of it. Now how long d'ye think I should carry on? I dinna want them to think I'm no' man enough to satisfy my bride, but neither do I want to go *so* long that they'll be looking on the morrow to see if ye're sore."

She merely shook her head, thoroughly disgusted.

Satisfied with his performance, Lachlan gave the bed a final, virile heave, and then stepped back. He assessed the frame with pride, as though he had constructed it himself.

"There," he concluded, "that should do nicely, I think."

He grinned conspiratorially, but this only earned him a narrow-eyed stare. God's bones, but the lass was contrary. Were they not friends after all? He stepped back to let her pass as she moved to the bed.

With her back turned to him, she began loosening the laces of her wedding gown. When it came time to shed the gown entirely, she turned her chin over her shoulder, fixing him with a pointed look.

"Avert yer eyes."

Lachlan thought her modesty amusing. Unless she had a third breast anchored to her chest, the lass couldn't possibly have anything he hadn't seen before. Nonetheless he obliged her, and pivoted to face the opposite wall.

The rustle and whisper of silk tantalized his ears, evoking images in his mind that emerged of their own accord: the caress of the gown's pearly sheen over the creamy flesh of a shoulder; the puddle of fabric around slender, bare ankles.

He was glad of his *feileadh mhor*, for the heavy wool disguised the evidence of his rather inconvenient arousal.

The sound of sheets being pulled back indicated she was finished, and he faced her again. He hoped that the sight of her— knobby bones, plain face—would remind his manhood that she was not an object of desire, that he had only to go searching among the servants for a plump, pretty lass more attractive than Moira MacInnes.

Nothing could have been further from his expectation. Moira MacInnes looked adorable, sitting in the bed with the covers pulled to her shoulders. She was so small; she nearly drowned in the many pillows and quilts. Her hair had been pulled free from its pins, and she'd shaken it out. It tumbled over her shoulders in glossy, alluring disarray. Lachlan saw that it wasn't flat and colorless as he'd first thought, but rather a rich fawn hue. A flush still stained her cheeks, and her eyes still glistened from the tears she'd been so determined not to shed. Those eyes, clear as a summer's day, stared back at him, their round, frightened innocence undermining the warning glare she was attempting to convey.

Perhaps he had judged her too harshly. Perhaps she was not as plain as he'd first thought her. This lass would make some man a fine bride one day.

Smiling inwardly, he unbuckled the clasp at his shoulder. The upper part of his plaid dropped to his waist. He made short work of his own clothes, unfolding the yards of fabric from his person with practiced efficiency. Once he had stripped himself down to his shirt, he rounded the bed on the other side of Moira, eager to slip between the sheets and lose himself in the oblivion of sleep.

"What in the devil d'ye think ye're doing?" she hissed when he pulled back the edge of the quilts.

"I'm going to bed. What d'ye think?"

"Ye'll no' be coming into *this* bed." Deliberately, she shifted to the middle of the mattress, and clamped her hand down on the quilt.

"And just where d'ye expect me to sleep, ye wee wench?"

Cocking a slender eyebrow, Moira reached behind her, shoveled up one of the feather pillows, and tossed it onto the braided rug in front of the hearth.

Lachlan stared at the pillow. "Ye canna be serious."

"I am," she answered, and settled herself into the mattress for sleep.

There was no denying it; Moira MacInnes was definitely in a strop with him. But he was too tired and too drunk to put effort into fighting with her. Grumbling audibly, he stomped to the rear wall of the chamber where a fine tapestry—one of hers, as it happened— hung. Dislodging the rod from its anchors, he yanked the tapestry free, wrapped it roughly around himself, and shuffled back to his pillow and braided rug.

Glowering at her, he flopped onto the rug like a selkie out of water, punched the pillow for good measure, and settled in for what was promising to be a very uncomfortable night. Whatever remained of his arousal died completely.

Perhaps the *shrew* wasn't as appealing as he had thought after all.

\*\*\*

Alex had only been asleep for an hour at best before the pitchers of drink he'd consumed made their way to his bladder. There was a chamber pot beneath his bed, clean and ready for him to use, but he'd never much liked the vile things. The thought of his own urine stagnating near the place where he slept—and worse, the poor servant who had to empty it in the morning—was not something he cared to think about.

Extracting himself from the covers, he rose from the bed. Hastily donning his plaid about his rumpled shirt, he left the chamber in search of a garderobe.

The corridor's cold draft snaked around him. He didn't mind. His chamber had grown rather stuffy, and he welcomed the fresh air. Besides, a wander would do his mind good, for his dreams had been rather vivid.

So vivid, in fact, that he was mildly surprised to find his bed empty upon waking. The feel, the taste, the scent of the woman who had lain in his arms had not been real. She'd been a product of his subconscious yearning.

Of *course* she hadn't been real—the Countess of Kildrummond, Lady Glinis, would never lie in his arms. She'd made it more than clear she was not interested in him. *And* she was married…perhaps Alex should have reminded himself of that point first (may God forgive him).

Yes, he prayed God would forgive him, though he very much questioned the likelihood of it. Married or no, Glinis had consumed every corner of his brain since the moment he'd clapped eyes on her. And for the first time in his adult life, he'd encountered a woman he could not have. A woman who would not have him—and not just because she was married. She truly did not desire him in any way.

A woman who did not desire him was an anomaly which Alex had never before encountered.

The irony of his situation amused him; he chuckled silently as he walked the darkened corridors of Glendalough. This must have been how that serving wench felt, for it was clear she was not often rejected, either. When she'd discovered that Lachlan had no intention of doing anything other than flirt with her, the wanton girl had turned her sights on Alex.

He could have had her, too. His bed would be warm right now if he'd taken her. But he could not. It was Lady Glinis, now, to whom he would forever compare all other women. Her quiet, composed, authoritative beauty would evermore be the standard to which all other women must live up—and to which no other woman could *ever* live up.

Twice knocked back, the lass had crept off with the first man of their accompaniment to indicate his interest. Likely she was still in his bed at this hour.

By this time, Alex had already passed at least one garderobe, the narrow enclave announcing its purpose by the musty reek of its recessed stones. But he'd been content to walk a bit farther, to find another, more remote spot in which to relieve himself.

Finding somewhere more favorable, he emptied himself efficiently. With a shake for good measure, he dropped his kilt, stepped back from the foul smelling drop, and continued on, aiming for a roundabout way back to his chamber.

Slains was a grander castle than Glendalough. It was the grandest castle Alex had seen in his lifetime. Before he'd taken his commission with Lord Erroll, he'd been a child at Byres Castle, in the lands of East Lothian.

Unlike Lachlan, Alex's father hadn't been a knight. He'd been a barrel maker. A tradesman. A lowly villager.

Lord Byres, however, had been amused by Lachlan, who was the son of one of his commissioned knights, a certain Viscount Strathcairn. Lord Byres had also been amused by the fast friendship which young Lachlan had struck with the barrel maker's son. A generous and good man, the Byres clan chief took it upon himself to grant Alex the same privilege of education that he granted Lachlan. As a consequence, Alex had been exposed to opportunities which his own father could never have given him.

And if he'd never had the opportunity to become a knight in his own right, Alex would not be wandering around Glendalough Castle right now, dreaming of Glinis Douglas, Countess of Kildrummond.

He'd become so consumed by his thoughts that the world around him had disappeared. When he wandered past a shallow, windowed alcove, the dark figure which blacked out the scant light of approaching dawn startled him more than it should have. With an audible gasp, he wrenched his *sgian dubh* from his boot, the base instinct to defend himself taking over.

Two or three galloping heartbeats passed before he realized the figure was that of a woman. A gracefully curved, dark-haired woman.

Lady Glinis.

She turned silently, unafraid of the blade aimed at her breast. An apparition silhouetted against the luminous dark, she had the subtle scent of wine about her. And from what dim light was available, Alex could make out that her eyes had the slightly unfocused look of one affected by drink.

Though she was not drunk. No, definitely not that. Her gaze, though glassy, was steady enough. She stared at him, challenging him, one eyebrow slightly raised.

"Forgive me, my lady." Alex returned the *sgian dubh* to his boot and straightened. He hoped she could not see how badly his hands were shaking.

"Sir Alexander." Her voice was smoky and sensual. "What takes ye from yer bed at this hour?"

What took him from his bed? Why *she* did. The thought of her; the ache for her. His body stirred, responding to nothing more than the *suggestion* of that ache.

"I couldna sleep. I thought to remedy that wi' some air."

"Are our beds no' comfortable enough for ye?" She raised her chin a fraction. "Or perhaps ye're in need of company for yer bed."

In need of—God's bones, what was the lady playing at? She leaned on the wooden sill, her hip raised slightly, which only accentuated her heavenly form. Her head tipped to the side in invitation, elongating the graceful slope of her neck. A subtle smile curved her full, pouting lips.

His thighs throbbed as he imagined taking her upturned face in his hands and kissing those lips.

But his warrior's instinct buzzed with warning. This was not the stoic, composed, disinterested lady he'd come to know. Not the lady who'd reprimanded him for his overtures as she had wrapped his wound in the great hall that day.

Something was amiss.

"I dinna wish for company, my lady," he answered uncertainly.

Her eyes narrowed a fraction. She pushed herself off the sill and slinked across the alcove to stand in front of him. Lifting a forefinger, she traced it from Alex's collarbone to his navel in a slow, deliberate line, enjoying the shudder it evoked in him.

"Perhaps we can change yer mind. Ye see, I myself am in need of company."

Alex's knees nearly buckled under the strain of resisting her. His manhood screamed at him from beneath his kilt: *Take her, ye bloody fool. She could be ours!*

His keen, calculating mind, however, kept its hold on his wits by a narrow margin. This close to her, with her maddeningly beautiful face inches away from his, he saw something which he hadn't picked up on from a distance.

It was her eyes. Those glittering gems of onyx were hard and brittle. Dangerous.

Oh yes, there was something amiss, all right. This was no invitation. It was a challenge. A dare. She may be affected by drink, but she was by no means inebriated.

He cleared his throat. "I imagine it must be difficult for ye, then, my lady, to have to resist that need. What wi' yer husband laying ill and all."

His remark had been pointed and cutting, though his tone had been gentle. From his experience with women (and he'd had plenty), he knew what to expect; he winced, waiting for the slap that should have come.

She did not raise her hand. Her face did not skewer itself into an expression of indignation, or wounded pride. To Alex's astonishment, his remark seemed to be exactly what she'd been looking for. The brittleness in her eyes softened.

But she was not done with him, not yet. Alex stood, transfixed, as her eyes took on a new quality: *pain*. The drink which affected her had loosened the reins on a hurt which, he'd no doubt, she'd spent a lifetime suppressing.

And as soon as the pain had loosed itself, another suppressed emotion blazed to the surface.

Rage.

"Ah, yes. My *husband*," she said through bared teeth. "The *husband* who this day flaunts the evidence of his adulterous deceit. The husband who takes my home, my lands away from me and gives them to the offspring of his whore. I expect I willna have a bed, nor a home, for much longer. It willna be long after my *husband* departs this world that she throws me out."

A quiver wrinkled her brow and her glassy gaze moistened with unshed tears. Alex's heart clutched, her pain affecting him far deeper than he would have thought possible. Gently, so as not to frighten her, he placed his hands on her upper arms, and peered down into her face.

"Whether or no' the new Lady Strathcairn would have ye out, yer Lachlan would never let it happen. Ye ken that as well as I do."

Glinis stared up at him defiantly, trying desperately to hold onto the anger which had roiled inside of her for so long. She lost the battle, and her face crumpled in despair.

Without thinking, Alex exhaled and pulled her into his arms. She stiffened briefly, her long practiced role as Lady Kildrummond at odds with this unprecedented intimacy. But when he pressed his lips to the top of her head, and breathed into her hair, she melted into him. And began to weep.

"I did everything I could," she sobbed openly. "Everything to make him love me. It was never enough; *I* was never enough. It was always Lilian, Lilian, Lilian!"

He rocked her like a child, uttering soothing reassurances. Not a word of her bitter tirade did he interrupt; not one tear did he stop from soaking the linen of his shirt.

After a time her sobbing subsided, then died. She straightened. Alex held his breath, uncertain of how she would react to his impertinence now that she'd regained her composure. He pulled his chin back so that he could see her face. On it, there was a look of confusion. And chagrin.

She stepped away, raised a shapely, warm hand to his chest and ineffectually wiped at the drenched spot where her tears had fallen. Sheepishly she raised her eyes to his, opened her mouth to say something, thought better of it and shook her head.

Whirling on her heel, she walked silently away.

Alex gazed after her, following her retreating outline until it was enveloped by shadow. His heartbeat roared in his ears, and his skin tingled where he'd held her body against his. He released a deep, heavy breath.

Thoughts of his bed were completely gone now. There was no way he would find sleep again this night.

## *Ten*

"And how are ye this morning, Lady Strathcairn?"

Moira raised her eyes from her trencher to see who was addressing her. Smiling down at her was a young man, a Highland Scot, and one of Glinis Douglas's acquaintances. If memory served correctly, he was also one of Lady Kildrummond's most ardent supporters, and had been quite vocal in his disapproval of the earl's long-standing affair with Lilian.

He seemed to be engaging her pleasantly enough now—whether this made Moira wary or at ease, she couldn't yet say. She chewed her mouthful of crowdie carefully, tactfully delaying her answer.

"I am well, Lord...?"

"Lord Murdoch, my Lady. My father is the Earl of Mar."

"Lord Murdoch. Of course. Of Invernochty, no? I am told it is a lovely place."

"It is, my lady. I am quite proud of it."

"Forgive my ignorance, but are ye first in line to inherit? Or have ye older brothers?

"I am the firstborn. Of course, when I inherit Invernochty, it will be honorably. I'll need no' weasel my way into power through the back door like *ye've* done wi' Glendalough. In any case, I wish ye success wi' Kildrummond. Do give my regards to the *current* lady of the castle, will ye?"

His verbal slap thus delivered, Lord Murdoch bowed, his smile now brittle, and strode from the hall.

Moira glared at the polished wood grain of the slatted table board. A hot flush spread up her neck and into her face. She was not unfamiliar with the sentiment which Lord Murdoch had so blatantly expressed; the noble men and women who came and went through Glendalough's gates all felt this way. Their whispered remarks, derisive glances, and the rumors they left behind for the servants to circulate attested to that.

But never before had someone been so openly hostile to her.

The cruel jibe had driven away her appetite. Her eyes slid to Lachlan, who sat at her side. He had not heard; his attention had been otherwise diverted by a fresh maid across the hall.

Humiliation ignited into anger. She shoved back from the table with such force that it nearly tipped the bench over.

Lachlan's head snapped to her, his dark brows raised. "Moira? Ye all right, lass?"

She ignored him, and fled the hall by a side entrance—at the very time Lady Glinis was making her appearance through the same doorway. The lady stood her ground and glared dangerously at Moira.

"Sorry," Moira mumbled, skirting her by a hair's width and fleeing the hall.

Lady Glinis pressed her hands into her velvet surcoate, smoothing out a legion of imagined wrinkles. Once her countenance had been restored, she crossed the hall to the dais.

"What were all that about?" Lachlan questioned.

"How should I ken? I've only just come in."

"How is his Lordship this morning?"

She waited until an approaching ghillie had delivered a fresh trencher of bread before answering. "He rests now. Though I'm told he's had a better night than he's had in a while."

"Well, there are bound to be good days and bad, no?"

"More bad than good of late." She took a delicate bite of cheese and chewed before speaking again. "I trust ye slept well?"

He gave her a wry smile. "It wasna as restful as I would have liked—and no' for the reason ye're thinking," he added when she grimaced.

"And Moira? Did she have a peaceful sleep?"

"I'm surprised ye'd ask. I thought ye despised her."

"I dinna ken what ye're on about, lad."

"Give over. Ye're as easy to read as a book, *Aunty Glin.*"

Lachlan's boyhood name for her touched her heart. She examined the contents of her trencher, considering.

"I despise her for *what* she is," she stated, "no' for who she is. And my feelings on the subject of *Lady Moira*, as she is now, are irrelevant. I am still mistress of this castle, and so long as it's mine, I must consider the comfort of all my guests, no matter who they be."

Lachlan dipped his head in a small bow. "Yer diplomacy is admirable, my lady."

"I should hope so. Sometimes I feel it's all I have left."

The conversation turned to other, more pleasant matters for the remainder of the meal. When he'd finished, Lachlan excused himself from the table and left the dais in search of Moira.

She'd been inexplicably contrary ever since the wedding feast. It was discouraging—one minute he thought they'd come to an understanding, and the next she seemed ready to clout him over the head. If her mood swung from one extreme to the other like this on a regular basis, he was in for a long battle until the union was annulled.

"I believe she's in wi' his Lordship, yer Lordship," said a small, elderly servant woman when Lachlan inquired about Moira's whereabouts. "Leastwise I saw her wandering about the keep in't direction of his Lordship's chamber."

Thanking the woman, Lachlan took the keep stairs two at a time and went straight for Lord Kildrummond's door.

It was ajar, and indeed, seated at his bedside was Moira. His Lordship slept soundly, a rattle of phlegm whispering past his teeth with each breath. Unaware that she was being watched, she slouched in the heavy oak chair in a most unbecoming fashion. Her forearms lay on the armrests, her knees hung apart, and she was slumped so low that her chin touched her chest.

As unbecoming as her posture was, however, it was somehow…sweet. Vulnerable. She watched her father's sunken chest rise and fall, unaware that she herself was the object of observation.

Lachlan was reluctant to interrupt her, but he had come here for a purpose, and he meant to address it. Announcing his presence with a quick rap on the door, he stepped into the room.

She looked up, startled. Wiping a hand across her face in a mannish gesture, she sat up so that her back was arrow-straight, her knees pressed together, and her hands folded gently in her lap. She may not use them often, but it was obvious that someone, at some point, had attempted to instruct her on the proper deportment of a lady.

"Forgive me, my lord," she mumbled thickly.

"There's nothing to forgive." He paused, his gaze skimming over the sleeping earl, before continuing. "Moira, lass—is everything all right wi' ye?"

"Of course, why shouldna it be?"

"Ye seem—how should I say it—*annoyed* wi' me."

Her lips worked together in silence, as if some private thing amused her. Or annoyed her even more. Her gaze swung back to her father.

"I dinna ken what ye're on about."

"Ye're certain?" Lachlan pressed. "I could have sworn ye were in a strop wi' me last night. And this morning ye ran off wi' no reason as far as I can see."

She inhaled long and slow, her lips drawing into a tight line. "Well then, my lord, please accept my humblest apologies for running off...*wi' no reason.*"

"I meant what I said, lass. I desire us to be friends. We only have each other in this."

Her eyes stayed on the earl, but a sarcastic half-smile pulled at the corner of her mouth. "Of course," she answered chillingly. "We are in this *equally.*"

Lachlan stared at her. He was not sure what else he could say to dispel her mood. But talking to her was proving to be useless, and he was not fool enough to push at something that would not budge.

"Right then," he said, giving up. "I'll be off. If his Lordship wakes, give him my regard."

He left her in peace. He did not hear the muttered words that followed him out of the room:

"Make no mistake, Strathcairn, there's nothing *equal* about the circumstances in which we find ourselves."

***

Lady Glinis had spent the morning preparing herself before descending from the keep to break her fast. She'd been determined to avoid Sir Alexander's gaze, and for that she'd put a great deal of thought into where she would—and more importantly, would *not*—look upon entering the great hall.

All her preparation had nearly been for naught when that fool girl Moira almost collided headlong into her. That one, unexpected encounter had threatened to dislodge her carefully composed countenance. Instead, she'd glared at the girl—to keep her eyes from scanning the room for the one face she didn't want to see.

Yet the one face she so badly *wanted* to see.

She hadn't meant to be so harsh to Moira; she felt somewhat sorry about it, in fact. It was strange, but her outburst the night before, as uncalled for as it had been, seemed to have unburdened Glinis of a fraction of her pain.

It was an odd feeling. Unsettling even. Her hatred for Lilian and her bastard offspring had been a constant through most of her adult life. But now…now the fires didn't burn quite so hot.

Perhaps she might seek out Moira and offer an apology. Perhaps not. Perhaps she might just avoid the lass, and forget the incident entirely.

As much as she might have liked to, Glinis could not avoid Alexander MacByrne. She needed to address her indiscretion— though what, exactly, she was going to say she hadn't yet worked out. But she had to say something, to dispel in some way what he must be thinking.

Come to think of it, what *was* the young man thinking now? How had his impression of the pitiable Lady Kildrummond changed? Did he think her wanton as well as wretched? Did he think her…

"Oh for heaven's sake, ye *foolish* woman, his opinion of ye matters not!"

"I beg pardon, my lady?"

Mildly embarrassed, Glinis dismissed the passing servant's puzzlement with a curt shake of her head.

Long after the hall had been cleared of the tables, and the castle was abustle with daily activity, she worked up her nerve and sought Sir Alexander out.

Her stomach was in knots with each corner she turned and each empty room she peeked into. And it was not only because of what she had to do.

The truth was, when she went to bed that night, the steel-and-flesh contours of his body pressing against hers, and the stir of his breath over her hair as he soothed her, was like a spell upon her senses. And his lips brushing over her head with that tender kiss— she shuddered pleasantly just recalling it.

Her reaction to this young, handsome man frightened her. The others she'd taken to her bed over the years (few though they were) had not gotten under her skin this way. They'd been entertainment;

they'd been revenge on her husband—in principle, at least. John had never found out.

Whatever else they'd been, those young men were also forgettable. They'd served their purpose to her just as she'd served hers to them.

Sir Alexander MacByrne, however…

Finally she tracked him down in the stables, where he was patiently attending his chestnut gelding. He brushed the animal so gently, and with such affection that Lady Glinis admired him silently for a minute or two. Long, sculpted arms stroked the equally sculpted body of his mount. His shirtsleeves were pushed back to the elbows; the icy March air had finally broken of late, and the days now warmed to a slightly more tolerable degree of cold.

Lachlan's bay gelding was stabled beside Alex's; the animal swished its tail contentedly in a freshly cleaned stall. Her nephew had obviously been here already.

"We have ghillies for that," she called from the doorway. "No need for ye to be mucking out stables yerself here."

Alex's back stiffened upon recognizing her voice, and his hand hovered mid-stroke a heartbeat before continuing to brush.

"Dinna worry, my lady. A lad's been already to do the dirty work. My mount, I handle myself."

"Ye sound like our Lachlan." She approached the edge of the stable, and leaned her shoulder against the mildewed, wooden post.

"Aye. I've learned much from *our* Lachlan."

Long seconds passed while Glinis searched for the words she'd prepared on the way here. Damnation—they'd fled her grasp now that she needed them! Alex brushed several more strokes before he faced her.

"Is there something in particular ye've come to see me about, my lady?"

His eyes were as green as the summer sea, and just as mesmerizing. They bore into her, melting her belly along with her wits. The same, smug confidence she knew of him was still there, still maddeningly…*maddening*. But now—curse his handsome face!—now, she couldn't force herself to take offense.

It was several seconds more before she realized she was staring. Glinis breathed deeply, and summoned the strength to do what she must.

"I want to apologize for…for what happened last night."

"And what happened last night, my lady?"

Glinis pressed her lips together. "Dinna be coy wi' me, sir. Ye ken well enough that my behavior were inappropriate, my station being what it is. I shouldna have spoken to ye in that way."

That irritating grin of his returned. Well…it would have been irritating if he weren't so damned appealing.

"'Tis only inappropriate if I hadna welcomed it."

She tossed her hands in the air. "Sir Alexander, I dinna ken what to make of ye. Just when I begin to think ye're different than all those other shallow young men who see me as a forbidden prize, just when I begin to think there might be more to ye—ye go and prove me wrong."

Her accusation only encouraged him. His grin deepened.

"I have two things to say to that, my lady." He sobered. "The first is that when I said I welcomed yer behavior, it were not entirely a glib remark. I've been told much about ye by Viscount Strathcairn, and if what he says is true, then ye've been handed a difficult lot in life—much more difficult than any woman should have to endure. Ye've handled it wi' grace and dignity yer whole married life. Ye're more than entitled to unlock yer suffering and let it out once in a while. I'm glad ye were able to do so wi' me, for I enjoyed offering ye what comfort I could."

Glinis's knees wobbled.

"And the second?" She hoped her voice did not wobble, too.

"The second, sweet lady, is that I am no foolish young man, and ye'll no' be a forbidden prize for long. Now, dinna mistake me: I dinna wish death upon his Lordship. But—and God forgive me for thinking it—he isna long for this world. That means ye willna be a married woman much longer."

Her stomach lurched. Words became a foreign concept. God forgive him, indeed. God forgive them both!

Sir Alexander meant what he said. It was clear from the soft authority in his voice and the certainty of his gaze. He'd stated his intentions, and he did not speak them lightly.

Yes, he was certainly no foolish young man; Glinis could not put him in his place like she had with the others who pursued her. She'd long ago made herself a sinner by taking a lover or two into her bed. But with Alexander MacByrne, her sins had achieved a new depth, for her desire was not for his body alone. She desired more. *Much* more.

She desired his soul. His entire being.

The realization was wonderfully terrifying.

She took an uncertain step back. Then another. She pressed her hands against her thighs, trying to rub off the stain of her impure thoughts through her palms.

"Er…excuse me," she mumbled.

Pivoting on her heel, Glinis left the stables in a daze. Her body moved on its own, taking her to the front entrance of the castle. Just before she reached the doors, she veered left, and followed the inner wall until she was out of sight of the bailey.

She could not go inside. Not yet. What if someone saw her, saw the telltale flush of her cheeks, the glazed look in her black eyes. They would know the wicked things that plagued her mind. They would know that her heart now, too, had sinned against her husband.

Alone, she leaned against the stone, welcoming the cold that seeped through the fur lining of her cloak and into her skin.

She was not in love; she could *not* be in love. Not with this ten-a-penny knight who had ridden through the castle gates and into her life for the first time less than a month ago. No, this was not love.

But how could she be sure? She'd never been in love before. She'd heard great things about it, of course. Love made a person act a fool; it made the heart race one minute and ache the next. Love made one blind to sense, and honor, and duty. John Douglas and Lilian MacInnes had taught her that.

If this wasn't love…what else could it be?

## *Eleven*

Moira MacInnes was undoubtedly, no two ways about it, in a strop with him.

She'd been unaccountably cool towards Lachlan the second day after their wedding, just as she'd been the first day.

The third day she'd been downright hostile.

Was the lady stark-raving mad, or had he managed to insult her in some unknown way?

He spent a good deal of time searching through his memory for what he might have said or done, but nothing stood out as particularly offensive…given that their marriage was a complete fabrication.

He'd had just about enough of trying to be friends with her. He should give up—God's bones, he'd tried hard enough. But one thing Lachlan Ramsay was *not* was a quitter. Not at least before he was convinced there was no hope. He'd give it one last try.

She unwittingly gave him the perfect opportunity when, one morning, she announced that she would be away from the castle.

"Oh aye? And what d'ye have planned for the day?"

Moira rounded on him. "Am I no' trusted to be out and about by myself? Very well, then. I must tend to my animals and the upkeep of my lowly hut. I've relied on young Master MacCormack for three days now, and 'tisna fair to trespass upon his friendship any longer."

"Easy, lass. 'Tis no' that I dinna trust ye. I were merely showing polite interest—d'ye ken the word *polite,* by the by?"

Moira lowered her eyes to Lachlan's chest, annoyed with herself for snapping so quickly. "Oh…well, I beg yer pardon, then."

"We havena spent much time in each other's company these past few days," he explained. "I thought perhaps I might escort ye. I'm good wi' animals, and would not mind lending a hand."

"We havena spent much time in each other's company because we've nothing in common."

"Aye, 'tis true. But that can be remedied, no?"

She considered his offer, her lips twisting up at the corner in a long-suffering—and rather endearing—grimace.

"Oh, go on, then," she allowed.

Within the hour they were mounted and on their way south through the swelling hills and valleys of Kildrummond.

Moira did not say much on the journey, and in the silence, Lachlan allowed his mind to wander.

He wondered how things were going back at Slains. He wondered if Lord Erroll had made a decision yet on whether or not he would stand with the Earl of Douglas against the king. Word in the Highlands had it that the move against the Crown by the notorious Douglas chief was imminent.

He shuddered to think what the impact would be upon the more isolated, less involved branches of Clan Douglas that wished only to be left alone.

Such gloom-and-doom thoughts. They gave him the chills. Lachlan forced his attention to other matters...

Like the difference between his and Moira's mounts. Yes, that was another matter he could distract himself with nicely.

His bay gelding was one of the handsomest he'd ever seen (and he wasn't just saying it because it was his). At fifteen handbreadth to the withers, the bay was on the larger side of horse. He would have made a great destrier, but early on in his life, before Lachlan had acquired him, someone had decided to remove the necessary male bit that gave the destrier a suitable temperament for war.

As a consequence, his gelding was gentle. Authoritative, tall and beautiful, he was a good warhorse because he was as loyal to his master as Lachlan was to him. He trusted his master to bring them both through battle—and was prepared to die alongside his master if it came to that.

As loyal and handsome a beast as ever there'd been.

Moira's beast, on the other hand...

"What d'ye call that thing?" he jested, reaching out to flip a lock of the mare's tattered mane.

She leveled a stern look on him and guided her mount away. "Her name is Beauty."

"Oh aye? Were ye having a laugh when ye named her?"

"Ye *would* say that."

Her accusing tone stung. "Come, now. Ye have to admit the name doesna really suit the animal."

"The name suits her just fine. She may be no beauty to look at, but she's a beauty on the inside. A kind, gentle soul she is, and that's worth more than any beauty the eye can see."

His amusement faded as his folly became glaringly clear. Lachlan groaned inwardly.

"Ye're right. A beautiful soul is, indeed, far better than a beautiful face."

She ignored him, carefully indifferent. Still, he could see how deeply his off-handed words had cut her. He regretted his remark more than he should have.

When they reached her hut, she hopped abruptly from her saddle. She did not wait for him to help her—a deliberate slight. Tying Beauty's reins to a metal anchor fixed into the stonework, she gave the animal a few strokes and soft words. Beauty responded with a gentle whicker, and nudged her wet nose into Moira's side.

A gentle soul, indeed. Lachlan felt like an even bigger arse.

He hopped from his own horse and tethered him beside Beauty.

The poignant thought came to him then: they were both so much like their mounts, he and Moira. Lachlan, like his horse, was overtly handsome. He'd known it all his life. He'd taken it for granted all his life, too. But he was a good person. He cared about others. He was a knight by trade, and fought when he must; when his master told him he must. But he had no real appetite for blood and combat.

*Un*like his mount, he had his ballocks still. He chuckled silently, pleased with his own joke.

He didn't know Moira well enough to say how alike she and Beauty were, though he suspected it was a great deal. Outwardly, the animal's scar was a distraction, her tattered mane and patchy coat ugly. Many people would not bother to see past these defects in appearance to see the soul beneath it.

It was the same with Moira...though the word *defect* was rather harsh. She was skinny. Too skinny for a female. She had no curves, no soft pillows to her. The stark outline of her body would put many men off; they were unlikely to look past it to see her marginally pretty face—all right, perhaps it was a tad more than *marginally* pretty. She had not the unearthly beauty of Lady Glinis, but her luminous eyes, and her rich tumble of hair were quite attractive.

And if word in the village was correct, she was a kind, gentle person on the inside, too...when she chose to be. If he could just get past whatever wall she'd put up against him. If he could only discover why she was so determined to be contrary with him.

Mulling these thoughts over, he followed her into the darkened hut.

The place was bare, but tidy. A half-finished tapestry was draped over a wooden stand, its ends hanging less than an ell off the dirt floor. The fireplace was cold and empty, but it had been swept clean. And the scent of fresh hay filled the place, giving it a warm, inviting feel which most village homes had.

It was obvious she loved her home; cared for it and took pride in it. His admiration for Lady Moira MacInnes grew.

"Oh, see now," she tisked, dragging her toe across the hearth through a trace scattering of ashes. "See now, I kent I should have been by earlier."

"What's that?"

"He's only gone and let the sheep wander around the place. Can ye no' see the hoof marks in the ash here?"

Lachlan edged closer and inspected the floor where she pointed. Indeed there was a hoof mark or two. Barely visible.

"And this is yer Niall MacCormack ye're talking about?"

"Och, I kent I couldna trust him, I *kent* it!"

Surprised by what he judged an overreaction, he rubbed her arm. "Calm yerself. There's no reason to be so upset, no harm's been done."

"But there *could* have been." She wrenched her arm from his touch. "They could have chewed my tapestry. They could have gotten into my pantry. They...they could have—"

"Moira, it isna something to get worked up over."

He reached for her again. Again she pulled back.

"Nay, dinna touch me. I kent I shouldna have left. I canna be away from my home. I need to be home!"

"Glendalough is yer home now."

"Glendalough is *no'* my home," she shouted. "It shall never be my home wi' that *Glinis* hating me at every turn. Wi' those *despicable* nobles whispering about me behind my back and even to my face. D'ye ken the things they say to my face?"

"Well, perhaps a little, but—"

"And *ye*," she spat, jabbing her forefinger at him. "Ye make it all worse, what wi' yer shameless flirting!"

"Flirting?" He stared at her, aghast. Was that what this was all about? "Ye're no' jealous, are ye? We agreed this wasna a real marriage."

"Jealous? *Jealous*? Dinna flatter yerself." She threw him a look of such undisguised contempt that he felt immediately foolish. "Jealousy has nothing to do wi' it. How d'ye think it makes me look when everyone at the castle sees ye being such a flirt? They dinna ken we're no' really married. All they see is a marriage that neither of us wants, a match that isna well suited, and a bridegroom who finds the female servants far more interesting than his own wife!"

Her accusations thus hurled, Moira MacInnes did something that Lachlan never imagined he'd see from her...

She cried.

Right in front of him. The last of her shattered control fell away, and she buried her face in her hands and cried.

Lachlan felt like he'd been hit by a battering ram.

She was right. Of *course* she was right. On some level he'd known that life in the castle was not comfortable for her. But he'd never given much thought to just how poorly she was treated by those above her station.

Thinking back, he recalled several instances where he had witnessed their derisive glances, overheard their snide remarks. At the time, he hadn't paid much attention. It wasn't because he didn't care. Not at all. It was because he thought of Moira as a strong, self-assured woman who did not let such insults affect her.

But it was clear she'd been hurt by every one of them. And by the countless others he'd not been around to see and hear.

And he, Lachlan Ramsay, Viscount Strathcairn, had only gone and added more fuel to the fire by flirting—no, *shamelessly* flirting, the insensitive arsebugger that he was—with all the lovely young lasses.

As if being the bastard child of Lord Kildrummond was not enough of a reason for those high-and-mighty nobles to ridicule her, he had to go and give them another one.

The thing was, though, his wandering eye was innocently meant. He was a man; he flirted. To flirt was as natural to Lachlan Ramsay as the rising sun was to the morning. He had never, not *once*, thought about how his actions would be perceived now that he was a married man...more or less.

He should have thought about it.

He'd never felt so ashamed in his life.

"Moira," he pleaded achingly, and pulled her into his arms.

"Let me go." She shoved against him with little success. "I dinna need yer pity."

"Please, lass, dinna fight me. Let me apologize. I am very much in the wrong. I never meant to humiliate ye, but I see that's exactly what I've done. Words canna tell ye how sorry I am, and I promise: there will be no more of it."

She was silent for a while, staring blankly at the red and black lines on the plaid over his chest. She held herself rigid, straining away from him in symbolic defiance, but she did not pull out of his arms.

"I want to come home," she said eventually, her voice so low that he could scarcely hear her.

Lachlan glanced about the hut. He pondered the word *home*; he'd never had one like this before. With his father commissioned at Slains, he'd lived in a castle all his life. Yet it had never been a home in the same way that Moira's simple hut was home to her.

This place was no more than a peasant's dwelling. But it was loved. Meagerly furnished, yet every piece of worn furnishing was cared for. The pantry was tidy, the dirt floor swept and tamped, and the rushes clean.

In a way that he didn't understand—and didn't particularly *want* to understand—he desired to know what having a home like this would feel like. To know what the word *home* meant to the heart.

"All right," he heard himself say. "We'll leave the castle and stay here."

Moira's head snapped up. "I beg yer pardon?"

"We'll live here while we're waiting for all this business to be over."

"What—just like that? We'll pick up and leave?"

"Aye."

"But...but what will his Lordship say?"

"It matters not. I am lord of my own viscountcy; I dinna need his approval. And ye are now my wife—in name at least. So if ye want to, we'll live here."

She stared at him, awestruck. "Aye. I do want to."

"Well then, that's settled. Although I do have two conditions."

"Which are…?"

Her wary gaze warmed him. A genuine, effortless warmth which lasses in general rarely brought out in him.

"The first," he said, "is that we must spend our days at Glendalough. I have business at the castle, after all. If the estate is to be mine, I must learn how to run it. Ye need no' make yer presence known there; ye can hide away in the solar, if ye wish. Or ye can bring yer Niall along to entertain ye."

"Why must I go at all?"

Lachlan frowned. "Well, I suppose ye dinna need to. Though d'ye no' wish to see yer father from time to time?"

Moira tipped her head to the side, considering. "Aye, perhaps. But that's really the only business I'd have there."

"Of course. And we needna take our meals there. I dinna imagine ye'd want that."

"Ye imagine right," she agreed. "Then…what be the second condition?"

"The second is that I may sleep in the bed."

"In the bed?"

"In the bed. I'm sick to death of sleeping on the floor, and I'll do it no longer."

"And where am I to sleep?"

"Ye may join me, if ye wish. I'm no' greedy, and I suspect our two bodies beneath the covers will keep us warmer than if we were to sleep separately. If ye dinna want to share, *ye* may sleep on the floor."

A reluctant grin spread across her face, and a giggle bubbled to her lips.

"All right then," she answered, her smile deepening.

Her relief was almost tangible. It pierced Lachlan's heart and made him want to laugh, too. Her happiness was infectious.

So infectious, in fact, that he nearly forgot he was still holding her.

He should let her go. She probably wanted him to let her go. Moira MacInnes didn't strike him as one of those lasses who delighted in casual intimacy.

His arms tightened, pulling her closer.

"Thank ye," she whispered against his chest.

"Ye're welcome," he answered, his throat unaccountably tight.

## *Twelve*

Lachlan's thoughts were in a jumble all the next day. Overnight, a touch of regret had settled in to tangle them even more. Was he really going to do this? Leave the comforts of the castle for a peasant's hut? He had a viscountcy to his name and the promise of an earldom on his horizon. And here he was, trading the luxury and prestige which came along with all that for wattle and daub, stone and mud, and the aroma of animals' hindquarters!

Yet still, when he thought of Moira, when he recalled the humiliation, when he remembered the hurt and loneliness on her childlike face, his chest tightened. In the end, what he knew to be right in his heart would not bend to the indignant protests of his head.

It had only been a day—less than that, even—that the decision had been made to leave the castle. But already, all of Glendalough knew of the arrangement. The highborn men and women of Kildrummond and beyond made no secret of their feelings on the matter. Least of all Archibald Douglas, the Lowlander baron who represented the Earl of Douglas. He remained at Glendalough, availing himself of the earl's hospitality for as long as he could. And he accosted Lachlan outside the great hall that morning, as soon as the meal had finished.

"My lord, ye canna do this," the fat little man protested. "'Tis no' dignified. 'Tis beneath yer station. Lord Douglas will never approve of a future Douglas earl living in a peasant hut. 'Tis an affront to the honored name of our clan!"

Lachlan waited patiently, allowing the man to make his statement. When he had, Lachlan considered his companion, who stood just behind and to the left of him.

"And ye, MacCraig? What say ye? Am I as big a fool as Arch here seems to think?"

"I am sure the baron did not mean to suggest ye were a fool, as such, yer Lordship," MacCraig answered in an even tone. "But I must agree. 'Tis no' appropriate. The future Earl of Kildrummond, a Douglas noble, mustna descend to living as the peasants live. It is shameful."

Their assertions were nothing Lachlan wasn't expecting. They were nothing he didn't already know everyone else was thinking. Still, they came like a punch in the gut.

In contrast to this noble outrage, the servants of the castle appeared to esteem him all the more, for indeed they had been fully apprised of this development, too. From whom, Lachlan couldn't imagine. But they knew. Oh yes, they knew.

"Can ye tell me where Lady Kildrummond is?" he inquired of a serving lass a short while later.

The girl, a young, comely thing with the flush of youth still upon her cheeks, curtseyed. "Aye, my lord. She is in the solar, I believe. Leastways I thought I heard her in there no' long ago."

"Thank ye."

"Yer Lordship." She raised a hand tentatively, begging him to remain. Her brow drew together, and she nibbled at her lower lip.

"D'ye wish to say something?"

The lass looked left quickly, then right. She hesitated a moment longer, then whispered, "'Tis good of ye, yer Lordship. I ken it isna my place to say, but 'tis good of ye."

Then the lass darted off and was out of sight before he could blink.

With that glint of pride and respect in the serving girl's eyes still fresh on his brain, Lachlan made his way up to the solar. Indeed, as the lass had said, Lady Glinis was within. The door stood half ajar, providing no barrier to stop her elevated voice from escaping into the corridor.

Lachlan stopped just beyond the threshold, and listened.

"I'll no' let it happen," insisted the lady. "He canna debase himself like this in front of his kinsmen. They'll never respect him after this."

"I'm nay so sure, my lady," answered a male voice which Lachlan couldn't place. "We may find they'll respect him all the more, once they accept the situation. If he does this, he'll prove himself to be a lord worthy of the comforts of his wealth, a lord deserving of his possessions and lands and titles. Ye of all people understand that a frivolous lord not only loses his wealth, he loses the respect of his people."

The reference which the unseen man made of Lachlan's grandfather, Lady Glinis's own father, hit its mark. Of course Lady

Glinis knew better than anyone else. It was the reason she'd been married off to John Douglas in the first place, and the reason her brother was forced to take a position at Byres Castle as a hired knight.

"But that is precisely why he must remain here, at Glendalough," she insisted. "He has lived wi'out the comforts of wealth for long enough. First at Byres then at Slains. He deserves this."

"I dinna doubt that, yer Ladyship. But begging yer pardon, is it no' the Viscount Strathcairn's choice? If he has decided that living wi' Moira in her home is acceptable, 'tis no' for us to say he cannot."

"Och, I could throttle that girl," Lady Glinis hissed. "I blame her for this. I dinna ken what spell she's weaved upon my nephew, but she doesna deserve his kindness."

At that point, Lachlan made his presence known, lest his aunt say something she could not take back.

"Aunty Glin," he chastised gently. "I ken ye've reason to dislike Moira. But she is my wife now. I must insist that she be treated wi' respect."

"And how long have ye been standing out there?" Lady Glinis, who had been pacing in front of the window, stopped. She cocked a dark eyebrow at Lachlan, unperturbed that she'd been heard.

"Long enough to know that I didna like what I heard."

"I'll no' take it back, what I said," she insisted. "Lachlan, lad, I dinna like this, and I'll make no secret of it."

Glendalough's steward, Eamon Douglas, was the unknown man with Lady Glinis. He folded his hands in front of him and looked away, expecting an argument to ensue. But an argument was not what Lachlan had in mind. Instead, he took the lady's hand and led her to the small sitting area by the window.

"My dear aunt." Lifting his chin, he motioned for Eamon Douglas to join them. "I canna begin to tell ye how much I appreciate yer concern for me. Ye've been concerned for me every day of my life, and I'll no' forget that. But Moira is no' to blame for this. 'Twas no' even her idea—it were mine. In fact, I think she were just as astonished as ye when I suggested it. But I think this will be good for her. For *us*. Ye ken she isna comfortable here, that there are people in this castle who make life unbearable for her. And ye ken *why*. Just as ye ken 'tis no' her fault."

Glinis pressed her lips together. "All right then. Moira aside, ye canna live away from the castle. What will our nobles think of ye? Our highborn people, our tradesmen and merchants? Yer kinsmen, yer allies? What will they think if the great Earl of Kildrummond goes traipsing off to live like a peasant? What respect can ye hope to garner from them if ye do that?"

Lachlan laughed. "My lady, I am a hired knight. I am no great earl just yet."

"Dinna play games wi' me, lad." She leveled her dark eyes at him. "Ye will be, and that is what matters."

Lachlan considered her for a moment. She did have a point, of course. His reputation among the nobles would suffer if he did this. Not that he was particularly concerned about what they thought. But still, it was the kind of thing he'd have to consider if he were to take John Douglas's place.

"Master Eamon? What say ye?"

Eamon Douglas, who had been silent throughout the exchange, gazed thoughtfully at Lachlan. "My lord, her Ladyship speaks the truth, and that truth must no' be ignored.

"However," he continued quickly when Lady Glinis straightened with satisfaction, "being a leader of one's people means being a leader to all of one's people. Yer tenants, yer common folk, they love Moira. They consider her one of their own. And it would raise ye in their esteem to treat their Moira so considerately. Now, I admit this is highly unusual. Perhaps it is even unprecedented—I dinna ken. But overall, I do no' think it to be a folly... necessarily. At least a folly wi' any long-term consequences. If ye show yerself to be a good leader of men in all things, whatever respect ye may lose from yer noble kinsmen and allies, I'd wager ye'll be able to win it back easily enough."

Lady Glinis glared at Eamon Douglas. Lachlan nodded appreciatively. "I thank ye for yer honesty, sir. I'll give yer words due consideration. And now I'll leave ye, for I think my aunt has a few choice words she'd like to say."

He rose, and gave Lady Glinis a kiss to the forehead. She sat rigidly in her chair, her fingers digging into the arm rests. As soon as

Lachlan left the solar and closed the door, her muffled shouts reverberated from within.

"How could ye, Eamon? How could ye put such a notion in the lad's head? You're just as bad as the rest of them."

Lachlan snickered at the thought of poor Eamon Douglas on the other side of the door, fending off his aunt's outrage.

Poor fellow.

\*\*\*

Alex slumped at a dirty, dilapidated trestle table that night, in a tavern two villages distant from Glendalough. Already three drinks in, he stared sullenly into the dregs of his fourth goblet of ale.

It had been quite a ride to get here, and once he reached the first small outcrop of huts that qualified as a village, he nearly turned back. But Alex had had enough of castle life. He'd had enough of the highbred ladies and their simpering. He'd had enough of the Douglas men flapping their jaws about "Old Fiery Face" and the good Lord Douglas's noble cause to avenge his brother's murder. He needed to have a drink somewhere, anywhere, that was away from all of that.

Hell, he just needed a good, far-off place to get raving drunk!

It was Lachlan's fault Alex was in such a foul mood. Damn him and his soft spot for big blue eyes and a pretty face… not that Moira MacInnes was pretty, exactly, but the result was still the same. Already his thoughts were mired in the very essence of Glinis Douglas, and now his dearest, closest friend sprang *this* on him?

"Another?" asked the serving wench who had been looking after him all night.

Alex glanced up to see her leaning over him with her hip perched on the edge of the table. She tilted her head coquettishly, offering him more than just ale with her eyes.

Grunting, Alex lifted his goblet. Unoffended, she filled his drink, then sauntered off in search of another, more interested prospect.

Good God. If this had been a month ago, Alex would not have hesitated to take the lass up on her unspoken offer. She certainly was merry enough. But Glinis had a hold on him, on his entire being. There was no room for any other woman but her.

No other woman but Glinis Douglas, Lachlan's aunt. Damn that man twice over!

Given his vocation as a hired knight, Alex had naturally chosen a seat that faced the door to the tavern. So when the door opened, he had a perfect line of sight to watch Dougall MacFadyen, Glendalough's captain of the guard, swagger in. He greeted the lasses who smiled warmly at him, and clapped a few of the men on the back. Then, obviously having known Alex was here, Dougall strode over to the corner table where he was sitting alone.

"Come now, Sir Alex," he said jovially as he sat down across from him. "It canna be as bad as all that."

Alex took a long swallow of his refreshed ale. "I take it ye ken, then."

"The whole castle's heard. But dinna worry. I'll make sure yer chamber is no' given away while ye're gone. Ye were so partial to it."

His jest made Alex smile, despite himself. "I'll no' lie. I were pretty upset about that at first. How did ye ken where I was, by the bye?"

"Davey on the wall said ye'd ridden off, muttering to yerself about getting drunk. I figured ye'd either be heading to the tavern here, or the brothel in Findochty. I took a chance and came here first."

"And what if I'd been at the brothel?"

Dougall chuckled. "I'd have been asking the mistress for a bed for the night."

"'Tis no' a bad way to spend a night."

"No' for me, lad. Some of the lasses there are as dear to me as my own blood."

Alex raised a brow. "How did ye come to think of brothel lasses in *that* way?"

Dougall shrugged. "Call it an uncontrollable need to protect the less fortunate."

"I didna have you down as a saint."

"Aye, that's me. Saint Dougall of Moray."

Alex looked back down at his goblet, swirling the contents about and sloshing some of the amber liquid over the edge.

"About Lachlan," Dougall pressed. "It really could be much worse. Think on it this way: now that ye'll be living over at Moira's wee home, ye'll be closer to the tavern here."

Alex traced the rim of his goblet with a forefinger. "So ye havena heard, then."

Dougall's brows drew together. "Heard what?"

Alex laughed without humor. "It seems as though I willna be losing my chamber after all. I'll no' be going wi' them."

"Dinna tell me ye've refused to go. Sir Alex, I'll no' believe that of ye."

"I'm glad to hear it. And nay, I've no' defied Lachlan. He's ordered me to stay behind."

Dougall shook his head, not comprehending what Alex was telling him. "But... but he'll be alone out there. Unprotected, unguarded—"

Just then, the serving wench chose to try her luck with the captain. Her timing couldn't have been worse.

"Well if it isna Dougall MacFadyen," she cooed, toying with a strand of his hair. "We havena seen ye in such a long time. Ye've broken my wee heart, staying away like that."

Dougall's jaw clenched. "No' now," he snapped. The lass pulled back, shocked, and Dougall, recovering his wits, softened. "I'm sorry, Anwen. Forgive my manners. If ye could give us a moment, I'd be grateful. But mind ye bring me some of yer fine ale shortly."

Appeased, the lass sashayed away, with a flirtatious backwards glance over her shoulder.

"She a favorite of yours?" Alex questioned.

"Anwen? Nay. Though she has tried over the years. But enough of that. What d'ye mean, ye'll no' be going wi' them?"

"'Twas Lachlan's order. I'm no' to be going wi' them."

"But why? I can understand that he's newly married and he wants his privacy. But surely he canna be so shy as to worry about—"

"It isna that," Alex interrupted. "And shy, Lachlan Ramsay certainly is no'. 'Tis for his bride's sake, he said."

Dougall ruffled a hand through his hair. "I hope that lass recognizes what she has in that man. Well then, it looks as though I've some work to do. I'll have to organize regular patrols, and reorganize the guard. I'll no' have the future Earl of Kildrummond so far away from the castle without a regular patrol in the area. If he objects, I'll take the matter straight to his Lordship."

"He willna object," Alex confirmed. "I insisted on as much, myself. I told him I wouldna allow it, that I would defy his orders if he didna consent to at least regular patrols."

"That's good, at least," Dougall agreed.

The two men sat in silence, bewildered, drinking cup after cup of ale to numb the shock of Lachlan's decision. Alex felt a little sorry for Dougall, for his bafflement was twofold—at least Alex understood Lachlan's underlying motivation to keep Moira happy. He needed the little ruse the two of them had cooked up together to go off smoothly if he wanted his earldom.

From Dougall's perspective, poor lad, it must seem as though the future Earl of Kildrummond was losing his mind.

## *Thirteen*

That night's meal was Lachlan and Moira's last at Glendalough, and it was nearly as great a feast as the one after their wedding had been. Though Lachlan promised they would no longer take meals at the castle, Moira could hardly object to this final one, for it was the last evening that Lord Albermarle would join them.

In the morning he was to depart for Kinross, and from there, he and his men would be travelling to Douglas Castle in South Lanarkshire to join Lord Douglas's forces.

James Douglas was preparing for war against King James to avenge the murder of his brother and the theft of the lands that were his birthright. And now, enough of his allies had answered his call that the strike was imminent.

"What says yer fair Rosamund of all this, my lord?" Lachlan inquired as they sat down to eat.

Lord Albermarle exhaled. "She understands the need for it. But she frets—as any good wife and mother would, of course. My eldest two sons shall come wi' me."

"I suppose there is no changing yer mind? 'Tis treason, this stand."

"Aye, 'tis. And if I live through it and we dinna win, I may lose my head. I ken that and have come to terms wi' it. This isna a decision I've made lightly, lad. 'Tis no' only my own life wi' which I play this game, 'tis the lives of other men, too."

"Then why, my Lord? The king has returned Lord Douglas's lands to him. What is there to fight for?"

"Aye, old Fire Cheek didna get away wi' those ridiculous confiscations for long, did he?" The earl's shoulders shook with laughter. "Scotland's nobles raised their objections loud and clear—and that were the king's supporters *and* his enemies, mind. The fool had no choice but to back down." The mirth died on his lips. "In the end, I find that to do *nothing* would be the greater risk. 'Tis no' all pride and revenge, lad. 'Tis a principle. What kind of Scotland are we helping to build if we allow our monarch to murder good nobles and confiscate legally held lands at a whim? A king's justice is his divine right. His temper and his fits are *no'*."

Lachlan was moved by Lord Albermarle's conviction. An acute mix of pride and sorrow tightened his throat. "Ye're a fine leader, Edward Douglas," he said roughly.

"As ye will be one day, my boy. If Glendalough isna mine to inherit as I had always thought it would be, I ken now it couldna have gone to a more deserving man."

"I'm nay so sure about that. I'll no' be wi' ye to stand against the king, after all. D'ye think me a coward?"

"Nay, lad, and dinna think it for one minute. Ye're no' to join, whatever may come. Ye've an obligation to our John to keep Kildrummond out of the fray. 'Tis the reason ye've been named his heir: the name of Ramsay isna a part of this conflict. Ye'll no' go shoving yer way into it unbidden, and risk losing John's lands."

The force with which the earl spoke drove home for Lachlan one indisputable fact: Kildrummond should have been Lord Albermarle's by right of lineage. The earl had bowed out of his inheritance gracefully, and allowed Lord Kildrummond to name Lachlan his heir. He could have contested the decision. He'd had every right to. But he hadn't.

The earl meant what he said: Lachlan had an obligation to remain out of the conflict.

"When does Douglas plan to make his move?" he inquired.

"In about a month. When the ground has thawed and the spring rains have ceased. 'Tis no good fighting on a ground thick wi' mud."

"May then. Or thereabouts."

"I pray that poor John leaves this world before then. I wouldna wish him alive to learn we've lost our campaign."

The earl's defeatist statement alarmed Lachlan. "D'ye think ye will? Lose, I mean?"

Lord Albermarle shook his great head, his thick mane of silver-streaked hair quivering. "Och, dinna pay me any mind, lad. Douglas has a great force behind him. There is no reason to think he willna be victorious. I'm only preparing myself for the worst, is all."

For Moira, who'd been listening to the conversation quietly, Lord Albermarle's words fell heavy upon her heart.

A move against the Crown. Treason. She'd known the earl for most of her life. She could not bear to think of him being charged with such a grievous offense—to be sentenced and executed, should they lose.

\*\*\*

Moira was quiet for most of the journey back to her home.

"Ye're no' cross wi' me again, are ye?" Lachlan quipped.

"What?…Oh, nay. I were just thinking."

"Of?"

"Of Lord Albermarle. And how he's joining Lord Douglas."

"Ah, yes." He nodded slowly.

There was a moment of tense silence before she spoke again.

"Lachlan, ye're a knight."

"Last time I checked."

"What…what happens in a battle? Will Lord Albermarle fight, too, or will it only be his men?"

"Typically the lords dinna fight, no. If they do, they fight from atop their mounts and so are more protected than the men on the ground. Mind, though, the battles I've fought havena been anywhere near the size of this one—if it comes to that. Ye'd best prepare yerself, though. This isna a petty battle between clans. William Douglas's murder is a deeply personal matter for all the Douglas lords. Albermarle may very well fight. I suppose it depends upon his nature."

"That's what I were afraid of. 'Tis most certainly in Lord Albermarle's nature to take up a sword and avenge the death of his chief. He isna likely to sit back and watch other men carry out his justice for him."

"Aye, I've got that impression of him," Lachlan agreed. "I suppose the only thing to do is pray Douglas is victorious."

By then they'd reached the door of Moira's hut. The windows were dark; no homey turf fire flickered in the burlap-covered window, no plume of smoke lifted up from the chimney into the brisk night air. From outside, the place had a feel of abandonment to it.

Handing him her mare's reins, Moira darted inside and lit the fire. Returning, she helped him guide the horses into the crude stable which took up half the hut. It was tricky, for the dwelling had been built to accommodate only one horse and a handful of sheep. But neither mount seemed to mind the warmth of the other, nor of the Highland heifer they joined. The sheep bleated a half-hearted protest at having to share their pen, but soon gave up the complaint. It was too late and too cold outside to raise much of a fuss.

The animals secured for the night, Moira scanned the hut to make sure it was still tidy. Niall had kept the place well in her short absence. Her meager collection of things was still tidy; her handful of surfaces—floor, table, pantry—was still clean. He'd been into the pantry, though: the space where she kept her bannock, between the salt pot and the rye flour, was empty. This didn't surprise her. That boy could deplete Moray of its grain stocks within a sennight.

"Are ye in the habit of keeping mead?"

Moira glanced quizzically in Lachlan's direction, and followed his gaze to the right of the hearth. There, tucked into a corner, was a small, wooden cask with MacCormack's mark branded into the side of the wood grain.

"Oh, isna that sweet," she exclaimed. "Master MacCormack must have brought it to welcome ye."

"Ah, yes. He does make a good brew. I've never tasted anything quite like it."

"There's a reason the castle commissions most of his product nearly as fast as he can make it. We've one or two other brewers in the village, but their ale and mead is nowhere near as nice as his...or, I should say *theirs*, for the whole MacCormack family is involved in the trade. Even wee Imogen does what she can."

Dispensing with such formalities as etiquette, Moira fetched two cups. She poured a generous draught into each one, and handed a cup to Lachlan at the same time that she took a sip from her own.

The liquid was sweet and fragrant; it warmed her belly and took the edge off the chill night air. She must be careful not to drink too much, though. Lachlan was watching her from over the rim of his cup as he drank; the way his eyes scrutinized her made her belly a little *too* warm. She looked away.

*Stop it, ye daft lass. Ye dinna want to go imagining things that aren't there, now.*

"Well, I'm tired," she announced abruptly, and drained her cup. Setting it on the edge of the pantry, she shuffled over to the single cot.

It looked narrower than she remembered.

"I'll sit up a while, if ye dinna mind." Settling himself into Niall's armchair, Lachlan stretched his long legs out in front of him.

The firelight flickered on his bare shins, and danced over his raven hair. The whole situation felt far more intimate than she imagined it would. It was unsettling.

"Suit yourself," she replied nonchalantly, and set about stripping off her gown.

Since their first night together, Moira had overcome her modesty. Being modest, she'd discovered, was an inconvenience. Besides, the billowing linen of her shift covered her well enough. And thankfully she was too thin, too shapeless, to encourage a man to conjure in his mind what his eyes could not see.

Tossing her gown over the bedpost, she crawled under the layers of quilts and moved as close to the opposite side of the straw mattress as she could. She was so absurdly close to the wall that she could feel the cold coming off the stones graze her nose and cheeks.

Exhausted, she laid her head on her pillow and closed her eyes. But the sleep she'd been so eager to find all evening seemed lost to her with Lachlan in such close and intimate confines. She remained awake, cognizant of every sound he made. God's bones, she could hear the rippling of his throat each time he swallowed his mead.

The mead in her own belly began working against her senses. The warm comfort that seeped through her body was a little too relaxing. A little too…delicious.

She did not want to be relaxed around Lachlan. They may be friends now, they may have gotten over their initial wariness of each other, but he was still an arrogant arse like all the other handsome men she knew.

Though perhaps…not quite like all the others. Unlike them, when Lachlan talked to her, he wasn't looking over her shoulder for a more interesting woman to entertain. When Lachlan talked to her, it was as if he was truly listening, as if he was committed to the conversation they were having at that moment.

It was a trait she noticed in him no matter who he was talking to: commitment. Now that she had occasion to think about it, such was not a common trait. One did not often come across a person— man or woman, it didn't matter—that made one feel important when they spoke.

It was the mark of a good leader; Lachlan *would* make a good leader someday.

And therein lay the problem with the mead. For Moira could easily let herself be mistaken that this rare trait in Lachlan Ramsay, a trait which he showed to everyone, was a sign that he enjoyed her company. She could easily lose herself in the illusion that he *wanted* her companionship.

No handsome man ever really wanted her companionship. For the sake of her pride, Moira needed to remember that in this respect, Lachlan Ramsay was no different. He was not interested in her and he never would be.

And dammit, she was not interested in him, either.

Yet still, when he climbed into the bed beside her, she could feel his presence like an unseen force upon her skin. Like the tickle of a feather or the patter of rainwater.

"Night then, lass," he whispered to her back.

She pretended to be asleep. With that unseen feather tracing the sensitive line of her spine, she did not trust herself to answer.

\*\*\*

The mellow scent of clean hay, mingled with the slightly sharper aroma of animal netherparts, greeted Lachlan as he emerged from a deep and luxurious slumber. It was not entirely unpleasant, and he'd certainly awoken to more offensive smells in the past— unless a man knew what it was to sleep in a tent with thirty other men during the height of summer, that man could not claim to know what a bad smell truly was!

He did not move, did not make so much as a sound that he might chase away this unanticipated gift, this state of complete bliss in which he found himself.

Most mornings, when he awoke in a strange place, he did not immediately remember where he was. Given his profession, and the frequency with which he found himself sleeping in unfamiliar places, he'd become accustomed to identifying his surroundings straight away for any sign of imminent danger.

This morning was different. This morning Lachlan remembered exactly where he was and exactly why he was there. Instinctively he knew there was no danger; these were not surroundings that needed identifying.

The hut was warm. Curiously warm. The fire had died in the night, and from the harsh whistle of wind at the door and the rustling of the thatch on the roof he knew it was cold. But within the crude walls of Moira MacInnes's little hut it was a kind of cozy which no castle, no stable, no finely furnished guest quarters could hold a candle to.

He'd never known contentment quite like this. Was it the close confines of two horses, several odd sheep and a cow that made the place so comfortable? Or was it the small, willowy lass in the bed next to him?

Whatever it was, he didn't give a rat's left ballock. He was content, and wished for nothing more than to simply enjoy the peace of this moment.

Gradually the fog which drenched his senses began to lift, and he realized that he and Moira were snuggled much closer than they had been when they went to bed last night. She still faced the wall, but had inched closer to him in her sleep. His body was tucked around hers, his knees drawn into the back of her legs, and his arm slung lazily over her waist.

Lachlan had awoken to many a lass in his bed over the years (he was oddly ashamed to admit it now). But never before had he found himself cuddled up to them so casually in the morning. That was on the occasions when he remained in the bed all night, which (he was oddly even *more* ashamed to admit it now) he didn't always.

If he had been more lucid, if he had been less comfortable and less at peace, it might occur to him to wonder: why Moira? What was it about this lass that contented him so?

As it happened, Lachlan was not entirely lucid. It did not occur to him to wonder about anything just then. Closing his eyes, he allowed the gentle rise and fall of Moira's narrow ribs to lull him back to sleep.

Leave the wondering for another time.

## *Fourteen*

March descended from its wintery throne for another year, and the gentle hand of April moved in to rule over the Highlands. Spring rains tumbled from the sky, nourishing the soil and the tender flora that slept beneath it. Brave new shoots of grass poked their sleepy heads through the dead, brown mat of the previous summer's bounty, eager for a taste of the sun. Soon the hills of Kildrummond throbbed and swelled with all the majesty of an emerald paradise.

Glendalough tried, for the sake of the season, to enjoy the long-awaited thaw, and the fresh scents of earth and rain and new growth that enriched the mild air. But the coming battle loomed over the castle like a dark specter, threatening the peace and tranquility of Kildrummond.

Arkinholm, it was decided, would be the battleground on which the Black Douglases would challenge the king. On that hallowed ground, on the banks of the river Esk, they would avenge the murder of their eighth earl, would strike at the Crown for the confiscation of their lands. At Arkinholm they would reaffirm, once and for all, that their might as a clan lay not only in the political arena—it lay in the authority of the sword as well.

Either that, or they would die in the attempt.

The men of Kildrummond talked grandly of the coming battle. They spoke of Douglas courage and Douglas skill, and endlessly toasted all the men that would fight.

Alex joined in their merriment. He tipped his cup and saluted each and every name that was uttered with reverence.

What else could he do?

He would not tell these men that he didn't feel good about the battle. Something wasn't right, something he felt in his gut. As a knight, where instinct was every bit as important as skill and strength, Alex knew well to trust what he felt in his gut.

His gut was telling him that the Douglases would lose.

He could not bring himself to tell Lachlan, though. He kept his inkling to himself as, together, they learned the ropes of Glendalough by day, and enjoyed the cozy atmosphere of Moira's peasant dwelling by night, before he headed back to the castle with the patrol that made regular sweeps of the area.

He spoke not a word of it now, saddled next to his friends Lord and Lady Strathcairn as the trio made their way to market. A cartload of Moira's smaller tapestries and other bits for sale was pulled along by her mare (as ugly a mare as ever he'd seen that went by the absurd name of Beauty). The wooden wheels of the cart hobbled over the rocks and ruts of the traveled path, filling the silence of the morning with a pleasant, rhythmic clacking.

"Ye're all set then?" Lachlan asked once they'd gone a distance.

"Aye. My things are packed; I shall be off at dawn."

They spoke of Arkinholm; Alex was to witness the battle—with strict instructions from Lachlan that he was *not* to join in. In blatant defiance of what a knight was, what a knight stood for, Alex had been asked—no, *ordered*—to stand by and watch as men died around him.

It chafed him something fierce to be prohibited from taking action, but as a known servant of Viscount Strathcairn, Sir Alexander MacByrne's involvement might be misconstrued as the Kildrummond Douglases' support of their clan's cause.

Though Alex hated the idea, he at least understood it.

Immediately after the battle, he was to return to Glendalough with news of a Douglas victory. Or he was to return with news of…with word that…

Lachlan had not been able to make himself say it when they spoke last. He didn't need to; Alex knew: news of a Douglas defeat. News of who had lived and who had been killed.

News of which survivors would be executed for treason.

"Ye'll send our love and best wishes to Lord Albermarle," Moira added timidly.

Alex's throat tightened. He gave her as sincere a smile as he could muster. "Of course, my lady. I'm sure it will do him good to ken he has such loyal family behind him."

"Oh, I wouldna say I were family, exactly." She lowered her eyes self-consciously.

"Lord Albermarle would, though." Alex glanced knowingly at Lachlan. His friend looked back at him with unspoken thanks.

He needn't have thanked him, for Alex liked the young lass a great deal. Since the newly-wed couple had picked up and left Glendalough, Alex had become well acquainted with Lord Kildrummond's daughter.

He'd discovered that she was a breath of fresh air. In the comfort of her own home, which she readily shared with Alex on the regular occasions that he stopped in to visit Lachlan, Moira was gay and funny. She laughed easily, bantered endlessly with Lachlan, and was as lively as a spring brae.

She also had a quick wit and a quick temper. But somehow, in a way that was uniquely Moira MacInnes, her temper only served to make her more endearing. Alex recognized its source: deep pride coupled with a lifetime of having that pride tested. He could not fault her for that. Besides, she was never angry for long. When she was wrong she was just as quick to admit it; when she was right, her temper was easily soothed by a simple apology or a token amends.

Sir Alexander MacByrne occupied a unique place within this merry threesome. While he grew to know and like Moira MacInnes from an objective perspective, he began to suspect that his friend's objectivity was slowly seeping away. Observing Lachlan's interactions with his new wife, Alex was amazed by the transformation in his friend. Gone was the cool, aloof Viscount Strathcairn that emerged when the lasses were about. Around Moira, Alex saw a different Lachlan: the carefree, unguarded Lachlan he'd known since boyhood.

There were only four people on this earth (if one did not count the omniscient eyes of God) who knew this marriage was false. Sir Alexander MacByrne was one of them. And so the transformation in his friend was even more confounding.

Of course when he mentioned his observations to Lachlan one night after Moira had fallen asleep, they were immediately dismissed as ridiculous.

"If I *am* different wi' Moira—which I dinna think I am—'tis because I've no interest in her as a bedmate, and she's no interest in me that way. There isna any expectation between us."

"Aye, but if she's only a friend, as ye say, then ye treat her like a very *special* friend. I've never seen the like in ye."

"Well…" Lachlan thought on it for a heartbeat, "I suppose that's because she *is* a special friend. I'll no' lie, I do like her. She interests me. We get on well. I've never kent it before: simply enjoying a lass's company. But dinna mistake what ye see, 'tis no more than that."

Alex had nodded gravely, though he was not fooled.

The market was lively by the time they arrived. The day had started out under a leaden blanket of clouds, but now thick streams of sunshine pierced the molten barrier. As though heavenly fingers reached through to bless the gaiety below.

Moira had not brought a tent beneath which to sell her goods. Instead, she found a place among a line of other vendors, unharnessed the cart from her horse, and thenceforth declared herself open for customers.

Being the first time either Lachlan or Alex had come to market with her, neither was particularly impressed with her setup.

"That's all ye do, plunk yerself down like that and expect people to walk by and notice ye?" Lachlan crossed his arms dubiously.

"Aye," she answered simply. When Lachlan remained unconvinced, she giggled. "Careful, now, yer face will freeze that way, and then ye'll be sorry."

Alex imagined it, and laughed heartily. Lachlan elbowed him in the ribs.

"Aye," Moira repeated. "I'm nay so fancy that I need to display my wares. People ken what I do and what I have to sell."

Alex had his doubts, too. But before he could voice them, a well-dressed man approached. In his middling years, with a thick helmet of gray hair, he looked dignified. Not a noble, perhaps, but someone of great importance.

Moira recognized him, and smiled. Lachlan backed off, allowing the transaction to proceed, though Alex noted the protective way he hovered at her shoulder. He uncrossed his arms, allowing them to fall to his side in a relaxed manner. But from the tension in his forearms, Alex knew his friend was not relaxed at all, that Lachlan was preparing to draw his sword at the first sign of a threat to his lady.

Alex turned his head to hide his grin.

"Lady Strathcairn," the man said in a deep rumble, bowing. "I've no' yet had the pleasure of addressing ye by yer new title. It suits ye, if I may be so bold."

"Sir Colm." Moira offered her hand. "I am glad to see ye. Ye're looking well."

"As are ye, lass. And is this the Viscount Strathcairn?"

"It is. Sir Colm MacKenzie, may I introduce Lachlan Ramsay."

"My lord." Sir Colm bowed again.

"Sir Colm comes to us from the house of Leslie," Moira explained when Lachlan's expression remained politely blank.

"I serve the Earl of Leslie normally."

"Normally?" Alex put in.

"Today I come on Lady Leslie's bidding, Sir—"

"Sir Alexander MacByrne," Lachlan offered on his behalf. "He is my lifelong friend, and has followed me to Glendalough from our previous employ wi' the Earl of Erroll."

"Ah, Slains," Sir Colm nodded.

"Ye ken it?"

"I've heard of it. And I ken Lord Erroll, though I've never been to Aberdeenshire myself. So then, from commissioned knight at Slains to the future Earl of Kildrummond. I'd say that must be a welcome change. Though under the circumstances, 'tis no' something to celebrate, is it? Oh, by the by, Lady Leslie sends Lord Kildrummond her best. Will ye tell him?"

"Of course," Moira promised.

"Speaking of Lady Leslie, I come today to retrieve her Ladyship's latest commission. I trust it's ready?"

"Indeed it is." Stooping over her cart, Moira began pulling the lighter items from the top of the pile. She handed them, one by one, to Lachlan, until only his eyes could be seen above the pile in his arms.

"Here it is!" She pulled the largest tapestry from the bottom and unrolled it for Sir Colm to see.

Lachlan dropped his armload of items back onto the cart, grunting. He rolled his eyes and shook his head as if to say "women." Alex grinned—but not for the reason Lachlan thought.

"Ah, that is grand, my lady," Sir Colm breathed. "Ye've a fine talent there. The countess will be well pleased."

Peering around Sir Colm's thick shoulder, Alex marveled Moira's her latest work. He'd seen her tapestries displayed about Glendalough, of course. Nonetheless he was still amazed by her skill with a needle, and the vision which directed it.

The scene depicted the Leslie crest—a recently developed crest, as Alex understood, since the earldom of Leslie had been in existence less than ten years. It rose proudly above a sea of heathered hills, and the colors of the threads were so artfully chosen that these two separate entities looked as if they belonged to one another.

What turned this particular tapestry from a merely exceptional one into...well, to be frank, a work of *genius*, was the brae that bisected the violet-and-green hills. Either he was going mad, or the intricate detail of the stitching appeared to ripple with the slightest movement of the fabric. And it was such a luminous blue that it appeared to spring off the tapestry.

Sorcery! Or as good as. Sir Colm was just as taken with it as Alex was.

"How did ye achieve that affect wi' the brae?" He inquired in a hushed tone.

"'Tis only trickery of the eye," Moira explained. "See here how the edges of the water lighten? It is many different blues stitched so small ye canna see it from afar. And it shimmers and shifts like that because of the silver thread woven in. It catches the light and makes the brae look as though it flows."

The work was a masterpiece, yet she spoke so casually of it. As if it were nothing more than a loaf of manchet. It pained Alex to watch her roll it up, knowing he would never lay eyes on it again. How did she manage it? She would likely never lay eyes on it again either, and it was a masterpiece borne of *her* hand and *her* mind.

But manage she did. She placed the tapestry in Sir Colm's arms with no more ceremony than if it were a sack of grain.

Alex wished the nobles of Glendalough could see her like this, could see her tenacity and her grit. At the helm of her own ship, so to speak. Moira's deftness as a merchant was admirable. They mocked her, of course, the nobles—especially the ladies. In whispers, they gossiped about how shocking it was that Lady Strathcairn, soon to be the Countess of Kildrummond, was selling needlework at market like a commoner. Though of course, no one was truly shocked by it. They snickered and ridiculed Lachlan, too. Smiled at him and curtseyed and said "my lord," as they passed, then mocked him behind his back for his failure to check the wild, unworthy Moira MacInnes.

Not that either Moira or Lachlan seemed to care. In truth, neither did Alex. It would not stop Lachlan from becoming Earl of Kildrummond, and it would not stop Moira from doing just as she pleased, as she had all her life.

Let the nobles snicker and ridicule, Alex thought. If it wasn't this, then they'd just find something else to mock, anyway.

Sir Colm pulled a small leather purse from inside his shirt. "Of course I bring the countess's final installment." Parting the drawstring, he tipped out a generous handful of coin.

Alex watched him finger the payment in his beefy palm, counting the coins with him. He had too much; Alex was certain he would put some back. Instead, the man shook out another two pieces before handing the lot over to Moira.

"With Lady Leslie's sincere thanks."

"Please tell her the pleasure were all mine, and send her my well wishes."

"Aye, I will." Sir Colm MacKenzie bowed to Moira, nodded amiably to Alex and Lachlan, and led his horse away, into the seething market crowd.

"I didna ken ye stood to make so much from a commissioned piece," Lachlan said when he'd gone, his eyes fixed on Moira's hand as she deftly pocketed her earnings. "He said that were the final installment? How many installments must one make? Two?"

"Three. Granted, the first two are mere pittances in comparison wi' the final payment, but they're nothing to sniff at."

"So I see."

"Well then," Alex declared, "since ye're wealthier than the two of us at the moment, how about ye treat us to a draught?"

"Oh, dinna beat about the bush, sir, if there's something ye want," she laughed. Then she leaned towards the vendor woman beside her. "Will ye be a dear, Agnes, and mind my wares for me? I willna be long."

The woman, one of the many Douglas villagers that flooded the market with a sea of blue and green plaid, winked. With her assurances, the trio threaded their way through the crowd to its very center, where Master MacCormack's permanent stall was erected.

Alex followed behind Lachlan, amused by the way his friend loomed over his lady. His head swept left and right. Alex could easily imagine the warning on it: any man that so much as looked at her wrong would be pummeled black and blue.

When had Lachlan become so sentimental?

MacCormack's stall swelled with happy villagers, cups dangling loosely from ale-warmed fingers. Interspersed among them were a few notable knights and lesser nobles from the castle. All stood cheek by jowl, the rules of class forgotten with the mild morning air and the best spirits in the Highlands. Behind the wooden counter scurried Master MacCormack and Niall, sloshing cups of ale towards their customers and catching coins flipped their way in payment. They moved with such precision that they might have been performing a well-rehearsed dance.

Spotting Moira and her companions, Dougall MacFadyen raised his arm and waved them over.

"Lady Moira," he called jovially.

"Dougall, I'm surprised to see ye here, so idle. Have ye no training this morning?"

"Ah, ye mock me. Ye forget, lass: if I do, then yer lord husband and his companion will be in as much trouble as I."

"Oh, all right. I willna tell, then."

"She is the measure of generosity, is she no'?" Lachlan declared with unintentional affection.

"Ne'er was there a more generous lass. And now let me buy the three of ye a draught. What will ye have?"

"Och, 'tis no' necessary," Moira informed him. "I've just sold my Leslie commission. The drinks are on me, and whatever ye'll have too, Dougall."

"No charge on this round," Master MacCormack interrupted from behind the counter. When this roused a round of protest from his paying customers, he shouted, "She is like a daughter to me. She doesna need to pay…for the first round, anyway. So what'll it be, gentlemen?"

"Three ales and a mead?" Alex suggested.

"Mead?" Niall snorted. "For Moira MacInnes? That there's no lady, Sir Alex. Our Moira can drink wi' the best of them, make no mistake."

"Four ales, then."

Niall poured the draughts from a large, oak cask at the back of the tent and handed them off. Receiving his cup, Alex took a long sip of the rich, dark ale within, savoring the unique flavor that he'd come to associate with Glendalough. He let it roll around his tongue, appreciating the subtle blend of heather and pine that had been infused into it. It made for a robust ale with a sweet finish.

"My compliments, Master MacCormack," he stated, raising his cup. "A fine batch, this. Have ye added something to it? I taste another flavor in there that I canna identify."

"Gooseberry," the brewer answered. "And as much as I'd like to take yer compliments, they belong to Niall. This be his batch. He were the one thought of the gooseberries. I'd say it turned out well, eh lad?"

"Aye, Da."

"Our Niall's well on his way to becoming a master brewer himself. Has a talent for it, he does. Runs in the family."

"This is fine, Niall, truly," Lachlan agreed, draining his cup.

"Careful now, men, ye're making the lad blush like a wee lassie," Moira teased.

"Shut yer gob," Niall muttered, but he flicked a wink in her direction. His eyes swept the crowd behind her, his face suddenly flushed red. He lowered his head and became intensely interested in his work.

What on earth had come over him, Alex wondered. He glanced in the direction Niall had been looking.

His question was immediately answered. Making her way through the crowd was a ripe, young maid Alex recognized from the castle. A lovely lass she was, with honey-colored hair and a fresh, bright face. No two ways about it, young Niall MacCormack was sweet on this lass—what was her name again?

"Good morning, Dougall," she greeted, approaching the gathering at MacCormack's stall.

"And to ye, Janet. How be ye this fine morning?"

"I am well, thank ye. This fine spring air does me good. And good morning, my lord," she added, addressing Lachlan, "and Lady Moira, and Sir Alex." Her bright eyes took on a hint of amusement when she turned them on Niall's bent head. "Niall, good morning."

"Janet," he mumbled, barely audible, and continued with his scurrying.

The small party of friends stared at the awkward young brewer, waiting for him to say more. He did not.

"Janet," Moira said tentatively, "this here is Niall's brew. We were all just saying how good it were."

"Is that so," Janet played along. "D'ye think he might let me have a taste?"

"Oh, I'm sure he would." Moira reached into her pocket and pulled out a coin. Slapping it onto the scarred counter, she said, "Niall, love, a draught for the lovely Janet, aye?"

Alex bit his cheeks, trying not to laugh as Niall poured the ale and handed it to Moira. He could feel Lachlan vibrating with silent laughter beside him.

"So, er, Niall," he ventured, "wi' this weather so fine, d'ye no' think this lovely young lass might like to walk sometime?"

Niall stared at Alex blankly. His eyes shifted to Janet, then swiftly darted away.

"Aye," Moira chimed in, "I think that'd be a fine idea. What say ye, Janet?"

Janet laughed lightly. "I am fond of walking, Lady Moira, 'tis true. But so often I find myself wi'out a companion. Will *ye* walk wi' me, Sir Alex?"

"Alas, I am bound for Arkinholm in the morning," he answered with mock gravity. "What about Sir Dougall?"

"Oh, no' me," Dougall said similarly. "Nothing would make me prouder, Janet, to walk wi' ye, but I…I have—"

"We both have too busy a training schedule to spare the time," Lachlan helped.

"That's right," Dougall agreed.

"'Tis a shame, that," Janet lamented, shaking her head theatrically.

Five pairs of eyes fixed expectantly on Niall. Long seconds passed with not a word spoken before Moira threw a coin at him in frustration.

"Ye daft lout, ask her to walk wi' ye."

Startled out of his wits, Niall blurted, "WILLYEWALKWI'MEJANET?"

He shouted so loud that the villagers in the immediate vicinity turned and stared. Poor Niall—his mouth hung open like a dead fish as he tried ineffectually to correct his error. The whole thing was so comical that Alex, who had taken an ill-timed sip of his draught, spit it out. Amber liquid sprayed from his mouth onto his companions.

"Oy, ye lummox," Moira accused, wiping her face.

Then she began to laugh. And Lachlan began to laugh. And then Dougall and Janet and everyone around who had witnessed the transaction—began to laugh.

"Oh all right, if ye insist," Janet sighed when she was able to catch her breath. "Call for me at my father's home on the morrow."

Bidding farewell to the others, she made her way back into the crowd.

Lachlan looked at Niall, amazed. "I have never seen anything quite like that," he exclaimed reverently. "Either ye're a great, awkward lout as ye seem—or that were a stroke of brilliance!"

The rest agreed, and a slow, sheepish grin softened the stunned look on Niall's flushed face.

"So, yer Lordship," said one of the villagers who had been drinking at MacCormack's stall when they arrived. "Will ye be putting an end to our Moira selling her tapestries and such at market?"

"*Lady* Moira," corrected the man to the right of the first. "She's no' 'Our Moira' anymore."

A look of hurt crossed Moira's face. "I'll always be your Moira, Keon."

"Aye," said the first man quickly. "But at the same time, nay. Ye'll be Lady Kildrummond when his Lordship passes." He crossed himself quickly from head to chest and shoulder to shoulder. Those within earshot did the same. "And Lady Kildrummond shouldna be selling at market," he concluded.

"Is that what ye want, sir?" Lachlan inquired.

The two men looked at each other meaningfully. The first man took a long swallow of his ale before answering.

"'Tis no' for us to say what we want, yer Lordship. 'Tis for *ye* to say. Moira— er, that is, Lady Strathcairn, is yer wife now. Surely ye'll no' be letting her sell her wares like a commoner anymore."

Alex stood back silently. He was interested to see how Lachlan would respond to this. None of the villagers knew that an annulment was on the horizon, and that Moira would go back to selling her tapestries at market soon after. His friend would need to know how the people he was called upon to lead would take such a betrayal of their beloved Moira. Lucky for him, these two men had unwittingly provided him with the perfect opportunity to find out.

"I'm sorry, sir, I didna catch yer name," Lachlan began.

The first man straightened. "I am Eramon. Eramon Douglas. And this be Keon Douglas. We've kent Moi— Lady Strathcairn, since she were a bairn."

Alex caught the look in Lachlan's sideways glance. They'd known each other so long they could nearly read the other's thoughts.

"Let me ask ye, friend," he jumped in. "What do ye think of the future Lady of Kildrummond selling her tapestries at market like a commoner? 'Tis true, she has an exceptional talent. But d'ye think you could respect Lady Moira if ye saw her selling tapestries at market in, say, a month's time?"

"'Tis no' a question of respect," put in an old woman, indignant at Alex's tone. She had been passing by, and had overheard the conversation. She stood now behind Alex, looking up at him from her stooped stature through a wrinkled face and keen, clear eyes. "We will always love and respect her. 'Tis a matter of wanting what's best for her. Wanting her to be happy. She shouldna be made to sell tapestries, of course, if she has wealth and position. But at the same time, that wealth and position shouldna prevent her from selling her tapestries, if it makes her happy. Maybe for other ladies of gentle birth it should. But no' Moira. Moira isna like any other noble lady. 'Tis what she's always done. And that shall no' change her in our eyes, whether she's a countess or no'."

The determination with which the old woman spoke surprised Alex. It surprised Lachlan, too.

"And is that how ye feel?" he asked Keon and Eramon, his voice strangely thick.

Keon shrugged. "As I said, 'tis no' my place to say. But since ye've asked, then...aye. I agree wi' Old Brigid."

"Aye," Eramon agreed. "I do also."

Their support of Moira was touching. Alex watched Lachlan struggle as he tried to reconcile in his head the fact that he and Moira were deceiving these people. Guilt flickered across his face. And regret.

And, was that...sadness?

Was Lachlan actually sad about the arrangement, sad that it would eventually come to an end? Was Lachlan Ramsay, of all people, sad that he'd be losing Moira when the grand deception over and done with?

Suddenly, Alex saw what was going on between them with a new kind of clarity. The unconscious protection of her, the way they were together... Lachlan Ramsay was falling for Moira. Really and truly falling for her.

Astonished at this revelation, he scanned the market absently.

His heart skipped a beat at something in the distance. He thought he saw...wait, *yes*, it was. A pair of dark, sensual eyes stared back at him across the grounds.

Eyes just like Lady Glinis's.

Before he could determine that it was, indeed, she, the crowd shifted, and in a breath, the eyes were gone.

Had he imagined what he'd seen? He must have, for what would Lady Kildrummond be doing at a common place like market?

Just to be sure, he searched the crowd. She was nowhere to be found. Dismissing the notion, he resumed the conversation with his companions, determined to believe it had only been a coincidence. But his thumping heart could not be convinced otherwise.

She'd been there. And she'd looked right at him.

## *Fifteen*

The door to Glendalough's rear garden swung open, its well-oiled hinges making no sound to disturb the still, morning air. A thick fog rolled across the threshold and into the stone corridor that connected the keep to the servants' quarters and kitchens. The pallid sky had not been light for long, but the twittering birdsong which rode the gentle breeze confirmed that night had passed.

Glancing left and right to ensure that no eyes had seen her, Lady Glinis pulled the wide hood of her woolen cloak over her head to conceal her face. Then she stepped onto the dewy grass and closed the door silently behind her.

She strode with haste across the rear grounds of Glendalough to the small gate on the north side of the curtain wall. It was the castle's only other exit point besides the main south gate. She prayed the guardsman there stationed had fallen asleep at his post, for she did not wish to be observed in this manner: sneaking out of her own castle—imagine what the servants would think.

Approaching the gate, Glinis muttered a foul word under her breath. Very much awake, and surveying the land over the parapet of the outer wall walk, was a lone figure. By his proud posture alone, she knew it was none other than Dougall MacFadyen.

Curse his loyal hide!

Though upon consideration, perhaps it was rather fortuitous that Glinis should find Dougall guarding the gate this morning. If anyone would hold their tongue and not tell John that she'd sneaked off it would be Kildrummond's captain of the guard. Lord Kildrummond's public betrayal of his wife had never sat well with Dougall, and though the lad was not in a position to voice his objection, neither was he inclined to inform on Glinis (and her occasional, minor indiscretions) to his Lordship.

Hearing the swishing of wet grass underfoot, Dougall turned and leaned his elbows on the edge of a merlon. He said nothing as she approached, simply regarded her.

"Lady Kildrummond." His greeting was louder than she would have wished. "Up this early and by yerself?"

"I beg ye, Dougall, keep yer voice down."

"Are ye well?"

"Of course I'm well, dinna be daft."

"Then what are ye doing wi'out an escort? Wi'out yer mare? Shall I fetch them for ye?"

"Nay, dinna do that."

He frowned. "Where are ye going, might I ask, wi'out a horse? Ye're no' off to some illicit tryst now, are ye?"

She raised one eyebrow in reprimand. He was not chastened by it; but of course, she'd not expected him to be.

"I wish to walk," she told him. "That is all. By myself—no mount, no escort."

Dougall shook his head. "I dinna like the sound of that, my lady. 'Tis dangerous out there. Ye could run into poachers, thieves, vagrants—"

"Ye ken better than anyone these lands are well patrolled. I've more chance of running into poachers and thieves in my own chamber than I do in Kildrummond's hills. Now let me out—and dinna say a word to anyone!"

Dougall hesitated. Unwilling, he raised the portcullis, taking care not to jangle the heavy chains unnecessarily.

"I *would* tell, my lady, if I werena so foggy-headed this morning. I should tell."

"Are ye foggy-headed this morning, Dougall?"

"Aye. I were enjoying myself a bit too much at MacCormack's market stall yesterday," he admitted. "I didna think I'd be on guard this morning, but one of my men fell ill."

"Nothing serious, I hope?"

"Och, nay. He'll be right as rain in a day or two. Now ye be careful out there. And I must insist, my lady, if ye're no' back by the time the morning meal is served, I'll send a search out for ye, and tell his Lordship where ye've gone."

"He'll tan yer hide himself if he discovers ye let me out alone."

"Never mind my hide. 'Tis yer safety I care about."

"That's why we love ye so."

Waving, Glinis crossed the rutted dirt beneath the arched wall and emerged onto the open ground beyond. The clinking of the portcullis being lowered again met her back as she walked away.

She was not at all surprised that Dougall was foggy-headed this morning. She'd seen him at market herself, enjoying the fruits of

MacCormack's labors in the company of Moira and Lachlan and Sir Alex.

*Alex.* His name made her heart skip a beat.

He'd seen her—she hadn't meant for him to, but he'd seen her. What a foolish woman she'd been, going to market just to catch a glimpse of him. But she had no choice; he made it so hard for her now that he was spending all his time with Moira and Lachlan in that wretched hut on Kildrummond's border.

She didn't know how or when it had happened, but suddenly, seeing him only at meals was not enough. At meals, he was across the room; at meals, people were watching. She was not free to gaze as long and as directly as she pleased—

Hellfire, *when* had she become such a lovestruck, empty-headed lass? *Shameful*!

After the meal he was gone for the day, out training with the men, or on patrol, or spending time with Lachlan and Moira.

It left Glinis feeling oddly abandoned. Deflated.

It was in this frame of mind (which could not be called *any* frame of mind, really, since she'd apparently gone and lost hers) she'd sneaked away to market with one of her handmaids as an escort. Her pretense was that she wished to purchase thread for her needlework, and did not know which colors she wanted.

When she glimpsed his face through the throngs of people, so carelessly enjoying the warmth and the ale and the general gaiety, she couldn't help but admire him. His golden hair had been tied in a queue, revealing the strong lines of his jaw and neck. It brightened the green of his eyes and made his skin shimmer like polished bronze.

Even from a distance his magic affected her, turned her knees to jelly and her stomach to a haven for butterflies.

When he turned those luminous eyes on her, the world ground to a halt. It was less than a second before she darted away, but it felt like a century. An eternity of falling into a void which she never wanted to find her way out of.

He was leaving this day. Leaving for Arkinholm and war. It was agonizing to know that he'd be so close to the fighting. Though Lachlan had forbidden him from joining, it didn't put Glinis's mind at ease, for she did not know Sir Alex well enough to say whether or not he would obey. She knew the minds of potent young men, knew the bloodlust that afflicted them when battle was near at hand.

Sir Alex was without doubt a potent young man. Would he be as helpless to the bloodlust when the fighting at Arkinholm began?

Her tangled thoughts kept her company on her journey north through the hillier regions of Kildrummond. Even in her one-and-forty years, she was as sure-footed as she'd been when she was a lass of twenty.

She knew this way, had traveled it many times. Beyond the next hill there was a small pool, not quite as deep as a man, and perhaps as wide as her bed was long. A mountain stream collected here briefly before continuing on its merry way down the other side. Who knew how many thousands of years it had been here, the water hollowing out this bowl for itself on its course into the rivers below?

It had been a long time since she'd been here last. She used to come as a girl, when she was first married and in need of solace. When the pain of her new husband's rejection, and his eventual betrayal of their marriage vows, cut too deeply to overcome in the presence of the castle's ever-watchful eyes.

She always came alone. At first, she'd brought her handmaid with her, but the stupid woman had run and told John, and John had forbidden her from going again for fear that she might drown or be swept down the mountainside. (He'd never come himself, else he would know that such a thing was improbable.) Young Glinis had agreed solemnly, and promised she would come no more.

From that day on she made this excursion alone, and in secret.

Standing over the pool, peering into its rippling surface, she wondered why it had been so many years since her last visit. In warmer days, Glinis would strip off her fine garments and the constraints of being a countess, and bathe naked. The feel of the water undulating past her bare flesh beneath the surface was soothing. She used to love ducking her head completely under, and letting the current move her hair and her body as it would.

It was too early in the season to do so now, though.

Although...perhaps not too cold to dangle her legs. It was nearly May, after all, and the air was warm by day...

She pondered briefly, before succumbing to the same, girlish abandon of decades past. Giggling aloud, she tossed her cloak from her shoulders and yanked her embroidered umber gown up over her head.

Hitching her sleeveless linen shift to her waist, she perched her bare bottom on the wet grass. A small gasp escaped her throat at the cool dew on her heated flesh. Slowly, she lowered her legs into the pool: toes first, then heels, then ankles and finally calves.

The water was crisp and fresh, not so cold that she couldn't acclimatize to it for a short while. In fact, if she were more adventurous she might take a dip...

Oh, what a coward she was. She flicked water into the air with her toes. Perhaps another day. Soon, though, for just as she'd needed distraction from the pain of her failed marriage as a lass, she needed distraction from the agony of Sir Alex's departure now.

Yes, she would come again very soon.

Giddy with a spontaneity she thought she'd lost long ago, Glinis kicked her legs vigorously, sending up a spray of water that sloshed onto the grass and dampened her shift. If she had her wits about her, she'd care what the servants would think when they found her wet undergarment.

But she didn't—neither care nor have her wits about her. The exhilaration was too great. She laughed, and raised her face to the sky.

A horse whinnied in the distance.

Glinis froze. Her heart thundered in her chest, and Dougall MacFadyen's warning sharpened in her ears: *thieves, poachers, vagrants.*

She listened to the air. Was it a Kildrummond crofter, one of her husband's tenants, going about his daily chores? No, it could not be that, for no land had been sectioned into farmsteads up here. Had she imagined the sound?

The slow thud of hooves on grass gave answer. Panic speared her breast. Someone was coming.

Scrambling away from the pool, Glinis snatched her cloak and gown, then scampered over the edge of a small dip in the land. She crouched behind the grassy knoll, barely concealed.

If she were lucky, whoever was coming would pass her by. The pool was not a visible landmark for travelers, so unless one knew it was here, it was unlikely to attract any notice.

She waited. The minutes were excruciating. Her limbs pulsed with the primal urge to flee; her trapped breath seared the tissue of her lungs.

God's bones, the traveler knew about the pool! The animal's footfalls came to a halt at the edge, and the sound of a man's feet hitting the ground was like an exclamation point upon her inner frenzy. Who was this man that had stolen the sanctity of her oasis?

And what horrible things might he do if he found her?

There were a few quiet rustling and shuffling sounds, then a great splash. A deep, male grunt rose in proclamation, followed by more splashing.

Glinis had no way out. She was surrounded by hills. To flee she would have to rise from her hiding place. Whereupon she would be seen.

Unless…unless his back was to her.

If his back was to her, she might have a few precious seconds to creep away. She would have to creep, for any movement quicker than that might alert the horse. Could she manage it?

Emboldened by the glimmer of possibility, she raised her head just enough that her eyes cleared the edge of the grass bank. She saw for the first time her uninvited guest—a yelp lodged in her throat.

Immersed to the shoulders in *her* pool, with his golden hair slicked back and his bare chest glistening…was Sir Alexander MacByrne.

Sir Alexander MacByrne! Of all the men that could have happened upon this place, at this time, it had to be him. Glinis didn't know whether to lament her misfortune or exalt her blessing.

She did neither, merely watched him duck and resurface, breathing sharply each time as his body grew accustomed to the cold water. His tunic, cloak, plaid and boots lay in a heap beside his gelding, which was peacefully grazing on the moist, fragrant grass.

He was fascinating to observe, a man nothing short of magnificent: his contoured chest gleamed in the dull morning light; long, powerful limbs skimmed the pool's surface with vitality and grace. As if he were water itself.

When he was finished bathing, Alex hoisted himself from the pool, unknowingly exposing his nakedness to Glinis. Emitting a strangled gasp, she ducked behind her knoll once more and prayed that he hadn't heard her.

But Sir Alexander MacByrne was a warrior and knight. He was trained to detect small sounds that did not belong in a place. He *had* heard. The scrape of his blade against its scabbard confirmed it.

"I ken ye're there. Show yerself."

His voice was harsh. A chill ran down Glinis's spine; a warrior's voice had made the command. It was a side of him she'd not yet seen. It frightened her...and thrilled her at the same time.

Muttering a prayer, she crawled out from behind her hiding place, her cloak and gown forgotten. She looked defiantly at Alex, every bit the countess she was, but for her traitorous cheeks which burned crimson.

He'd hastily fastened his tartan around his waist, but other than that he was still naked. He brandished his sword, the steel gleaming against the steel grey sky. When he saw her, his fierce expression melted into one of bafflement.

"Lady Glinis?"

"Aye, Sir Alex. I....em....I do say, this is rather awkward."

"What are ye doing here, and by yerself?"

She bristled at the question. "I am countess of Kildrummond, these are my lands. I should be asking *ye* what *ye're* doing here."

"I discovered this place soon after I arrived at Glendalough. I've been coming here most mornings since the weather's grown milder."

"Well *I* discovered this place nigh on twenty years ago. I'd say that makes the claim of it mine."

"Then I concede." He bowed low, but his eyes stayed on her.

Glinis shifted from one foot to the other. The way he was looking at her made her nervous. The fact that he made no move to dress himself made her even more nervous. She was keenly aware of her lightweight shift, which skimmed her skin with each wisp of breeze.

He knew the effect he was having on her. "Why d'ye keep yer distance, my lady?" he purred, his voice like velvet. "Are ye afraid of me?"

"Afraid? Nay, I am no' afraid. I keep my distance because I dinna trust ye." *Nor do I trust myself.* "Ye'd best dress yerself; ye'll catch yer death of cold."

"'Tis nothing. The water is cold, aye, but the air is warm enough once ye're out of it. Besides, I've warm blood." When she gave him a disapproving look, he lowered himself to the edge of the pool.

Tossing his broadsword behind him into the grass, he dangled his bare legs in the water. His hand thumped the grass at his side in invitation.

Glinis's conscience begged her not to entertain the idea. *No good will come of this, woman. Dinna be a fool, ye ken what he wants.*

Her heart hammered madly at her ribs. It made a different plea, in a language that had no words.

"Oh, very well," she sighed. She stepped lightly, closing the gap between them. Raising her shift to her knees, she sat and slipped her own legs back into the pool. She tensed at the icy throb, then relaxed as the cold subsided.

Alex laughed. "Aye, ' tis no' summer yet, I suppose."

"'Tis beautiful here in summer." She smiled wistfully. "I have many regrets in my life, but becoming lady of these lands has never been one of them. 'Tis a beautiful place."

"And what regrets *do* ye have, if I may be so bold? D'ye regret marrying his Lordship?"

Glinis chewed her lip. "I used to—no' that marrying John was ever *my* choice, mind. I were barely fifteen, and my father wasna one to dote on his daughter. He bartered my hand away in exchange for kinship wi' the Douglases as easily has he would have bartered a horse for seed grain."

"'Tis common of noblemen," he offered.

"Aye, and I dinna wish for yer sympathy, Sir Alex. Many women of my status end up in situations worse than mine. I'm no' fool enough to be ungrateful for the comfortable life I've led. But there was once a time when I did regret. It was long ago; I were a young, silly girl, and thought I'd stay young forever, as silly girls do."

"What was that regret?"

She glanced sideways, then away again. "I regretted that I didna defy my father and run when I had the chance. And later I regretted that I didna run from John, when he betrayed his marriage vows and took up wi' that—"

The word *whore* died on her lips before she uttered it. It was a strange word now, felt strange to say it without the force of her hatred for Lilian MacInnes behind it. Oddly, that rage was gone now.

There was an empty place where her heartache had been. The word held no significance anymore, no power.

Seeing her thoughts flicker across her face, Alex slid closer. Only a sliver of space remained between them.

"I'm glad ye didna run. I never would have met ye otherwise."

The lull of his voice made Glinis tingle from her forehead to her toes.

"I dinna wish to be a young man's prize," she said, almost pleading.

Alex slid closer still. His thigh grazed hers. "Aye, ye've said. 'Tis a good thing I dinna want a prize."

"W-What do ye want?"

He leaned into her, and slid his arm around her back. Bending his head to her neck, he brushed his lips along the length of her jaw.

Glinis closed her eyes; a tremble started in her core. She felt like she was drowning, being pulled under by the sensuous spell he was weaving over her. She held still, seeing nothing but the darkness behind her lids, waiting for his lips to find hers...

A shove at her back wrenched her from her spell, and she was propelled into the frigid water. Her head went below the surface, and she pushed against the rock bottom to stand. Her lungs pulled in sharp, shallow breaths at the sudden shock, and before she could take stock of what had just happened, Alex's strong arms wrapped around her, pressing his warm body to hers.

She opened her eyes to find him gazing intently at her. Then her eyes slid to the edge of the pool where they'd been sitting...

His plaid lay in a heap on the wet grass.

"Sir Alex, this i-isna app-ropriate," she stuttered through chattering teeth.

"Then let go of me," he whispered, rough-tender.

He did not wait for her to answer. Or perhaps it was she that did not wait—it was unclear who had made the move. But he was kissing her, devouring her with an urgency that took her breath away. And she was kissing him back with a fury to rival his. The water drew a deep shiver from her, but she didn't stop. Never wanted to stop, even if she froze to death where she stood.

They were not in the pool long. She was vaguely aware of being moved through the water as Alex pulled her to the edge and onto the grass. His lips parted from hers for only the briefest second to hoist her out of the water. Then he climbed out himself. His hard, lean body came down on her with a delicious weight.

Glinis's head disintegrated; every inch of her skin surged under his hands, which skimmed her body with insatiable need. Her need matched his; her own hands drifted over the ridges of his chiseled back, the slim line of his waist, the hardened swells of his buttocks.

He moaned against her lips, a rumble that came from deep within his chest. "My God, woman, I've wanted ye since I first laid eyes on ye."

She believed him. And knew that his want of her was more than plain lust. Of course, Glinis had heard such declarations before, but had dismissed them out of hand. Those foolish, handsome young men had thought to flatter her with their inflamed sexual urges. Their flattery had meant nothing to her; their lust for her had meant little more.

Alex did not flatter her now. His declaration was a statement of fact, his want for her far deeper than carnal desire.

Or perhaps her own want of him made her willing to believe it. If that was so then she didn't care. When he tugged at the neck of her shift, drawing it down over her shoulders and her breasts, she wriggled the rest of the way out of the sodden garment.

Her naked skin, stippled like gooseflesh, melded with his and was warmed. The evidence of his desire, rigid between his thighs, pressed into her belly.

He did not claim her, though. Not right away, for he was not one to seek only his own satisfaction. His mouth roved over her bare flesh, moving downward as he shifted his body atop hers. His tongue teased the peaks of her nipples, slid below the soft, plush mound of her breasts: first one, then the other, then to the base of her sternum before dipping lower to her navel.

The cold was forgotten. Glinis's entire body blazed with unseen flame. She released a tiny cry of surprise when his tongue flickered over her womanhood.

*Sinner*, shouted the voice in her head. *Your husband is still alive, yet you give your heart another man.*

*My husband gave his love to another woman, and this man gives his heart to me*, she shouted back.

Defying the voice and the last of her reservations, she yielded to the pressure of Alex's hands upon her knees, and allowed them to part. When he put his mouth to her fully, she bucked upwards. Her eyes flew wide and her hands threaded through his hair, clasping him to her. An unbidden moan wrenched from her lungs.

He was skilled. He knew where the most sensitive flesh lay, knew how to tease by pushing and withdrawing in a seemingly endless, pleasurably frustrating rhythm. Her legs moved restlessly against him, and her gasps came short and sharp, making her grow light-headed.

When she could stand no more, when she thought she would die without fulfillment, she coaxed him back up.

Alex obliged. His eyes met hers, heavy lidded and dark as a stormy sea. Her body was racked with a new kind of shiver that had nothing to do with the cold. Nonetheless, Alex reached for his rumpled plaid and blanketed them both with it.

Beneath the cover of his *feileadh mhor*, he eased himself inside her, gentle but deep. A shudder rippled through his body, and his mouth was on hers again. His lips moved, urgent and demanding, mimicking the rhythm of his hips against hers. Soft grunts pillowed at the back of his throat; driven wild by the sound, Glinis dug her fingers into his back, demanding that he move faster. He obeyed, bringing her closer and closer to the edge of a climax.

She was too close, too mad with need to notice that he held back his own pleasure for the sake of hers.

Her climax crested in a blaze of light and heat. She buried her face into his neck, crying out against his skin. Her body convulsed against his manhood as he continued to thrust, determined to wrench every last ounce of pleasure from her.

When it was over, she leaned her head back and looked into his eyes. The heat of his own need burned in him, his brows were pulled together with the intensity of his torture.

She nodded. "Now," she whispered to him.

Yes, now. He closed his eyes, giving himself over to the sensation which had built and strained within him. His breath came hot and fast over her skin, and his fingers threaded through hers, gripping her hands above her head as if for dear life. The moan which tore from his chest when he found his climax was nearly deafening; it echoed off the rocky hills surrounding them. The evidence of it came slick between her legs. She hugged her knees to his waist so that he might gain the most satisfaction possible: a carnal reciprocity.

Spent, Alex collapsed against her, trembling as much from the exertion as from his release. When he'd caught his breath, he rolled onto his side, and gathered Glinis into him. Laying her head on his broad chest, she listened to the frantic beating of his heart. It matched the pounding of her own. The plaid which he'd tossed over them trapped the heat of their bodies, warming away any remaining shivers that were left from the cold water of the pool.

"Ye're no' sorry, are ye?" he asked after a while, trailing his fingertips up and down her arm.

Glinis smiled—a small, private smile. Shoving against his chest, she raised herself into a sitting position and reached for her sopping shift. She wrung it out as best she could and pulled it down over her head. The fabric was still cold; she flinched when it touched her heated skin.

Pulling her knees to her chest and wrapping her arms around them, she looked at him.

"Sorry? Nay. I am no' sorry. *Nervous*, perhaps, but no' sorry."

He raised himself on his elbow, the plaid slipping to his waist. Glinis felt a ripple of excitement tease her shoulders at the magnificent male body displayed so casually and intimately before her.

"Why nervous?"

She regarded him warily. "Well, I dinna ken where we go from here, do I?"

"And what d'ye mean by that?"

"Dinna toy wi' me. Ye ken what I mean."

"Aye. But humor me."

She rested her cheek on her knee. "Do we bury this as a forgotten incident? Carry on in secret? When Lord Kildrummond passes, I dinna think I'll stay on at Glendalough whether or no' Lachlan will have me there, so there is only so long this can last."

Alex stared at her, incredulous. "Stay on at Glendalough? Are ye mad, woman? I dinna want some silly affair wi' ye, for God's sake. I want ye for my *wife*."

Glinis snorted. "Is that so? Come now, Sir Alex, I'm too old for these games."

He sat up, and raised her chin from her knees with his forefinger. "I play no games, my love. I want ye to marry me."

"Dinna be daft."

"I'm never daft."

"I'm one and forty. I've ten years on ye at least."

"Ye're beautiful, and I dinna give a rat's arse hole how many years ye have on me."

"I have nothing to give ye but a dowager's living."

"I only want *ye*, and I can make my own living."

Glinis laughed, and looked away. Her heart throbbed, and she felt as though she could squeal and flutter up into the sky. It was the young lass in her that had been denied the joys of first love. The jaded, disillusioned part of her that had been forged by years of disappointment, however, was more wary.

"Let's no' get ahead of ourselves just yet." She stood, and reached for her rumpled gown. "First ye must concentrate on the task ahead of ye, and that is to come back from Arkinholm safe and sound."

Alex conceded, though from the glint in his eye, she knew the debate was far from over.

The ride back to Glendalough was a silent one, though the silence was not uneasy. Alex kept his sure, strong hand tight against Glinis's belly. The gesture gave her a contentment she'd never imagined could be had from a lover. She gave in to it, and let her head rest against his shoulder for most of the journey. The rise and fall of his chest, his breath upon her hair, the beating of his heart deepened this sense of peace which was entirely new to her.

She hardly knew what to make of these feelings. She'd always wanted to be loved by John, but he'd never given her any reason to hope as she did now. She'd shared her bed a few times, and though she'd enjoyed the activity, nothing had remained once those young men had left her chamber. No peace, no contentment, no deep-seeded need for anything else they might have to give.

Not that they had anything else to give; they'd wanted no more of her than she'd wanted of them.

She could hardly deny now that it was love she felt for Alexander MacByrne. And her heart told her that he did not lie, that he loved her too. Her head, however, warned her that if her heart were wrong, the pain would be excruciating.

Alex, it seemed, could read her mind. Or else her face gave her thoughts away.

"I mean it, my lady," he said when she dismounted a short distance away from the rear gate. "I want ye for my wife. And I'll return to ye from Arkinholm wanting nothing different."

She breathed deeply, checking the excitement which threatened to burst from her chest. "Aye, so ye said. Ye be safe."

Dougall MacFadyen was still on the wall walk when she came into view of the castle.

"Lord in heaven, my lady, what has happened to ye?" he called down to her.

"Dinna ask. And if ye can keep hold of yer tongue about it, I'd much appreciate it. I'll even see a handsome reward make it to yer purse."

Dougall leveled her with a look of disappointment. "My lady, ye should ken well ye dinna need to bribe me. I've no' seen ye this day at all, and that's my final word on the matter."

## *Sixteen*

Moira had been dreaming. A terrible dream of a galloping horse; a destrier as black as midnight. Its hooves were forged of steel, and they pounded the dirt as if they were pounding the drums of hell. Above, the sky was red with fire. The unholy light gleamed off the destrier's slick, black body, and was reflected in its flat, dead eyes.

In the dream she had stood, petrified, as the destrier tore a path directly for her. She tried to run, but her legs would not move. Her limbs were held ransom by the white-hot fear that surged through every part of her body. She tried to scream, but the ragged pull of her breaths was the only sound other than the terrible drumbeat of the destrier's steel hooves.

The beast rode forward, bringing carnage with it. And Moira could do nothing to halt its advance.

She awoke suddenly. Her eyes met not the light of a fire-red sky, but the mellow light of a grey dawn. Birdsong twittered beyond the covered windows, carried into the hut on a current of damp, cool air.

Beside her, Lachlan snored softly. His large body lay close beneath the quilts, providing warmth and comfort and safety. The frantic thrumming of her heart died as the fear ebbed from her body.

Awake and able to reflect on her dream, the cause of it was easily explained. Sir Alex had been gone for a little over a sennight, and for days, all of Kildrummond had been wondering when the battle would be—or if it had already taken place. With Arkinholm being the main topic of conversation for miles, Moira was bound to have such nightmares, was she not?

Thus soothing her frazzled thoughts, she allowed herself to drift back to sleep for another precious hour. She dreamed again, but this time it was not unpleasant.

This time, she dreamed of a man.

There were no clear images in this dream, nothing but sounds and tastes, colors and scents. And desire, a flame of desire that burned in her veins and made her loins ache. She felt a strong, firm body press against her, and then move over top, trapping her with a pleasant weight. Moist, soft lips slid along her jaw; sure hands knitted into the sleep-dampened strands of her hair, traced the line of her arm and stroked the curve of her small, pert breast.

Then the lips melted into hers. She succumbed, knowing nothing except that she wanted to drown in this dream. She opened her mouth to this unknown man, kissed him back with a passion to match his.

This was not the first time she'd dreamed of making love. Many times had the dawn taken the nameless, faceless lover of her nights, and left behind the ache that she was forced to satisfy for herself. It was the first time her dream was so real, though. It was the first time scent and touch had been a significant feature. This dream was too wonderful to wake from; she could stay asleep for the rest of her life if all her dreams were like this.

But sleep was not a thing to be commanded. Moira could no more choose how long she stayed asleep than she could choose what she dreamed about. As it always did eventually, sleep ebbed away, bringing reality with it.

And in reality, she discovered...she'd not been dreaming.

The body that hovered over her was no nameless, faceless lover. It was *Lachlan*.

It was Lachlan's lips that were kissing her now, Lachlan's hands that skimmed the bare flesh beneath her shift.

It was Lachlan who took her breath away with the things he was doing to her.

The sleep that lingered in her brain stole from her the command of her own body. It was clear Lachlan was at least half asleep himself, yet she could not make herself rouse him. Of how much or little he was aware, she could not say. It made no difference; she could not make him stop. Could not make *herself* stop. The throb of desire was too strong, the need for satisfaction too great.

A part of her wondered: would it really be so terrible if they broke the terms of their agreement? *Let it happen,* said that devious little voice in her head. *You want it, he wants it. Don't fight it.*

But another part of her argued differently. The proud, wary part that had suffered a lifetime from the stigma of being John Douglas's bastard daughter. John Douglas's *plain* bastard daughter.

*He does not really want you,* it taunted. *He only wants your body because he is not yet awake. He would regret it afterwards.*

Panic seized her. No, this could not happen. She was foolish to have even thought it might. When he woke, he would be sorry. He would reject her.

Well—she'd be damned if she'd let that happen. If anyone was to be rejected here, it would be *she* that rejected *him*.

"Lachlan, Lachlan wake up." She shook his shoulders.

"No lass, let me no' wake," he murmured against her lips.

She pushed harder. "Lachlan—no!"

Her urgency broke through his curtain of sleep, and he stared at her, confused. Then astonished.

"God's bones, I am sorry. I—I dinna ken what came over me."

Just as she'd thought: he regretted it. It was clear by the shocked look on his face.

It was no more than Moira had been expecting, and yet…his regret stung more than she imagined it would.

That sting soon turned to anger—anger at herself for being hurt in the first place. Of *course* Lachlan had reacted no differently than she expected he would, the arrogant sod! What right did she have to hurt feelings? She'd saved her pride; that was the important thing. Her heart had no business being bruised.

"Moira?" He searched her face, anxious that she should say something. His body still straddled hers; his weight still pressed her into the mattress.

"Dinna fash. Ye didna ken what ye were doing." She smiled a tight, awkward smile.

He made no move to release her. "Ye ken I'd never hurt ye, lass, right? Not so much as a hair on yer head, I swear it. I didna mean to frighten ye."

"Ye didna, and there is no need to say anything more about it. 'Tis forgotten."

Eager to put the incident behind them, she squirmed out from under his body. This, however, put her between him and the wall. To avoid climbing over his body, she crawled over the foot of the bed.

She kept her eyes away from him as she dressed herself and set about her business. But the whole time she was keenly aware that he was watching her. She did not want to see the expression on his face—whatever it might be.

She did not want *him* to see how much she was hurting.

The rest of the morning passed in an uncomfortable silence. What little words they did exchanged were forced, overly polite. The animals were let out of their pens, the breakfast was cooked and the peat logs stacked. All the while, the pair worked as though they hardly knew each other. As though they were right back at the start of their liar's marriage.

Niall offered a reprieve from the tension when he paid them a visit. They were both outside in the yard—she scrubbing the laundry over a steaming barrel of water and lye soap, and he cutting new turf logs from a stack at the side of the hut—when the eldest MacCormack lad cantered in on his family's lone mare.

The grin on his face might have been the light of dawn itself.

"Moira!" He jumped down from the saddle and ran the short distance to her, not even bothering to tie up the speckled grey animal. "Moira, ye'll never believe what happened."

"What? What is it?" She shook the water from her hands. Curious, Lachlan came around the side of the hut to hear the news.

"I called for Janet—ye remember she said I should call for her? And she were home as she said she'd be, and we took a walk as she said we should, and we talked—Moira, I *talked* wi' her, actual words and all. We talked about so many things, we did, and…well, she kissed me. She *kissed* me!"

Overcome, Niall swung Moira into a huge embrace and whirled her around.

"Oh, Niall, that's grand. I'm so pleased for ye." And she was. Her heart soared for her friend, forgetting for a moment the dull ache she'd been trying to put behind her all morning.

"Where'd she kiss ye, lad?" Lachlan put in, raising one dark eyebrow suggestively. His remark earned him a disgusted huff from his wife.

"Behind my da's brewing shed," Niall answered, oblivious to the viscount's lewd insinuation.

Moira and Lachlan looked at one another, and laughed.

From that point on the awkwardness between them lessened. They accompanied Niall back to the MacCormack home in the village, and stayed awhile to visit with his family. Niall chattered the entire way, describing everything from the way the sun glinted off Janet's honey hair to the titter of her giggle when Niall had stupidly thanked her for kissing him. Poor Mary MacCormack had to shout over his babbling to offer her guests a drink.

Warmed by the ale and the hospitality, they set out for a day at Glendalough. Most of the journey was passed in a more amiable silence than had been earlier, and Moira hoped Lachlan would say nothing more of the incident.

She was not so lucky.

"Moira," he hedged as the castle came into view. "D'ye forgive me for what happened? I mean truly forgive me?"

"I told ye, 'tis forgotten."

"Ye say that, but is it really?"

"D'ye no' believe me?"

He paused, raking a long glance over her that smoldered far more than it should have.

"I wouldna say I dinna believe ye, exactly."

"Then what?"

"I think ye're determined to believe yer own words. Ye're a woman of great pride, lass. I think ye'd no' wish to admit ye were frightened."

She stared ahead, one eyebrow cocked and the other furrowed. "Well, dinna ye just ken everything, my Lord Strathcairn. Am I allowed to remark upon the fine weather we're having, or would ye think I were deluding myself in that also?"

Her terseness did not have the effect she intended. He laughed.

"Have mercy upon me, sweetling. If I didna ken any better, I'd say ye're harder on me than ye are on any other man in the Highlands."

"Perhaps," she admitted reluctantly. "We are married, though, so ye should hardly be surprised."

"Ah, Moira. Ye've a sharp wit, that's for sure. In all seriousness, I didna mean to offend ye. And I meant to tell ye that…that I respect ye greatly."

"I'm flattered," she answered dryly.

"Nay, hear me out. I have come to respect and like ye a great deal. I would never wish ye to be afraid of me. I'd never wish for ye to think that I might harm ye, or disrespect ye in any way. I want ye to ken that."

She had not expected him to say such things. He certainly hadn't been obligated to, but his declaration made her feel a touch better. So he did not desire her—it was nothing she didn't already know. But he respected her, and liked her. She could be satisfied with that.

"Thank ye," she said simply.

"Ye're welcome. And thank ye, in return."

"For what?"

She raised her eyes to his, and was rendered senseless by his intense gaze. How did he *do* that?

"For being a friend. I think ye must be the only lass on earth that desires me for my company alone. I'm glad I've met ye."

"Well…em…likewise," she muttered, her cheeks flushing scarlet.

Soon after they reached the bailey, where awaiting ghillies rushed forward to take their horses. Eamon Douglas, Glendalough's steward, was waiting for them too, and once they'd dismounted, he rushed forward with a list of items which needed the viscount's immediate attention.

Moira stepped aside and let the man of accounts whisk Lachlan away. Once she was alone, she headed to the same place she went every time she came to the castle: Lord Kildrummond's chamber.

As she walked through the empty halls, she went over their recent conversation in her head. What a curious thing for him to have said. *I think ye must be the only lass on earth that desires me for my company alone.* Had he meant to say he was tired of being handsome?

Her first inclination was to scoff at such a ridiculous notion. What a thing to complain about, as if being handsome were a curse.

But a small, private part of her saw logic in the idea. Was she herself not frustrated that handsome, silly men like Lachlan had no interest in her company? The earl's illegitimate daughter with neither looks nor title to recommend her?

Now that she thought about it, she was no better than them. Where she did not wish to be dismissed by virtue of her appearance, she'd done just that to Lachlan by virtue of *his*.

The thought was slightly depressing.

When she reached her father's chamber, she was startled to find Lady Glinis seated at his bedside. Normally she was not there this time of day. They'd made a routine of avoiding each other these past few weeks, and she'd not expected to cross paths with the lady anytime soon.

"Oh, er…I'm sorry, my lady. I'll come back, shall I?"

Lady Glinis glanced in her direction. But instead of the derision with which she normally regarded Moira, her face held only mild curiosity.

"Nay, dinna fret. I'm just about ready to leave anyway."

Moira's mouth fell slack.

Vacating her seat so Moira could have it, Lady Glinis made for the door. Moira entered the room, giving the lady a wide berth, just in case. When she had seated herself and took her father's hand, Glinis did not leave as Moira thought she would. Instead, she hovered at the foot of the bed and continued to watch her husband.

Her presence made Moira nervous. Did Glinis expect her to do something? Talk to the man? Moira seldom ever talked to Lord Kildrummond anymore, for he slept almost all the time now. And when he was awake it was no use talking, for her could not talk back. He had too little strength and there was too much phlegm rattling in his chest.

She snuck a glance at Lady Glinis. The woman gazed wistfully upon the wretched form in the bed.

"He breathes so queer," she whispered. "'Tis almost painful to watch."

"Aye," Moira agreed tentatively. "I keep telling him he must let go, but he hangs on."

"He were always stubborn," she said affectionately.

"He never spoke ill of ye, ye ken. Quite the opposite, in fact, even to my mother. Even when she spoke ill of ye, and railed at the fact that ye had his hand by lawful right...even then, he'd no' speak ill of ye. Whatever else he might have done, he respected ye greatly."

For a moment, she worried that she'd overstepped her bounds, that the mention of her mother would darken Glinis's mood. But the lady simply smiled. A sad, lonely smile.

"I ken."

Glinis paused. When she spoke again, Moira could scarce believe what she was hearing.

"Ye must forgive me, Moira. I dinna think I can change overnight. Twenty years of anger is a difficult thing to bury, and I'll no' be able to overcome it in a day."

Moira eyed her warily. "Change, my lady?"

"Change," Glinis nodded. "I dinna want to hate ye, lass. I've never wanted to hate ye. I dinna think hate is even the right word for it. I dinna want to…to *blame* ye—aye, that's a better word. Blame."

"Why change now, my lady, if I may be so bold?"

Glinis frowned, thinking. "I'm…I'm weary," she answered. "Weary to my bones. I dinna have it in me to hold onto that hurt anymore. For so many years I thought that life held nothing new for me. I thought there would be nothing else but marriage to a man that didna love me. A good man, true, but still, a man that was not in love wi' me. I've only now been able to see that I've still so much life to live. I dinna want to spend the rest of it with a bitter heart."

The two women studied each other. There was no hatred in Glinis's eyes. Moira had never dreamed the lady would ever look at her like she was now—like a person, an equal, rather than a blight. A small glimmer of hope burned deep in her chest.

"I thank ye for saying so," she said simply.

Glinis gazed at her a touch longer. "Well, I'll leave ye be, then."

She departed the room, and Moira watched her retreating back. For a long time after that she stared at the empty doorway.

When she turned back to Lord Kildrummond, it seemed as though the old earl's breathing had eased. And perhaps (she might have been imagining it, but just perhaps), he looked a little more peaceful. As though he'd been aware of what had just transpired at his bedside.

Of course such a thing was impossible. Fanciful thinking…

Though it seemed that his hand, once limp and unresponsive, gripped Moira's ever so slightly.

## *Seventeen*

The fallout from the Battle of Arkinholm descended upon the Douglases with a fury as swift and terrifying as the destrier of Moira's dream. And it fell on Sir Alexander MacByrne's shoulders to warn Lachlan of what was to come.

On a cool, rainy evening in early May he returned to Glendalough. The sentry atop the wall walk spotted his sodden silhouette against the twilight sky, and shouted to a ghillie to alert Viscount Strathcairn.

Lachlan had been in the treasury all that afternoon, combing the records of the previous year's modest prosperity. Perhaps it was not necessary to give the figures such singular attention, but he found it was the best excuse to avoid the tension that pervaded the castle of late. Everyone wanted to know how the battle had gone, and they all looked to Lachlan for an answer.

An answer he did not have.

He was just about ready to give up for the night—his eyes were now burning with strain—when the ghillie's knock came.

"Come," he invited.

The ghillie, a boy of perhaps fifteen summers and as gangly as Moira's friend Niall, stood in the entrance. He was anxious; his rigid posture and the waver in his deepening voice attested to it. Lachlan's senses heightened.

"My Lord Strathcairn, Sir Alexander MacByrne has returned. He is being attended in the bailey.

Lachlan rose from his chair, his hands braced on the edge of the oak desk on which a roll of parchment lay open. "And?"

"And...and what, my lord?"

"How does he look, lad? What can ye tell me of his face? Is he excited? Worried? What?"

The lad's eyes darted around the room, and his hands twisted together in front of him. "I dinna ken, my lord. 'Tis no' my place to say."

Lachlan pulled in a breath, willing himself to calm down. He was making the young fool nervous.

"Fear not, lad," he said evenly. "I am no' one to hold the messenger responsible for the message he brings. I only wish to ken yer impression of him, so that I might prepare myself. Please—how did he look?"

"He looked…grim, my lord," the ghillie admitted.

Grim. So Kildrummond's fears had come true; it was the worst. What, exactly, did the worst mean for Edward Douglas, Earl of Albermarle? What had his fate been…or, more horrible, what might his fate yet be?

"I shall wait for him in the solar."

Relieved at the discharge, the boy bowed hastily and scampered off, leaving the door open behind him.

In the close, still air of the treasury, Lachlan listened to the patter of rain against glass. The scent of parchment and dust was so heavy he could nearly taste its musk. How many years, how many lives of Douglas men and women were stored here? The details of their existences: their harvests, their commerce, their births and deaths…had their collective story officially come to its end?

Abandoning the open parchment, Lachlan snuffed out the single candle and locked the door behind him.

The solar was cold when he arrived. A modest fire burned low, having been lit just ahead of him. He didn't much like this room, and came here seldom. It was large and hollow. Finely furnished, yes, and decorated with enough tapestries (Moira's by the look of them, or her mother's) that it should have been comfortable. But there was something about the room that put Lachlan on edge. The few times he'd been in the solar alone he had the unsettling notion that the ghosts of Kildrummond lords past—Douglases, all of them—were watching him. Disapproved of a Ramsay taking their beloved realm.

It was fancy, of course. Yet the rain tapping at the windows and the bleak, grey light that suffocated the room did nothing to dispel it. The feeling was especially acute this night, as Lachlan waited to hear the fate of Clan Douglas.

He was grateful that Alex did not keep him waiting long. He appeared at the open door and stopped at the threshold. His hair and cloak were sopping from his journey, his face a canvas of defeat. Lachlan's pulse quickened.

"What chance is there that ye mean to play me a trick wi' that face of yers?"

Alex shook his head.

"Ah." Lachlan breathed. "I thought not."

He gestured to the two large chairs positioned in front of the hearth, and took one. Alex followed, and took the other. They regarded one another, both men weary. Not for the first time over the years, Lachlan reflected on his friend's devotion. The strain of the Douglas feud was etched on Alex's face as if it were his own family that suffered it. Lachlan's future earldom meant as much to Alex as it did to him. One day he would find a way to tell his friend how much he meant to him.

Now was not the time, however. With reluctance, he spoke.

"Give me the news then, for I'll hear it sooner or later."

Alex's eyes trailed to the fire. He perched his elbow on the wide, polished armrest, and his forefinger stroked his upper lip absently.

"Lost," he confirmed. "Lord Douglas's men faced a force equal in numbers, but they were outmatched."

"Whose force did they face?"

"The Earl of Angus."

Lachlan blanched. "The Earl of Angus—as in *George* Douglas?"

"One and the same."

Lachlan slumped in his chair. George Douglas of the Red Douglases. Kin to the Black Douglases. James had been opposed by his *own kin*.

"So Red takes Black," he murmured.

"Aye. These noblemen ken nothing of blood loyalty…that goes for both sides, by the by."

Lachlan looked up. "Oh?"

"It were over before it began," Alex said gently. "Lord Douglas's greatest allies abandoned him—the Lindsays and the MacDonalds both. When he learned of this, and when he learned that the lesser clans loyal to his allies were refusing to fight as well, he fled to England before the battle. In the end, his brothers took on leadership and led the fight. James Douglas, the coward, saved his own neck, and left his own brothers—his *blood*—to suffer the fate that should have been his."

"Lord in heaven," Lachlan whispered.

"Ye certain ye wish to be a noble?" Alex jested without humor.

He then proceeded to tell Lachlan everything he knew about the three remaining Douglas lords that had stayed to fight the battle. Archibald Douglas, Earl of Moray, killed. Hugh Douglas, Earl of

Ormonde, captured. John Douglas, Lord Balvenie, escaped to England. The lands of the Black Douglases had been declared forfeit by the king. Heaven knew what would happen to the clan now.

"And what of Lord Albermarle?" Lachlan asked when Alex had finished.

The knight inhaled. "Captured, too. He is imprisoned at Stirling wi' the Earl of Ormonde, and awaits trial."

"And his sons?"

"His eldest, Edward, were killed near the end, and his second son, Brandon, escaped wi' Lord Balvenie to England."

They lapsed into silence. A draught from the hall whispered through the room; the tapping of the rain and the crackle of the fire were the only other sounds. Lachlan felt sick as he contemplated what he'd heard.

This may very well be the end of the Black Douglas clan.

"Lady Rosamund will have to be told," he said heavily.

"Should I have a messenger sent?"

"Nay, this I must do for myself. I am Lord Kildrummond's heir. 'Tis time I started acting the part. Lord Kildrummond would have told her himself if he were well enough to do so. I am sure of it."

"And how does Lord Kildrummond fare?"

"He's in his last days," Lachlan affirmed. "It willna be much longer now, I think."

"Will ye tell him? About Lord Albermarle?"

Lachlan knew the answer already, for he'd spent much time thinking on it. "Nay. There is no purpose to that. Besides, I doubt whether he can hear us anymore."

\*\*\*

Lord Kildrummond's last hours came the next night. The sky had cleared, revealing a spray of stars and a brilliant moon. It was as if the heavens had parted the bounds of earth, ready to receive the earl's soul.

His family gathered in his chamber, and waited for him to take his final breath. No one spoke. Moira sat in the single chair beside his bed and held his hand. Glinis sat on the other side, perched on the edge of the bed by his withered knee. Lachlan and Alex stood solemnly against the wall as a priest gave the final benediction. A handful more Douglas clansmen rounded out the watch.

Moira swallowed thickly. "I canna stand the sound of his breathing," she whispered to Glinis. "D'ye think he's in pain?"

Glinis gazed at Moira. There was not a trace of the animosity which had existed for years between them. Then her eyes fell to her husband, and she listened to his irregular, shallow breaths which rattled sharply in his wasted chest.

"I dinna think so," she said evenly. Taking his other hand in both of hers, she leaned over him, and spoke quietly to the dying man. So quietly that only Moira was close enough to hear over the priest's murmured prayers.

"John, love, can ye hear me? My love, 'tis time to let go. Ye've done all ye can in this life. No one could have asked more of a man. Ye've secured the future of Kildrummond, and yer people will live and prosper under our Lachlan's hand. Yer daughter will have a home, and will be protected for the rest of her life. And…and I will be fine as well. What we had wasna love, but I ken ye cared for me. Ye did everything for me that was in yer power to do. I ken that now, and I thank ye for it, John. But there's no more ye can do for any of us. 'Tis time ye went home now."

Several minutes passed, long minutes in which there was nothing but the sound of Lord Kildrummond's breathing and the whispers of the priest. Then, even the priest fell silent as the earl opened his eyes. He gazed across the chamber, seeing not the brick and mortar and faces of those present. Whatever it was that he saw was not of this world. A smile of wonder crossed his parched lips and his blue eyes shone with love.

"Lilian," he whispered.

With the name of his love hanging in the air, John Douglas, Earl of Kildrummond, closed his eyes for the last time.

Glinis slumped, and released his hand. Her onyx eyes filled with tears, and she allowed them to wet her lashes and cheeks. Her obligation to her husband had been fulfilled; no one could say she hadn't done her duty—not in his time of illness nor in their fruitless marriage. Neither could anyone fault her for the relief she felt. Her grief was true, but her burden was lifted.

Moira, though, began to sob. Her shoulders shook, and her chin lowered to her chest.

"Papa," she cried quietly.

Unable to stop a few wayward tears of his own, Lachlan went to his young wife's side. Gathering her into his arms, he pressed her head to his shoulder, and rocked her while she poured out her grief.

"I wasted so much time," she moaned, the words muffled against his tunic. "I canna make it better. I canna tell him that I love him anymore. I'll never have another chance."

"He kent, love," Lachlan soothed, stroking her hair.

"Aye, he did," Glinis added. "And ye gave him a wonderful gift—ye gave him the love of a daughter in his final days. Ye sent him to his Blessed Father a happy man."

The mourners in the room huddled together, offering each other condolences for the loss of a great man.

Beyond the chamber wall, the clear night sky twinkled one star brighter.

## *Eighteen*

"I'm coming wi' ye," Moira stated. She had been grinding rye flour when Lachlan announced his plans to depart for Kinross the next morning.

Still barefoot and rumpled from sleep, he joined her on the bench in front of the fire. It was still early, the twitter of the morning's first birdsong a recent addition to the still, cool air inside the little hut.

Already the day was promising to be warm—though a thick mist rolled over the ground outside, the low-lying sun, which burned halo-like through a transparent layer of cloud, would likely evaporate it well before noon. The window coverings were drawn wide to admit as much of the fresh, spring breeze as possible before they had to be lowered again to keep out the heat and the bugs.

"Here, let me help wi' that." Lachlan's large, capable hands took the crank from Moira's small, equally capable ones. Rhythmically he began turning the two circular stones. The fine silt of rye flour began to fall from between them, pillowing in the awaiting pan below.

"Ye make that look so easy," she commented, observing the flex and pull of his warrior's arm. *I shall miss this when our marriage has ended.*

"Does it impress ye, lass?" He wiggled one eyebrow at her. "And ye dinna need to trouble yerself by coming along. I wasna planning on taking a carriage, 'twill only slow down the journey."

"Carriage," she snorted. "I've never been fond of them. I'll go on horseback, like ye."

Mesmerized, as she was, by the rhythm of his arm, she missed the small, affectionate smile that touched his lips. "Of course ye shall. What *were* I thinking?"

Within the hour they departed south for Kinross, a small guard of three men trailing them. Happy chatter, normally the song of travelers, was distinctly absent amongst the party—no one was feeling particularly happy, nor chattery, given their reason for traveling.

At mid-day, when the sun was high in the sky, which was dotted with white, powdery clouds, they stopped to eat the travelers' fare that had been sent with them. Inside bundles of crude linen were hard cheeses, bread of mixed grain, and ginger cakes. Several skins of ale had been pressed into Lachlan's arms by Mary MacCormack when they stopped to ask if Niall wouldn't mind looking after Moira's animals for a night or two.

On a bank by a fresh, fast-running stream, the group dismounted and sat in the grass to enjoy their meal. The new Lord Kildrummond seated himself among his men as casually as if they were of the same station.

It did not escape Moira's attention that it was *she*, in particular, beside whom Lachlan chose to sit. This he also did casually; perhaps his choice had been an unconscious one. Because Lachlan didn't seem aware of it, and because the men didn't seem to think anything amiss in a husband sitting next to his wife, Moira pretended not to notice as well.

Privately, though, she was very aware of his proximity. She liked how it felt, this notion that a husband's companionship was an unspoken understanding. Never, in all the time she'd spent at Glendalough over the years, had anyone sat beside her so willingly—other than the various Douglas crones of course, the aging relics of minor noblewomen past. Diminished by time, and by the succession of their lesser titles to their sons with the deaths of their husbands, they were outcasts of a sort, like Moira. But they at least were trueborn, and were therefore less wretched than she. They were the only ones to favor her with their pity, with their kind smiles and wary glances.

Yet another thing she'd miss when her marriage to Lachlan ended: the constancy of his companionship.

By evening they reached the northern border of Kinross, and by nightfall they were upon the gates of Glen Craggan.

The seat of the Albermarles for countless generations, Glen Craggan was three times the size of Glendalough. Kinross was richer in arable lands than Kildrummond, and though it did not have direct access to the sea, it was better established along the inland trade routes than its northern neighbor. Glen Craggan's size and ornament was a testament to the commerce which Kinross enjoyed.

Whichever House was granted Kinross after it was taken from Lady Rosamund would enjoy that commerce now. Glen Craggan was the seat of the Albermarles no more.

Their arrival, it would seem, had been expected. As soon as they handed their horses over to the castle's stable lads, they were escorted directly to the keep where, they were told, Lady Albermarle was waiting for them in the solar.

The strain of the past fortnight had done Rosamund no favors. Though her clothing was as fine as ever and her golden hair neatly arranged and bound in a pearl-sheened satin ribbon, she was indisputably haggard. Deep shadows marred the milk-white skin beneath her eyes, and she looked as though she'd hardly eaten a thing in all the time her husband had been away.

She was standing by the window. When Lachlan and his party entered the chamber, she spun slowly on her heels, wringing her pale hands so intensely the veins at her knuckles stood out in sharp contrast.

Moira, tucked unobtrusively behind Lachlan and between his men, scanned the castle's solar. Accompanying Lady Rosamund were her four remaining children. She recognized them, having met them on occasion when she was much younger. She could recall only one of their names, though—Eleanor, the eldest girl who was only two or three years younger than she. It was Lady Eleanor around whom the other children were gathered. Moira did not doubt by their arrangement that it was she who had shouldered the burden of caring for her siblings in this time of great tension.

Confronted by Lachlan's grim countenance, Lady Rosamund began to tremble.

"D-Dead? Or…" A well of tears turned her eyes to glass.

"Captured. And awaiting execution," Lachlan answered gravely.

One of the younger girls began to cry.

"And my sons?" Lady Rosamund whispered.

"Lord Brandon has fled to England, my lady. And young Lord Edward…has been killed."

*Killed…* the word hung in the air, dreadful and thick. An awful silence lingered before the lady made a sound. When she did, it was a keening wail so horrible it was almost unearthly. It shredded the silence, a mother's anguish wrenched directly from the heart. Lady Rosamund staggered, and sank to the wooden floor.

Lachlan rushed forward to embrace her, forgetting his tentative grasp on the finer points of noble deportment.

No one blamed him, not in the face of Lady Rosamund's agony. He pressed her face to his breast, muffling her cries, and she clutched at his tunic. Her hands clawed at the fabric and at the mortal flesh beneath like some grotesque, feral animal. He suffered the lady's blind fury with neither a word nor a flinch of pain.

Lachlan's men hung their heads, deeply affected by the spectacle. Frightened by their mother's display, the younger children began to weep, and sought solace in one another.

All except Eleanor. The girl stared blankly at the sight of her mother, crumpled and broken. She looked empty, as though she'd been expecting this outcome. With only a single, steady glance directly at Moira, she slipped from the room.

Moira waited a short time, and then followed her. She found Eleanor not far away, leaning over a stone balustrade that looked down upon Glen Craggan's great hall. The grand space below was empty, save for two of the castle's dogs that rooted through the rushes for scraps dropped at the most recent meal.

Moira approached, and took a spot beside the girl, leaning similarly with her elbows resting on the railing and her wrists dangling over the edge.

"Ye look as though ye're not surprised by our tidings." She spoke carefully, watching for the lass's reaction.

Eleanor continued to gaze upon the dogs. Her golden hair, like her mother's, was plaited, and hung over her shoulder. Her face, so much like Lord Albermarle's, was neutral. She was taller than Moira, almost a head taller, and her shoulders were broad for a woman. She was her father's daughter, Moira thought; she carried herself with the same graceful strength that Lord Albermarle always had...

That Lord Albermarle still *did*—he was not dead yet, she reminded herself stiffly.

"I heard Mother and Father arguing, the night before Father left." Eleanor's voice was naturally husky; a low, soothing voice, not at all unattractive. "Mother begged him no' to go, pleaded wi' him to see sense. But Father wouldna. He said he couldna stand by while the king murdered nobles at will, and wi'out repercussion."

"He were an honorable man."

"To his detriment. And he were determined to bring Edward and Brandon wi' him. Of course, Brandon is headstrong, always has been. But Edward were a gentle soul. He didna want to fight. He told me so the night before they left for Arkinholm."

"Did he?"

"Aye. And ye ken what else he told me? He told me he kent he would die. He didna expect to survive the battle. If ye kent our Edward, ye'd trust these inklings of his. He were always right, had some kind of dark talent for knowing these things. And that's how I kent, ye see. I kent it would end badly."

Moira breathed deeply, speculating as the dogs fought over a piece of mutton bone. "I am sorry," was all she could say in the end.

"What about the others?" Eleanor's tawny eyes slid sideways to Moira.

"The Earl of Ormonde has been captured also, and awaits trial at Sterling wi' Lord Albermarle. The Earl of Moray was killed, and Lord Balvenie escaped to England."

"And the Earl of Douglas?"

"He…fled. To England, before the battle. When he realized his strongest allies had abandoned him."

Eleanor's upper lip curled viciously, and she spat over the balustrade. "Coward."

"I dinna disagree." Moira hesitated, sorry to tell her the rest. "Douglas lands are now forfeit to the Crown." When the lass merely nodded, she added, "Of course ye and yer family will always be welcome at Glendalough. Lachlan wouldna have ye go wi'out."

"I'm sure Mother means to leave Scotland."

There was something about the way she said "Mother" that made Moira uneasy. Almost as if the girl had not included herself in that outcome. She nearly inquired if Eleanor had other plans for herself, but thought better of it. The inquiry might be taken as an insult.

It was true that Lady Eleanor Douglas reminded Moira of herself, in the restrained defiance that shone from her eyes, in the proud set of her shoulders. But it did *not* follow that Lady Eleanor Douglas would *act* as Moira would under the circumstances. She hoped not—if she were in Eleanor's place, Moira could not say what she'd do.

Though she *could* say what she *wouldn't* do. And skulking away to England to lick her wounds, as Lady Rosamund intended, was at the top of that list.

*** 

Though she tried, Moira couldn't shake the ill feeling left behind after her conversation with Lord Albermarle's eldest daughter. An innate instinct warned her that the girl had more on her mind than she was letting on.

When she retired to her and Lachlan's guest chamber for the night, she fell into a state of brooding so deep that she almost didn't hear Lachlan come in behind her.

"Ye're here then?" Lachlan dropped heavily onto the edge of the bed.

She glanced up from her place on the floor by the hearth. "Ye look like a lad whose pony's just died."

"Next time I'll let *ye* be the one to tell a woman her beloved husband's about to be executed, and her first-born son is dead, shall I?"

"I'm sorry, I didna mean to mock ye."

Lachlan rubbed his face with one hand. "Nay, of course ye didna, lass. I'm the one that's sorry."

"It sounds as though Lady Rosamund is settled now. Was it very hard to calm her?"

"It were her personal physician that calmed her. Fixed her a rather large draught of wild poppy milk, he did. I wouldna be surprised if she sleeps the day away tomorrow."

She rose from the hearth and came to sit next to him. "'Tis probably best. The more she sleeps, the more time she has to forget."

"I'm nay so sure forgetting is the best thing. It only delays the grieving process."

"She's a delicate woman. The more delay for her the better."

Lachlan was silent; his jaw moved as though he were chewing over her wisdom. A tug of pity exerted itself on Moira's heart as she watched him grapple with his thoughts. The weight of his duty as the Earl of Kildrummond was already an enormous burden.

She slipped her hand into his. He responded by closing his fingers around hers.

"'Tis the cruelest twist of life, is it no'?" He tilted his head towards her, his dark eyes searching hers.

"What is?"

"That the want of the heart is so strong, it causes the body pain when it is denied."

Moira grimaced. She'd been thinking something similar for a while now, and Lachlan's comment had hit a little too close to the mark: the annulment of their marriage. It hadn't even come to pass yet, but already the pain of losing him was raw. The knowledge was frightening.

In a queer way, her fright combined with a sense of compassion for his burden. Moved by it, Moira leaned in to kiss his cheek…

And missed. Her lips landed firmly on his, as bold as if she'd kissed him on purpose.

*Had* she done it on purpose?

*What are you doing?* her brain shouted. *He doesna need yer awkward kisses to add to his turmoil. Stupid lass, let go of him. Let go of him and run.*

She pulled away, intent on doing just that—fleeing from the room like the fool that she was.

But before she could do so, he kissed her back. Intently!

At first she was too surprised to react. She held still as he molded his lips to hers with conviction. When his arm slid around her waist, pulling her body close, she was astonished to find her mouth moving with his. His tongue caressed her lips, urging them to part. And God help her wanton soul, she acquiesced.

More than acquiesced, in fact—she kissed him with equal need. With the same passion which had begun that one morning in their small, cozy hut. But this time, he was awake. And he kissed her like a man fully aware of what he was doing.

Like a man fully aware of *whom* he was kissing.

His urgency made the voice in her head feeble. Moira willingly ignored it, and when Lachlan urged her to lie back, she did not resist. She allowed his weight to carry her down to the bed, and his strong arm to swing her legs up onto the mattress.

Settling himself beside her, Lachlan's lips began trailing down her jaw and to the soft, sensitive flesh beneath her ear. She shivered, and twined her fingers into the fabric of his tunic, which was damp from Lady Rosamund's tears. His body was hard beneath her fingertips, the contours of his shoulder ridged where it met the crest of his chest.

Her touch, hesitant though it was, seemed to please him. His kisses came faster, and his hands took possession of her body, exploring the ripple of her ribs, the slope of her waist, and back up to the small, firm mound of her breast.

Emboldened by his obvious need of her, she found his belt, and tugged at the worn leather.

"Ye sure, lass?" he whispered.

Moira knew what he was asking. Was she sure she could lie to the priest when they annulled the marriage?

Was she certain she could blaspheme and say the union had never been consummated?

Was she prepared to be made a liar in front of God's servant? In front of God Himself...?

*Yes.* She was sure, and to hell with all of it! If Lachlan was prepared to lie, then so was she. In answer, she pulled the leather of his belt through the buckle, allowing the cloth of his *feileadh mhor* to fall from his hips.

A prickle of alarm set in. Only the thin linen of her shift remained between her bare flesh and his. The evidence of his need was rigid between them. What if she did not satisfy him? What if he expected something of her that she was not prepared to give? She'd heard horrible tales of what men did to women in the whorehouses of Edinburgh and Berwick...granted, most of those tales had come from Niall, and Moira was sure the daft lout had never set foot in a whorehouse before. But still...

Determined not to ruin the moment between them, she pushed the thought aside. She was no ripe, fresh lass of sixteen tender summers. Women her age had been long married and had borne several children by now. She was old enough to know what she wanted of the man in her arms—and *far* too old to be frightened by it.

Allowing her curiosity free reign, she brushed her fingertips against the warm, tender spot between his thighs. He held still for her, and let her explore as she wished. He was patient, even chuckled when she tested his girth and gasped in surprise at what she found.

"Are ye...that is, I mean, is yers...bigger than..." she stumbled.

He tipped his dark head to the side. "I am no' small, love, if I do say so myself. But neither am I unnaturally large."

"Oh—I didna think they were so...so thick. So Niall, and Lord Kild—" Moira shuddered. "Never mind. I'd rather no' ken."

A rumble of laughter shook his chest, but was swiftly silenced when she wrapped her fingers around his width. The discovery intrigued her. He was soft and pliant, yet hard as stone. Each touch, each change in pressure made him shiver against her. *This* intrigued her also—his response to her touch.

"God's bones, lass, I'll no' be able to hold on if ye keep going like that." His eyes were clenched shut, and his hands gripped the pillow behind her head.

"Oh, aye...em... Sorry?"

He traced her lips with a fingertip. "Sorry, sweetling, is the last thing on earth ye should be right now. In fact, it would be me that's sorry if I were to take my own pleasure before I've had the honor of giving ye any."

She frowned dubiously. "Honor?"

"Aye, honor."

To illustrate his point, he slid the hem of her shift up along her legs. The soft linen tickled her skin, and when he'd lifted it up past her breasts, she folded her arms over her chest and crossed her knees.

"Nay, dinna hide yerself," he pleaded. "Let me look at ye."

"Lachlan, I am skin and bones. Ye dinna need to flatter me that I am any bit desirable to look at."

He started, astonished, and searched her face. "Flatter ye? Moira MacInnes, are ye really so daft that ye canna see the effect ye have on me? 'Tis no flattery, love. 'Tis sheer, uncontrollable *want*. I want ye, Moira. And I mean to make *ye* want *me* just as badly."

Whatever doubts she had were silenced the instant his mouth began to travel southward. First he brushed his moist lips along the line of her sternum, tracing the ridge of each collarbone. Then he moved farther south, outlining the soft, small globes of her breasts with his tongue. He teased her nipples, licking and nibbling at them with the edges of his teeth. Her breaths came heavy, and when he led her hands to his head, she willingly slid her fingers through his thick, black hair.

When his hand descended past her ribs, over her belly, and to the tender flesh at the crest of her pelvis, she instinctively batted his hand away.

"Nay, lass. I'll no' hurt ye."

His voice was throaty and low. It lulled her into a state of bliss, both terrifying and wonderful. When his fingers began sliding expertly over the most, intimate spot of her womanhood, her brain grew hazy, and she forgot the reasons for her protest. The mild shame that had initially spread through her at his touch gave way to a spreading of another kind—a blossoming; a delicious ache which she'd never known in the presence of a man. Moira pressed her eyes together, her hands moving restlessly over Lachlan's naked back, waist, buttocks.

He nearly had her, and he knew it. Soft moans escaped her lips, and her quick breaths turned to gasps.

"Open yer eyes," he urged when she was nearly there.

Rendered senseless, unable to think rationally, she responded. His deep, black eyes pierced hers and held her captive. The blossoming ache intensified, crested, exploded, and still he commanded her gaze, would not let her look away. She convulsed with pleasure, seeing nothing but the dark orbs of his irises. His hand still sought her pleasure, and her convulsions turned to shudders before he slowed.

Only when they'd turned to weak, intermittent spasms, and the haze cleared from her brain, did she see the full effect she had on him. His gaze was heavy-lidded and burning with lust. It lit a fire in her belly, and suddenly the pleasure he'd given her was not enough. She needed more.

"What say ye of flattery now?" he whispered.

The flame of his desire blazed in his eyes. There was no mistaking his need for her—skinny, shapeless body or not. He wanted her.

"I say that I think lust is blinding," she quipped. Then she pulled his head to hers and kissed him with abandon. All her fears, all her doubts and her self-conscious reservations were forgotten as she parted her knees beneath him. An invitation.

He accepted.

Knowing that she'd never received a man before, Lachlan moved slowly. When he slid himself inside her, he did so with care, penetrating only a fraction at a time. She adjusted to him, accommodating his width until he reached the physical barrier of her virtue.

There was a slight burst of pain when he broke through; her back stiffened, and he winced in sympathy. When her face relaxed, Lachlan relaxed too, and slowly began to rock his hips.

She was bolder now. Her body moved with his, her arms clutching him to her and her legs wrapping around his narrow waist. Encouraged by her unspoken demand, he moved faster, driving her pleasure higher at the same time that he drove his own.

It felt different this time, the sensation of fullness as she climaxed again. She cried out, wilder and less guarded than before.

"Dinna hold back," she breathed.

"I couldna if I tried, love," he responded.

His declaration was followed not long after by a moan that tore from his chest. Even sated as she was, the sound of his release made her lust flare.

And there was something else which she hadn't expected, something deeper than just a physical joining of bodies. She felt something almost...*protective* at his helplessness, at his submission to her.

It was overwhelming. She ground her teeth together, determined that she would not cry for the beauty of what she'd just experienced.

The beauty which she would likely never experience again.

When it was over, he held her. Moira rested her head against his chest, and Lachlan nuzzled his face into her hair. His heart raced beneath her cheek, and the deep whoosh of his breath in and out was like an ocean tide.

In those quiet, drowsy minutes before sleep took hold, she pondered what they'd shared. They'd shared each other's grief, had been each other's solace.

In the afterglow of their lovemaking, she understood with a heavy heart that they'd been nothing more than each other's passing pleasure. A man like Lachlan Ramsay did not fall in love with the women he made love to. Moira was well aware of his history on that score. And she was well aware that she was just another in a long line of women who had shared his bed and his passion.

She did not know what she'd say to him in the morning, but she knew she must not let this change their friendship, nor their arrangement. She must not mistake his lust for love. If she did, if she declared her feelings for Lachlan, she would be made a fool when he put her back in that line.

She would not, *could* not let that happen. Moira was determined that she would find a way to treat their shared passion for what it was—*convenience*.

Nothing more.

## *Nineteen*

Lachlan had hoped their intimate encounter would be the impetus that changed how she felt about him. But the next morning, Moira MacInnes said nothing. In fact, she gave not even the slightest acknowledgement that anything had happened at all. She simply rose, washed her face and hands, and dressed herself. She hardly even glanced in his direction.

He was disappointed. More than disappointed, if truth be told. What they shared last night had been special. Special in a way he'd never had with any other lass. But because Moira said nothing of it, Lachlan said nothing of it.

It was clear she did not share the sentiment, that he *hadn't* managed to close the distance between them after all. If anything, last night's encounter had only added to it.

*I'd say I think lust is blinding*, she'd said. The statement, which hadn't made sense to him at the time, made perfect sense now. She'd been blinded by lust. And in the sharp light of day she saw once more that she did not care for him. Not enough to stay married to him.

The fact of the matter, though, was that *Lachlan* wanted to stay married to *Moira*. He'd felt it for quite some time now, only he hadn't realized it until last night. The respect he'd come to hold for her, the enjoyment of her presence, the laughter and silly moments in that little hut of hers—at some point, without even being aware of it...all those things had grown into love.

Lachlan *loved* Moira.

Moira, however, did not return Lachlan's love. And he respected her too much to force her to remain married if she did not welcome it.

But that was *if*. It did not mean he wouldn't try to persuade her, to change her feelings towards him. He resolved to talk to her on the journey back to Glendalough.

They broke their fast in Glen Craggan's great hall. It was nearly empty; only a handful of Kinross's Douglases, mostly guardsmen, were present. Given that their clan had just been destroyed, they ate in gloomy silence.

The only noble presence at the morning meal was Lady Eleanor. It was the first time Lachlan had gotten a chance to take a look at the girl; he'd hardly noticed her last night in the solar. She was a handsome lass, he decided. Perhaps near twenty years, with hair as golden as her mother's, and a manner as regal as her father's.

The lady chewed her pottage with disinterest; her head remained bowed to her trencher. She looked as though she were deep in thought.

***

Lachlan mentioned this to Moira on the journey back to Kildrummond.

"I didna like the feeling I got from her," she admitted. Her voice was low, and she leaned towards him so the other three men wouldn't hear.

"What feeling is that?"

She tilted her head, squinting at the dull clouds above. "When she told me Lady Rosamund was likely to leave Scotland...I dinna ken, but I had the impression that she wasna planning on going wi' them. Perhaps it's a daft notion."

"Daft," Lachlan echoed, though Moira's inkling niggled at him, too. "Where would she go—a lady of her station? The Douglases have few friends in Scotland that would shelter them now, after what's happened. And what reason would she have to stay?"

"There. Ye see? Daft."

No more was said on the matter. No more was said at all. Moira spurred Beauty on, distancing herself and her mount from Lachlan and his.

Now she didn't even wish to hold a conversation with him? No lass had ever been so determined to keep him at arms' length before. The slight stung. Why would anyone want to keep their distance from him? He was handsome. Desirable. And he held a title and land now on top of it all. What was it about him that Moira MacInnes found so objectionable?

More concerning was, how on earth did such a wee thing succeed in making a strong, capable man like himself—a knight, at that—feel so...*insecure*?

Dammit all to hell. He promised himself he would talk to her, and if there was one thing Lachlan was good at, it was keeping his promises.

He dug his heel into the side of his mount, and closed the distance between them once more. When Moira noticed him pull up beside her, she cocked an eyebrow.

"About last night," he began.

She shook her head. "Dinna speak of last night. 'Tis forgotten."

"Forgotten?" Lachlan reached out and touched her arm. "'Tis no' forgotten, love. I've forgotten nothing."

She offered no response to that, and Lachlan thought he saw a tremble in her lower lip. But it was too fleeting to say for certain.

"I were thinking," he pressed, "I ken what the arrangement was between us, but I'm wondering now if it might no' be the worst thing in the world to stay married."

"The worst thing?" Moira pulled her chin back as if she'd been slapped.

Lachlan winced. "Poor choice of words. What I mean to say is… is that we've set a precedent with this ruse of ours, an expectation of sorts. As laird of Glendalough and Earl of Kildrummond, I'm meant to have a wife. And heirs. Am I really so objectionable that ye couldna stand the thought of staying married to me?"

She looked at him then, with her blue eyes full of emotions he was unable to interpret. "Moira, I'm getting this all wrong. I want to say…well, what I mean to tell ye, is that… that I—"

He had been about to tell her that he loved her. It had been on the tip of his tongue to ask her to reconsider the annulment, to give herself a chance to learn to love him. But she cut him off before he got the words out.

"Lachlan," she said gently, but with finality. "Staying married isna what either of us wants. If this daft offer is yer way of assuaging yer guilt over what happened last night, then dinna fret. Ye've nothing to feel guilty for. It were nothing more than a liaison of convenience—for both of us. I wanted ye for solace then, the same as you wanted me. I'll no' hold that against ye, and demand ye stay married to me when neither of us wants it."

She might as well have thrown him into a spring brae. He felt the shock of her words over every surface of his body. So that was it, then. She wasn't even willing to try. She didn't love him, and she never would.

Lachlan allowed himself to drop back, feeling like his heart was being cut in two.

The layer of clouds grew heavy. By the time they reached Kildrummond it had started to rain. The party stopped at Moira's hut to see her safely deposited, before continuing on to Glendalough.

"I've business at the castle," he lied as soon as she'd dismounted.

Moira shrugged, and disappeared into the hut.

Such indifference. The hurt it caused made it feel like a weight was pressing on his chest.

The rain pelted the travelers for the rest of the journey, soaking their clothes and putting a chill in their bones. Lachlan hardly noticed it.

Back at the castle, Alex had taken shelter in the granary when the rain started. Having been alerted to the returning party, he trotted over the open ground to the bailey, and sheltered beneath the raised portcullis to meet them. Even at a distance he could see the dark expression on Lachlan's face.

"Ye're back then?" he said, taking the reins of his friend's bay as he dismounted.

Lachlan nodded. He glanced up from beneath his drawn brows as he passed Alex on his way inside.

"That bad, eh?"

"Aye, that bad. Meet me in the solar, will ye? No, wait—meet me in the treasury. I hate the solar. I'll be there shortly; I only want to sneak a bite from the kitchens and a good, strong shot of whiskey."

"Bring some for me when ye come."

Soon after the pair was seated in the treasury, in two small armchairs that were light enough to be moved, though were rather uncomfortable on the backside. Since the chamber had no hearth, they'd pulled the chairs close to the single window to watch the downpour. Lachlan held a heated stone wrapped in crude linen, which he tucked close to his stomach for maximum warming. His clothes were still drenched, and an occasional shiver rippled up his spine.

"I can have dry clothes brought for ye," Alex offered.

"Nay, I'm all right."

"Will ye tell me how Lady Albermarle took yer ill tidings then?"

He listened with rapt attention as Lachlan recounted the lady's anguish. Alex, too, found Lady Eleanor's behavior curious, and expressed sympathy for the remaining Kinross Douglases.

"Will ye take them on at Glendalough?"

"Aye," Lachlan affirmed. "I believe we can accommodate them. Strengthen the guard and add to the servants. I've enough empty land to rent to crofters and tradesmen. 'Tis no' that I'm worried about."

"'Tis Lady Albermarle."

Lachlan shook his damp head slowly. "I tell ye, when she cried, I felt as though it were *my* heart being ripped from my chest. Not a man in that solar wasna affected by her pain. Imagine that: being told yer eldest son is dead and yer husband is soon to follow."

"And ye'll lose yer home and titles shortly."

"Indeed. Though in truth, I dinna think she cares about that. I think she would trade all her wealth and nobility in a heartbeat if it meant having her men back. Can ye imagine loving someone so much ye'd give up everything for them like that?"

The remark nicked Alex's conscience, reminding him of what he needed to tell Lachlan.

"Em…actually…I can. I've been wanting to speak wi' ye about something, and have been waiting on yer return."

"Oh, aye?" Lachlan raised an eyebrow. "What is the matter— and why d'ye look so worried all of a sudden?"

Alex squirmed in his chair; he could feel a cold sweat breaking on his forehead. Well—no time like the present.

"Lachlan, ye ken the love I bear for ye is like that of a brother. Ye're my closest, most trusted, most *honored* friend in the world, and I've an unconditional respect for ye. Ye ken that, aye?"

"Aye, I ken that. What are ye on about, man? Spit it out."

Alex breathed once, and measured Lachlan with a long, wary glance. "I wish to marry."

"Marry?" Lachlan's brows shot up in surprise. "I hadna thought ye were the marrying type."

"I wasna before now, 'tis of a certain."

A slight smile reached Lachlan's eyes. "This is the first piece of good news I've had all day."

"And I have yer blessing?"

"Blessing? Ye dinna need my blessing, ye're free to marry as ye see fit."

"As it happens, I *do* need yer blessing—in this."

Lachlan's expression turned wary, and Alex found his extremities had gone distinctly cold. Pray God that his friend would understand.

"Tell me," Lachlan pressed when Alex faltered.

"I wish to marry the Dowager Countess Kildrummond."

He didn't immediately comprehend; John Douglas's death so recent, Lachlan didn't at first connect the title to any face in particular—

And then suddenly, he did.

A slow creep of understanding smoothed his furrowed brow, and he looked upon Alex with guarded reserve. Knowing him as well as he did, Alex knew that Lachlan was hanging on by a thread, keeping himself in check for the sake of their brotherhood. If he was to convince his friend of his genuine intentions, Alex would have to move quickly.

"We both ken my reputation wi' the lasses is just as bad as yers, but I assure ye, by all that I hold dear, this isna the same."

"Why?" Lachlan's tone was brittle.

"Because I love her."

"Ye love her."

"Aye. I love her. I've loved her the instant I laid eyes on her. Ye remember, that first day here at Glendalough, when I barged into yer chamber wi' that damned piece of bread shoved into my mouth like a heathen?" He chuckled warmly at the memory. "I tell ye, I thought the earth had fallen from beneath my feet when she turned and raked me over wi' those eyes of hers. Full of contempt, they were. I kent my life were forever changed in that instant. For better or worse, I'd never be the same."

"Ye love her now," Lachlan pressed. "But what about when ye want sons? She's barren, remember. In more than twenty years she never bore his Lordship a child. What happens when she is no longer enough, when ye realize there's no one to carry on yer name?"

"D'ye no' think I havena considered that already? That I'd leap so carelessly into marriage—marriage wi' *yer* aunt, and a noblewoman at that—wi'out considering everything I might face? MacByrne is a name of no consequence. I have no ambition that it may one day be graced wi' a title, whether in my life or beyond it. I am a selfish man, Lachlan. My heart wants Glinis, and it wants her for life. I'll no' deny my heart because the woman I love canna bear my children."

His earnest plea warmed Lachlan's cool facade. The hard glint in his raven black eyes softened as he digested Alex's declaration.

"Does my aunt return your love?"

"Aye, she does. She pretends she doesna, but she does. I've told her I wish to marry her. I wanted to tell ye before I ask her finally."

Lachlan smiled sadly. "Then I suppose it shall be her choice that decides the question of whether ye will, or willna, marry. I'll no' stand in yer way."

"I have yer blessing?" Alex's heart leaped in his chest.

"Ye have my blessing." He breathed, and adjusted the stone in his lap. "So, the death of one earl, the succession of another, two weddings and an annulment. What a year Kildrummond has had so far, and 'tis no' even half over yet."

"So ye do mean to go through wi' it? The annulment?"

"That were always the plan."

"But things have changed."

Lachlan threw his friend a challenging glance. "Have they?"

"I ken ye well. Something has changed."

Alex waited patiently as Lachlan grappled with the accusation.

"Aye, things have changed," he said finally. "But they've no' changed enough. Or they've no' changed for her as they have for me. The marriage will be annulled because it's what she wants."

"I dinna believe that."

"'Tis true. She doesna want to stay married to me." When Alex fixed him with a dubious look, Lachlan explained. "I didna tell ye, but about a fortnight back, maybe a bit more, I…em…well, I tried it on wi' her. In a manner of speaking."

This certainly was a surprise. In fact, Alex was rather taken aback that he hadn't been told until now. He sat forward in his chair. "And?"

"I didna set out to seduce her, if ye can believe that—and dinna look at me like that. 'Tis God's truth." He paused, slightly embarrassed. "I were...I were asleep. I were dreaming. I dinna need to tell ye *what* I were dreaming about, but when I woke, I found it were no dream at all. I were on top of her, kissing her, and...and more. Right there in that wee little bed of hers."

Alex's eyes were wide as he took in Lachlan's tale. He did not say so, but privately he was amused by the way Lachlan spoke.

Lachlan Ramsay, Viscount Strathcairn, had never been delicate when regaling Alex with the stories of his exploits in the bedchamber. Nor Alex with Lachlan, for that matter. They were fast friends, and the lasses they'd enjoyed in times past hadn't meant anything other than sport.

And *they* had never meant anything but sport to the *lasses*, if truth be told.

Alex knew now what it was to be with a woman he loved. He recognized the same knowledge in Lachlan.

"I take it our Moira didna look too kindly on what ye were trying to do to her?"

Lachlan lowered his head, ashamed. "Alex, ye should have seen her face. I frightened her something fierce. I've never had a lass look at me like that in bed."

"But she is a maid, aye? Surely it were only her inexperience that frightened her."

"That's what I told myself. Later, ye see, when I couldna stand the guilt of having so terrified her. But then, last night—"

Alex slid further forward in his chair. His knees bumped against Lachlan's.

"Eh, get off!" Lachlan shoved his shoulder.

"Sorry," Alex laughed, and sat back in his chair.

"I were going to say—last night she kissed me."

"She kissed you?"

"I'm sure she only meant to comfort me, what wi' my having to deal wi' the Countess of Albermarle. Only, when she kissed me, I pushed it further. I couldna just let it be a kiss, I had to see if I could have more." He sighed heavily. "She *let* me make love to her. I hoped it might make her feel differently about me, and I was determined that she would enjoy it. And believe me, I did everything I could to make her enjoy it."

"And did she?"

"Aye, she did. At least I think she did. But this morning she said no' a word about it—at first."

"At first?"

Lachlan lowered his head. "I spoke to her on the journey back. Asked her if she might want to stay married to me. She made it clear she did no', and that she were no' interested in trying.

"I canna complain, though, can I?" he concluded. "It were the bargain we both made. 'Tis time that I upheld my end of it."

Lachlan's version of the story perturbed Alex. He'd known for some time how his friend felt about the lass he'd married, even if Lachlan hadn't known it himself. And he thought Moira might feel the same. They got on so well, and what Alex saw between them, as one standing outside looking in, was a man and a woman who harbored secret affections for each other.

He did not believe that he'd been wrong about what he'd seen. There must be something Lachlan was missing, or something he wasn't telling him.

The story simply made no sense otherwise.

\*\*\*

That night Moira sat in her chair, in her little hut. Alone.

Lachlan had not come back from Glendalough. Deep down, she knew he would not be coming back ever again. She'd offended him with her remark, wounded his pride that he'd not been able to make a lass fall in love with him.

But it was for his own good that she'd done it, and he'd get over the initial shock. After all, he would not thank her for trapping him in a marriage he did not want. His offer to remain married had been borne of guilt—of that she was sure. She suspected he'd meant to talk to her that morning about what passed between them, and she'd taken the time to prepare what she would say.

Well, she certainly had accomplished her goal. Moira had released Lachlan from any sense of obligation he felt towards her. She'd set him free.

Her own heart, though, felt like it was being squeezed bloody. Tears streamed down her cheeks as she watched the peat fire flicker and smoke. Up until now, Moira had always prided herself on being a selfless lass. Until now, she'd never known what being selfless truly meant.

Selflessness had never hurt this much before.

## *Twenty*

Despite Sir Alexander MacByrne's misgivings, the end of the
marriage between Lachlan Ramsay, Lord Kildrummond, and
common born Moira MacInnes came to pass.

The highborn Douglases of Kildrummond, who had never
accepted John Douglas's illegitimate scrap of a girl, nodded their
heads in satisfaction. The harlot Lilian MacInnes's urchin would not
be the one to take the Dowager Countess's place at Glendalough.
That was as it should be.

Though it perplexed more than a few noble brows that Glinis
herself avoided sharing in their satisfaction. It was as if she no
longer hated the girl, which surely could not be the case.

The people of the village nodded their satisfaction also. They'd
come to respect Lachlan as lord and leader of their land, but he was
not for Moira. No, their Moira was a good, honest lass. One of them.
Let the new Lord Kildrummond have his castle, his title and his
riches. They would welcome their Moira back into their folds with
open arms. That was as it should be.

Though it perplexed more than a few common brows that Niall
MacCormack was spending all of his time with that Janet lass now.
They would have to find some other, hardworking lad for their
Moira to marry, if the brewer's lad would not have her anymore.

Within a sennight of their return from Kinross, a priest was
summoned to take their statements, and hear their accounts.
Unfortunately, it was the same priest from the abbey at Inverness
who had married them, and the holy man remembered well the
spectacle the bride and groom had made of themselves on the
occasion of his first visit to Moray.

In Glendalough's quiet solar, with the ghosts of long-ago
Kildrummond earls watching silently, the old priest listened with a
stern face as Lachlan told the truth about the marriage.

Or, at least, a version of the truth.

"So ye see, father," he concluded, "I never intended to remain
married to the Lady Moira once Lord Kildrummond passed. It were
the only way his Lordship would let me inherit a land and title of my
own."

The priest looked upon Lachlan with undisguised contempt. "And the Lady Moira went along wi' this blasphemous plan, did she?"

"No," Lachlan was quick to put in, "she didna. I kent she wouldna agree, so I kept my designs to myself."

Moira stared at Lachlan, baffled. She had not intended for him to take all the blame. The part of her that was proud and defiant demanded that she correct him, that she must not allow him to debase himself like this. But one warning glance from Lachlan silenced her. If she protested, the priest might wash his hands of the affair and declare the marriage sound.

"I must say my Lord Kildrummond, disappointment doesna even begin to describe how I feel about this. This isna what God designed the sanctity of marriage for. I dinna lie, I fear for yer mortal soul, lad." He sighed dramatically. "But it would seem that I've no choice other than to put through yer petition for the annulment— unless, of course, the marriage was consummated?"

Lachlan swallowed thickly. He could stop this annulment if he wanted to. All he would have to do is tell the truth, and Moira would have to remain his wife. But he could not—this was what she wanted. And he respected her choice.

"Nay, we never consummated the marriage."

The priest looked to Moira. "And ye, lass, what say ye? Can ye confirm what yer lord husband says?"

Moira's stomach felt like lead. She was about to lie to a priest, to tell a lie that would break her heart. But she had to do it. It was what Lachlan wanted, and she respected him too much to keep him locked in a marriage he did not want.

"Aye, 'tis true. The marriage was never consummated."

The priest gave them both a stern glare. "So be it. It grieves me to do it, but I shall take yer testimony to the Bishop. I imagine his decision shall reach ye wi'in a fortnight. In the meantime, I suggest ye both make haste to the nearest chapel ye can find and pray for His holy forgiveness. For in the end, 'tis our Lord God's forgiveness which is the only one that matters."

The priest shuffled out of the room, a model of piety. Once he was gone, Moira gazed poignantly at Lachlan. Her throat was tight, and she felt like she was about to cry. "Ye didna have to do that. Ye didna need to fall on yer sword for me."

"Aye, I did. It were me came up wi' this mad scheme. It should be me to shoulder the blame for it."

They looked at each other for a very long time, two hearts breaking simultaneously. Two hearts being sacrificed to make the other happy.

"Ye take care of yerself, aye?" Lachlan said. "I imagine we'll see each other now and again, at market and such. Ye'll come to a feast at the castle soon, won't ye?"

"Aye, I will," Moira promised.

They both knew it was a lie.

## *Twenty-One*

The days passed into weeks, and the weeks into a month. Moira lived each day, each *hour*, mechanically. Work became her solace, the agent by which she numbed her mind and her heart. Her little plot of land had never been so well maintained. Her animals had never enjoyed such hospitality. And in the long, empty evenings, Moira wove more tapestries than she had in a year.

Yet none of those tapestries made it to market. Not, at least, on her creaky little cart, for she avoided the place. Market had people, and people had eyes. No matter how much she might have wished it, Moira could not make herself invisible to their pitying glances.

Instead, Niall went for her, bringing her wares with him and returning with admirable coin. Moira simply added the profit to her growing collection which she never spent.

It was Niall who remained faithfully by her side during those times of heartache—a heartache which she staunchly denied. But her visible deterioration spoke a truth she *couldn't* deny. In the past month, Moira had dropped a significant amount of weight. There was now a distinct joylessness to her. Her bright, blue eyes, which had always sparkled with life, were curiously dull. As if her soul had been drained away.

He had wondered aloud on one occasion if seeing Lachlan again might raise her spirits. It had only been one occasion, though, for she swiftly snuffed the idea—and any possibility of its future resurrection.

She would *not* see Lachlan. There would be no purpose in it, for he was not the cause of her ill turn. And besides, there was no ill turn to speak of. Could a person not work hard without drawing speculation? Niall's fears were clearly founded on idle village gossip. He need only use his own eyes to see that she was perfectly all right.

And of her unnatural thinness, which she was forced to admit…well, Niall received her solemn promise that she'd make more of an effort to eat.

It was a promise she couldn't keep, for Niall could not be there at night to distract her from her dreams. Dreams of Lachlan, each and every one. And every morning she'd wake from her dreams to that same, hollow throb in her heart that only work could numb.

The summer days brought glorious warmth, and the green hills of Kildrummond blossomed with heather. On a morning as fine and bright as any, Niall made his usual ride out to see Moira on his family's knobby old mare.

Only this day, there was nothing usual about his purpose for coming.

He found her mucking out the animals' pens. Again. For the third time in twice as many days.

"Ye'll run through yer rushes by autumn if ye keep that up," he observed when she emerged from inside, brandishing a heaping pitchfork with both hands.

"They stink. I canna stand the smell."

"The smell never bothered ye before."

She stopped, and wiped her brow with the back of her wrist. "Well it does now."

With a great heave that would have been admirable for a person twice her size, she flung the forkful of rushes onto her growing pile. A smaller pile sat next to it, the clean rushes which she'd reclaimed and would return to the stalls. An even smaller pile sat next to that— Niall gave *this* particular pile a wide berth as he followed her back into the hut.

"D'ye have anything to eat? I'm half starved."

Stabbing the pitchfork into another heap of rushes, Moira rolled her eyes.

"Ye're always half starved, Niall MacCormack," she said dryly. Nevertheless, she dropped the fork and obligingly led him to the pantry. "There's some bannock up there," she pointed. "I'd fetch it for ye, but I'd wager ye'd no' appreciate the manure."

Niall grimaced at her dirty hands, which she held up in illustration. Reaching for the fresh loaf on the top shelf, he took a large bite.

"Have ye any treacle?" he said through an overstuffed mouth.

She nodded, and let him root through her various jars for himself until her found the fired clay pot with the thick, black syrup.

"Divine," he declared, scooping up an indulgent dollop with a chunk of the bannock.

Feeling suddenly drained, Moira collapsed onto the bench in front of the hearth. No fire burned in the charred dirt. She hadn't a need to bake any bread, and it was far too warm to light the turf logs merely for the sake of it.

Finishing half the loaf of bannock, Niall took his customary place in the chair beside the bench. "So, how are ye faring?"

"Ye ask me that every time ye come here."

"That's because every time I come here I want to ken how ye're faring."

"And every time, I tell ye I'm fine." She let his skeptical gaze pass without comment. "Have ye been to the castle lately?"

Niall stretched his long, spindly legs out in front of him, examining an errant scrape on his shin. "I have. Lady Kildrummond sends a message, by the by."

"Oh?"

"She bids me to tell ye that she hopes ye're no' avoiding Glendalough on her account—I suppose I should be calling her Lady MacByrne now, shouldna I?"

Yes, it was Lady MacByrne now. Shortly after Lachlan and Moira's marriage was dissolved, Sir Alex quietly married Lady Glinis in Kildrummond's village kirk. The resident priest officiated, and the only guests in attendance were Lachlan and Eamon Douglas, the castle's steward.

Moira, too, had been invited. But she declined.

"I dinna avoid Glendalough," she insisted unconvincingly. "'Tis only that I have no business there."

"No' even to visit wi' Sir Alex? He asks about ye at market, ye ken."

"Now that ye mention it, I had a rather peculiar visit from Sir Alex a sennight ago. Or thereabouts"

"Did ye now." Niall feigned surprise. "And what did Sir Alex have to say?"

"I dinna quite ken, to tell the truth. He merely appeared one afternoon, came inside, and proceeded to ask me a handful of daft questions."

"Daft, ye say?"

"Aye. Things like what do I do wi' myself in the evenings, and what did I think of Lord Erroll making a journey to Kildrummond wi' his eldest daughter. They were all so odd that I couldna make sense of them, and I canna remember half of them now. But the thing that's odder still is that he were staring at me the whole time, like he were expecting me to answer one way or another. Only, I didna ken what answer I was expected to give. After a while it began to feel awkward, and then, just as suddenly as he'd come, he up and left. I havena spoken to him since. D'ye have any idea what that could have been about?"

"Nay, I canna imagine."

It was not the least bit true; Niall barely managed to hang onto the wicked grin that threatened to betray him.

Of course he knew why Alex had come to see Moira. More importantly, he knew why he'd up and left so abruptly. It was because she'd given him the very answers he'd been looking for. Unintentionally, of course. They were in the veiled hurt when he'd suggested falsely that an eligible maiden might be paraded in front of Lachlan. And they were in the loneliness in her eyes when she recounted her evenings spent without Lachlan's company.

There had also been another answer, one which Moira had not mentioned just now, and one which had tipped the scales for Alex.

"D'ye regret what happened at Glen Craggan?" he'd asked.

"What d'ye mean by that?" had been her swift reply. A fierce blush had instantly mottled her fair complexion.

"Oh, only that it must have been difficult to accompany Lachlan and his men on their mission. I thought perhaps ye might regret having been a party to it when it wasna necessary."

Later, when Alex caught up with Niall to report on his findings, he'd recalled how she stumbled her way through every sentence, and every answer after that. It had been enough to convince them both of one certainty: the impression Moira had given Lachlan after Glen Craggan was not a faithful account of her true feelings.

Alex had exalted in his own cunning, and together with Niall (and the rest of the MacCormack family who insisted on being a part of it all), he hatched a plan.

"I believe I need some air," Niall declared, rubbing his sticky hands on his plaid. "Ye're coming for a ride wi' me."

"Nay, I dinna much feel like riding."

He stood. Taking her by the hand, he pulled her to her feet. "'Tis no' a request, lassie. I'm telling ye: ye're coming wi' me."

"Dinna be high-handed wi' me, Niall MacCormack," she snapped. "I'm no' fit for riding. I'm right dirty, and I have no desire to go."

"Ye're right dirty because ye've been working far too hard, and ye've no desire to go because ye've hidden yerself away in this little hut for far too long. I fear that if ye stay here any longer, ye'll grow roots to the ground, and then ye'll be stuck forever. Now take yer bony wee arse outside. Ye're coming for a ride."

Seeing that further argument would prove fruitless, Moira unwillingly let Niall pull her outside to his mount.

"Why are the pair of us going on one horse?" she question when he offered to help her up. An offer which she pointedly ignored.

"Because I said so, that's why."

More like because she wouldn't be able to turn around and ride away when she saw where he was taking her, Niall thought smugly.

Swinging himself up behind her, Niall took the reins and set them off at a walking pace in the direction of the village.

Moira allowed herself to settle into the rhythm and sway of the beast as they went. Though she hated to admit it, Niall was right: it did feel good to be outside in such fine weather. The hills were an explosion of color and scent; they shimmered green and violet with every rush of breeze that ruffled the blanket of heather.

This time of year was her favorite. But ever since Lachlan left, she hadn't been able to enjoy any of it. Shame, that. Here she was, blind to the brilliance of the Highlands around her, insensate to the warmth of the air and the scents of the greenery, and for what? Because her heart had been crushed irreparably? It was her own fault, falling in love with a man when she had no right to. They'd had an understanding at the outset of their arrangement.

Lachlan likely never thought of her. Probably didn't miss her one pinch.

Thus occupied by her thoughts, Moira didn't noticed when Niall took a turn away from the village. Not until he stopped abruptly.

"Village is that way," she pointed behind her.

"Aye," he replied vaguely. Then he hopped down.

"What are ye doing?"

"Let's walk a while, shall we?"

She looked down at him with suspicion. "Ye're acting queer. Ye sure ye havena been into yer da's ale this morning?"

"Oh, I never said that."

Too glum to engage in their usual banter, Moira followed. Together they walked aimlessly over the scrub and crags of the wild landscape.

At least she *thought* their wandering was aimless. That was, until they rounded a small hillock which dipped to a flat stretch of purple ground.

She halted abruptly, and her heart lurched in her chest when she saw what was there. Or, rather, *who* was there.

Standing in the center of the clearing…was Lachlan.

He was dressed in finery—the same finery, she recalled, that he'd worn the day of their wedding. His raven hair was pulled back from his temples and tied in a neat queue at the nape of his neck, and his jaw had been scraped clean. Once more the savage knight had been transformed into the regal viscount—now earl—by the mere difference of a scraped chin. It took her breath away just as it had those months ago when they'd stood side by side in Glendalough's great hall. The only difference about his appearance now was that, in addition to his *feileadh mhor*, which was of the Ramsay plaid, he wore a band of the Douglas colors around his upper arm.

Lachlan was not the only one waiting for them in the clearing. Behind him were Sir Alex and Lady Glinis, side by side, her arm tucked proudly into the crook of her new husband's elbow. And behind them were the MacCormacks—all of them. Several villagers that Moira knew and loved filled out the gathering, as well as a select handful of Glendalough's guard, with its captain, Dougall MacFadyen, at the helm.

Positioned next to Lachlan, in simple robes of undyed wool, was one more figure: the priest from the village kirk.

The first thought which came to Moira was that she'd stumbled upon something she wasn't meant to see. When she began to back away, Niall grabbed her arm.

"Niall, let me go," she said shakily.

"Now Moira, ye dinna want to be rude to yer guests, do ye?"

Her head snapped to him. "*My* guests?"

It was then that Lachlan came forward, approaching her like one might a wounded starling.

"Moira," he said, in a voice that was as rich and sultry as she remembered.

"W-What is this?"

"It's for ye," he told her. "Moira, I want to beg yer forgiveness."

"Forgiveness?"

"Aye, forgiveness. I were such a fool to let the annulment pass through. I thought it were what ye wanted, ye see. I thought ye didna want to stay married to me, so I went through wi' it to make ye happy. I've been miserable every day since.

"Now I hear from yer Niall, and from Alex, that ye love me. Or at least they think ye love me. I hope to heaven it's true. If it isna, if they're wrong, just say the word. I'll let ye leave here now, and I'll never ask another thing of ye. But I canna do that before ye ken how *I* feel about *ye*."

Her cerulean eyes widened, and she looked nervously towards the guests behind him. He took her hands in his and gave them a firm squeeze, commanding her gaze back to him.

"Moira, I love ye. I love ye like I've never loved anyone before. If ye'll let me, I want to spend the rest of my days bound to ye in matrimony, and loving ye each and every one of them. I ken we didna marry for the right reasons the first time, but if ye'll have me, I will spend the rest of my life making sure that we *stay* married for the right reasons. Marry me, Moira MacInnes?"

Moira couldn't breathe; the air was trapped in her chest. She looked to Niall. Then to the anxious faces in the clearing. Then to the priest, who smiled benevolently at her from the head of the gathering.

When her eyes returned to Lachlan, they fixed on his with...*fury*.

"Ye stupid lout," she shrieked, and smacked him in the arm with her open palm. Then she shoved angrily against his chest, and smacked him in the other arm. Her hands went wild as she slapped and shoved and hit, accompanied by a tirade of livid accusations which echoed through the hills in an unending stream.

"I canna believe ye've dragged me here. I'm dirty, I smell like my animals. What were ye thinking? Ye're just as daft as Niall. Look at me; I'm nay fit for a wedding. I'm utterly mortified. How could ye do this to me?"

The audience watched, horrified, as she abused Lachlan mindlessly. For his part, all Lachlan could do was shield himself from the worst of her blows.

But the horror of the audience turned to astonishment as Moira's angry tirade somehow transformed into a passionate embrace. It wasn't entirely clear to anyone how it happened. One minute she was berating him shamelessly, and then next she was kissing him with a fury of a different kind.

Just as astonished, Lachlan pulled away, and searched her face. Her eyes shimmered with tears, and a smile which she could not control spread across her lips.

"Marry me," he repeated. "Please say ye'll marry me."

She emitted a sound somewhere between a sob and a giggle. "I'll no' forgive ye for this, ye ken."

"I'd be sorely disappointed if ye did. *Marry* me!"

Moira was dizzy as she gazed into his smoky eyes. Even though her vision was swimming, and the world had grown hazy around her, there was one thing which she could see with undeniable clarity: he loved her.

He *loved* her. He had all along.

Hesitantly, she nodded. "Yes."

Overjoyed, Lachlan swept her into his arms and twirled her around. Behind them, a rousing cheer lifted into the summer sky as he brought her back down and kissed her again, tenderly this time. A kiss to seal a promise.

That day, a wedding took place. No honored priest from the fancy abbey at Inverness was in attendance. Instead, officiating was the local priest from the local kirk—a simple and honest man for a simple and honest wedding. The vows were exchanged in the purity of nature, rather than the grand arches of a great hall. And though the highest-ranking of Scotland's nobles were not there to witness, those who were looked on with true happiness and admiration for the bride and her groom.

The ghosts of Kildrummond lords long past smiled down as they watched over their beloved land.

And perhaps...just perhaps...one Kildrummond lord in particular smiled the widest. With his Lilian at his side, to share in the joy of his daughter's happiness.

It was all he'd wanted for her, after all.

*Don't miss the second installment of the Douglas Clan series:*

# A Noble Treason

Stirling, Scotland, 1456. The traitorous Earl of Douglas has fled to England, leaving his clansmen to die in his place on the battlefield of Arkinholm. Two Douglas lords have been captured, and await execution: the earl's brother, Lord Ormonde, and his distant kinsman Edward Douglas, Earl of Albermarle.

Eleanor Douglas, eldest daughter of Lord Albermarle, is a noblewoman by birth, but a rebel at heart. When her family, stripped of their titles and thrown from their lands, flees to England, she does not follow.

Sir Dougall MacFadyen is captain of the guard in the Highland realm of Kildrummond. His master, Lachlan Ramsay, presides over a branch of the Douglas line that is close kin to Lord Albermarle. Suspecting that Eleanor has remained in Scotland to find a way to free her father, Lachlan sends Dougall across the land in search of her.

When he finds her, will Dougall be able to sway Eleanor from her course? Or will Eleanor's conviction sway him? Her intentions may be noble, but if she fails in her mission, Eleanor could lose her head a traitor to the Crown—and Dougall along with her.

# A NOTE FROM VERONICA

My Dear Friends,

Your readership means the world to me. I want to thank you for coming with me on this journey of the Black Douglas clan.

Though this novel is a product of my imagination, it is based on actual historical events. William Douglas, the eighth Earl of Douglas, was murdered in 1452 by King James the Second of Scotland (also known as Fiery Face for the prominent birthmark on his cheek). At that time, the Douglas clan enjoyed a powerful alliance with the earls of Clan MacDonald and Clan Lindsay, and when the king demanded that William Douglas put an end to the triad, the earl refused. As a result, King James flew into a rage and stabbed William twenty-six times, then threw his body from a window at Stirling Castle.

Three years later William's successor, his brother James Douglas, waged war on the king, which culminated in the Battle of Arkinholm on July 1st, 1455. When he realized that his allies abandoned him, James Douglas fled to England before the battle commenced, leaving his brothers to carry on the campaign. They failed. Archibald Douglas, Earl of Moray, was killed. John Douglas, Lord of Balvenie, escaped and fled, and Hugh Douglas, Earl of Ormonde, was captured, tried and executed. This marked the beginning of the end for the Black Douglases.

Within recorded history, there are always untold stories that never made it to the books. Though Lachlan and Moira's story is a work of fiction, there is no telling what countless, ordinary stories were played out on the sidelines of these milestone events. I like to think that, by breathing life into these fictional characters, I am, in some small measure, breathing life back into those whose tales were not put to parchment.

Though I may be a die-hard history fan, I do so enjoy living in this modern era of social media. It means I get to interact with you directly and instantaneously, and hear firsthand what you think of my stories. I pay attention to everything you have to say, and endeavor to learn from your insight—you are the experts, after all, the ones who make or break a book's success.

I would love to hear from you, whether it's to tell me what you thought of *A Noble Deception* (or anything else I've written), or just to say hi. Stop by my webpage to connect with me on social media: www.veronicabale.com.

Until next time, my friends, hugs to you all. And as always, happy reading!

Cheers,
Veronica

# ABOUT THE AUTHOR

Veronica Bale is a freelance writer, book reviewer, *Coronation Street* junkie and author of cracking-good love stories set in the Highlands of Scotland. She lives in Ontario, Canada with her husband, son, and three spoiled cats. When she's not writing, Veronica likes running, reading, or spending time with her family. What Veronica loves most about being an author is hearing from her readers.

Did you enjoy this book? Drop us a line and say so! We love to hear from readers, and so do our authors. To connect, visit www.boroughspublishinggroup.com online, send comments directly to info@boroughspublishinggroup.com, or friend us on Facebook and Twitter. And be sure to check back regularly for contests and new releases in your favorite subgenres of romance!

Are you an aspiring writer? Check out www.boroughspublishinggroup.com/submit and see if we can help you make your dreams come true.

29659406R00115

Printed in Great
Britain
by Amazon